STICKS AND BONES

MEREDETH CONNELLY MIND HUNT THRILLERS
BOOK 5

E.H. Vick

DARK TRIAD PUBLISHING
NEW YORK

Dark Triad Publishing
2080 Nine Mile Point Road, Unit 106
Penfield, NY 14526

Publisher's Note: This is a work of fiction. Names, characters, places, and incidents are a product of the author's imagination. Locales and public names are sometimes used for atmospheric purposes. Any resemblance to actual people, living or dead, or to businesses, companies, events, institutions, or locales is completely coincidental.

Sticks and Bones/ E.H. Vick. — 1st ED.
ISBN 978-1-951509-22-4

TABLE OF CONTENTS

DEDICATION

For Paul Martin, Ryan W. Fox, Anthony M. Strong, Sonya Sargent-Strong, and, of course, Supergirl, each of whom, in their own way, contributed to the timely completion of this novel when I thought I couldn't make the deadline due to my battle with COVID-19.

I hope you enjoy *Sticks and Bones*. If so, please consider joining my online community—details can be found at the end of the last chapter.

CHAPTER 1

AND GET THE PRIEST AS WELL

Ukiah, CA

NERVOUSNESS AND FEAR wracked Jamie Wenstrom, which in itself wasn't anything unusual—he was almost always anxious in social situations. In this case, however, he was alone, standing at the curb of 1408 Rosemary Lane, staring up at the abomination of a house, listening to the raucous combination of a multitude talking at once at full volume, shrieking laughter, and possibly honest-to-God screaming. A shiver ran down his spine.

The house had once been white with black trim, but even the white paint seemed sullied, dirty, and urine-yellowed. There was a stench coming off the place that he'd noticed from a couple of houses away as he approached on foot from the south. The guy he'd met at the party earlier that evening had said he couldn't miss the house and had then laughed. Now, Jamie got the joke. The rest of the houses on the street were immaculate—though small. None of them smelled of vomit, urine, feces, and worse. None of them had large, hand-lettered signs stuck to the front door.

Jamie forced himself to step up onto the curb, then advance toward the door until he could read the sign. It said, "No gang members allowed. No one representing the so-called government of this land—which was stolen by terrorists two hundred and some odd years ago—has permission to enter this domicile. That includes cops, social workers, deputies, feebs, drug-addicted enforcement agents, IRS criminals, Department of Homeland Silliness, or anyone else. If you don't know whether this applies to you or not, *it does*. Turn around. I will not be presumed guilty until proven innocent. If you can make laws in a land you stole, so can I. So be it. Punishment for disregarding this notice is death." Beneath that strange proclamation, something in Arabic chipped out of the thick black paint that coated the door. Years of faded or ripped-off stickers decorated the edges of the door. Above the peephole, someone had applied a crucifix sticker upside down. Below it, was another handmade sign that read: "Evil will always triumph over good." On either side of that, three-inch square pirate flags had been taped. In the upper left corner, a giant skull covered in Halloween spiders had been affixed. In the upper right corner, a mundane "BEWARE OF DOG" sign hung above "ARE YOU THREATENING ME?" in white stick-on letters.

The last two items brought a grin to Jamie's face. The guy at the party had had a wicked sense of humor, and he took everything stuck to the front door in kind. He quelled the turmoil within and tried to stride confidently to the front door. He looked around but could find no cheerily lit doorbell, and the door's knocker lay against the front wall of the house, ripped from the door and discarded. He didn't know what to do. It seemed unlikely anyone inside would hear him knocking over the din of the party. He backed away far enough to double-check that the window shades were all drawn down tight, then put his hands in his pockets and let his shoulders slump. The guy had no doubt known this would happen. It was just another snub, another joke at Jamie's expense. He turned away, blowing his cheeks out with a released sigh.

"Just go in," said a woman's voice.

Jamie jumped and spun his head from left to right and back again but saw no one. He whirled around to face the house, but the front porch was empty, as well.

"Up here," said the girl.

He looked up at the roof, and there she was: an elfin blonde girl—though her roots gave lie to her hair color—wearing nothing but a pair of once-white panties and a pair of Keds. His gaze strayed to her chest, and heat came to his cheeks in a rush. "Uh, sorry..."

"If I didn't want you to look, I'd wear a shirt," said the girl. She took a final pull on a joint that seemed as big as Jamie's little finger, then snubbed it out on her palm. "No one can ever hear the door around here, so Kahin just leaves it unlocked."

"Oh. I, uh... I'm..."

"He invited you, right?" she asked.

Jamie found himself staring at her breasts again and blushed again.

She laughed. "Want to feel them?"

He forced his throat to work, swallowing hard, and once more moved his gaze to her own. "I apologize. I don't know what's come over me."

"What's come over you is that I have great boobs." She shrugged, making the organs in question bounce.

"Um, yes, you do."

She smiled at him. "Then look, touch, *caress* them all you want. The evening is looking up." She jerked her chin to the side. "How old are you, anyway?"

"Uh. I'm twenty."

A sly grin slid across her features. "No, you're not." She cocked her head to the side. "I'd say you're seventeen or eighteen but still at Ukiah High School."

His blush burned bright. "Um, yeah. I'm a senior, but it's all bullshit."

"Can't say I'd disagree with that assessment, but I was homeschooled, so my opinion's probably not worth much." She shrugged again and grinned as his gaze dropped to her chest. "Go on," she whispered. "Lay hands on."

Jamie looked around, feeling sneaky, raunchy even. No one was out on the street. "I can't exactly reach you up there, but if you were down here with me..."

"Yum," she crooned. "I like a man who's not scared of touching what he wants. Stick around, and we'll have some fun. So go on in. I'll meet you inside."

"How did..." Jamie frowned at the single-story home. "How did you get up there? A ladder in the backyard?"

Her face twisted with a half-grin. "Why do you want to know? I'm coming down."

"Just... Just curious."

"Kahin cut a priest hole from one of the closets and put in a wooden ladder. He calls it the 'escape hatch' as if the cops wouldn't notice us up here." She turned and walked up the gentle slope of the roof. "Meet you in the kitchen. Just go on in."

"Okay," said Jamie. He approached the front door and lay his hand on the doorknob, which felt loose and somewhat greasy, but it twisted easily, and the door swung open to reveal what would be the formal living area in any normal home. In Kahin's house, however, it was hard to tell what the room was intended to be.

The floor was covered in garbage, and by the smell of the carpet, urine and feces. The walls had once been white, but between the thousands of stickers affixed everywhere there was space, the color could better be described as industrial grime. The stench he'd detected from half a block away grew to impossible proportions inside the place, and his eyes watered a little while his stomach did slow flip-flops in his gut. Mold, waste, body odor, and drug smoke wafted through the open door and slapped him in the face.

Twenty people lounged in the room—some on a beaten-down old couch, some in chairs pulled from the kitchen, and some right on top of the layer of garbage. There were more men than women, which wasn't unusual at a party, and Jamie was glad he'd had a moment outside to meet the girl on the roof. He'd almost certainly have shut down in this room, talking to no one until it was time to go. The people were in various states of undress, though the ones with the most clothes on also had the clearest eyes.

The man he'd met at the earlier party came through a door that Jamie figured was the basement door. The man's eyes lit when he saw Jamie, and a large grin split the lower half of his face. "Hey, man!" he shouted over the din of the thrash metal screeching from the stereo speakers, of the television blaring "American Ninja Warrior" at full volume, as well as the shouted conversations. "Glad you could make it!"

"Yeah, um, thanks," said Jamie.

The man's eyes were even more glazed than they had been earlier, and something crimson and wet glistened on his lips and chin. He'd stripped to his underwear and age-

and dirt-grayed athletic socks since Jamie had last seen him. He'd also wrapped his greasy dreadlocks in a green silk cloth wound up like a turban. "I forgot to get your name."

"Jamie Wenstrom," he said. "What's yours?"

"I'm Kahin Alshaytan. Welcome to my home. There are no rules once you're inside. Do whatever you want; stay as long as you want. Beer's in the fridge, and there might even be some food, but generally, everything but the water is BYO."

"Thanks," said Jamie. "It's a"—his eyes cut away from Kahin's—"nice place."

Kahin threw back his head and laughed. "It's a piece of shit! But it's *my* piece of shit." He grinned.

"You mean *your mother's* piece of shit," said a waxy-faced guy on the couch, who seemed to be doing nothing but staring at a shadowy corner and nodding.

"Shut up, Jack," said Kahin. He threw his arm around Jamie, and a wave of emetic body odor washed over him. "Let's go into the kitchen with the civilized folk." He glared at the one he'd called Jack for a few heartbeats, then turned and headed into the kitchen without releasing the hold he had on Jamie's shoulders. As they walked, he said, "That guy's on my last nerve. I'm going to kill him at sunrise."

Jamie laughed—it was just another instance of Kahin's black humor—but the man only looked at him askance. As they turned the corner into the kitchen, the girl from the roof squealed and danced over to slip under Kahin's other arm. Two other scantily-clad women watched in silence— one sitting on the corner of the counter, the other laying on the floor, her head propped in her hand looking up at the other.

"Hey, girls," said Kahin. "Meet Jamie. He's new."

The girl from the roof took half a step forward and looked him in the eye. "I get first dibs," she said. "Jamie and I are old friends."

Kahin arched his eyebrows at him, then grinned with one side of his mouth. "Where did you meet Anya?"

"Uh, outside. She was on the roof when I came up."

Kahin laughed long and hard, then slipped out from between them and shoved them together. "You kids have fun." He walked toward a hall that led to a darkened room on the backside of the house. Just before he entered it, however, he turned and looked back. "Unless you want to help me kill him, Jamie?"

"Who?" asked the girl on the counter.

"Jack," said Kahin with a sour look.

"Being a jerk again?"

"Being disrespectful, and we all know where that leads him."

The girl on the counter nodded. "He's a selfish lay, anyway."

"So? Jamie? Are you in?"

Laughing, Jamie nodded. "Yeah, of course."

Beside him, Anya made a face and squeezed his waist. "He's asking a serious question," she said. "Don't say yes unless you mean to help him."

Jamie glanced down at her, then looked at Kahin, who nodded. "Oh," said Jamie. "I thought... I thought you were joking."

A slow grin spread across Kahin's face. *"Of course* I was." He beckoned. "Come on. You can screw Anya later."

Jamie thought that might earn a rise out of the beautiful girl beside him, but she only gave a throaty chuckle and soft shrug. "Don't go telling him stories about me," she said.

Kahin only grinned.

CHAPTER 2

WHAT DO YOU MEAN, MISSING?

Quantico, VA

JIM MCCUTCHINS FLAILED for the jangling phone, frantic to grab it before it could wake half the house. His calibrated internal chronometer said it was *late*—just that late, no sense of the actual time, which was why he ignored that internal chronometer most of the time. Well, that and the fact that it was also wrong as much as right. Beside him, Nerida mumbled something about trees and rolled over.

His fingertips danced across the cool, glass surface of his cellphone and he pulled it toward him, loath to leave the comfort of his pillow-top mattress even for a moment. He spun the phone around and peered at the caller ID. "Jenna Wenstrom," it read. Jenna Wenstrom née McCutchins—his baby sister.

Concern flickered across his expression—Jenna was conscious of his life, his job, and his sleeping habits. She lived on the West Coast—and he on the East, of course—and always paid special attention to the time difference. His bleary eyes went next to the time above the caller ID—11:57 p.m.

He silenced the ringer, intending to get up, get downstairs to the kitchen, put on a cup of coffee in the Keurig, then call back. With a glance at Nerida, he peeled back the covers carefully and set his feet on the floor with the least amount of noise he could manage. At least the floor was jacketed in a nice, warm frieze instead of the cold hardwood that planked the main areas of the house. He pulled on a terry robe against the incipient chill and stepped out into the hall, closing the door with a quiet click as the ringer squalled again.

"Geez, give me a second, Jen," he muttered even as he thumbed the accept button. "Hold on a second, Jenna. Let me get downstairs."

"Jim!" she gasped. "I don't know what to do!"

Jim frowned. Of all his siblings, Jenna had the tightest grip on reality, on her emotions. He didn't like hearing her so on the edge of panic. "Let me get downstairs so I can talk without waking everyone up, okay?"

"What..." Jenna sighed. "Must be midnight there. I'm sorry, Jim, I...I just don't know what else to do. It's been—"

"Start from the beginning. Then I'll have something to say that's worthwhile." His no-nonsense tone had the desired effect—not quite command voice, but not big-brother voice, either—and he heard her draw a deep, calming breath.

When she spoke next, she sounded much more like the Jenna of his memories than one of his other sisters. "Jamie's been... Well, I've told you about some of the trouble he's been giving us these past couple of years. It's much worse now. He's—"

"I thought he was doing better?"

"Ups and downs," said Jenna, "and your ideas do help, they just don't stick."

Jim grunted. Adolescent drug abuse was hardly his specialty, but a few words from Uncle Jim *had* seemed to wake his namesake up a little.

"He goes along for a while, doing well in school again, hanging out with his old friends, even spending time with Danny and me, but then one little thing goes wrong, and he'll just sort of go off the rails again. We can sometimes get him back, but sometimes it's like he just has to get out there and swirl in the drain a little before he's ready to come back."

Jim stepped into the kitchen and nodded. "And he's in mid-swirl?"

"That's just it, Jim!" she cried, all semblance of calmness gone. "*He's been gone a week*!"

Frowning, Jim took a step back from the counter, from the Keurig, from the empty mug, and frowned at them. "What do you mean, gone for a week?"

"Jim, I..." A sob escaped her. "We don't know where he is, and the cops say he's on a bender because of his past, but no one's seen or heard from him and—" Her words began coming faster and faster, flowing into each other, becoming a stream of panic and fear and motherly-love.

"Hold on, hold on," muttered Jim, but it was as if she didn't hear him.

"—he's been hanging out with a really strange crowd of druggies and who knows what, staying out all night and all that, but never like this. I mean he always called, always texted so we knew he was okay, but now...but now...nothing, and his phone goes straight to voice mail, our texts go unread, and the tracking app you told us about reports it can't find the phone, and I'm scared, Jim, I'm *scared* and so is Danny, and we don't know where to turn, but we do know we can't go on like this! We need help, Jim! We need someone to help us!"

"Of course you do, Jenna, and I'm here. I've got resources to put on this—the very best—and I can swing my weight around with the locals. What's more, *I'm going to do all that*. Don't worry about that one little bit."

A sigh of relief gusted out of his sister, sounding like the apocalypse over the phone. "I knew you would, Jim. I'm sorry I'm so—"

"Understandable, Jen," he said in a quiet voice. "I'm halfway to joining you."

"You? You're always so calm."

"Presence training, Jenna. On the inside, I'm a whirlwind. And speaking of that, I need to start asking you questions. I need you to be succinct—don't edit your answers, just tell me the plain, honest truth, no matter how painful."

"Oh...okay."

"Let's start at the beginning of this episode. What set Jamie off?"

"An argument with Danny, of course."

"About what?"

"About his future plans. Danny presses him too hard."

"College? Work?"

"Or military. Danny thinks he should have a firm plan for after graduation. Jamie wants a year off. He says he needs to relax after high school."

"Okay," said Jim in a noncommittal tone. "What happened next?"

"Well, you know. The more Danny pushes an idea, the more Jamie has to rebel. So, he snuck out that night—it's as if he wants to prove how wrong his father is when Danny says he's mature and ready to take on life."

"And this was a week ago?"

"Last Saturday night. He said his friends were having a small get-together to watch movies and stay up late. No drugs. No booze, even, and we decided to put our faith in what he was telling us. He said he'd be late, but we couldn't very well come back and say he had to be in by midnight while telling him how mature he was."

"No, I suppose not," Jim said, though he thought anything but that. "And Sunday morning?"

"That's just it, Jim. He never came home from that party."

"And you called? Texted?"

"Of course. Voicemail. He did read the texts, but no response."

"*Someone* read the texts, anyway," said Jim. "And you've had no further contact from him?"

"Nothing. Not even asking for some money."

"Okay. Then what?"

"Well, I called the police, didn't I?"

"And they classified him as a runaway?"

"Well, they didn't say as much, but he has run away before, and they know that. They *suggested* waiting a few days to proceed."

"Not what I would do."

"No, me neither, Jim," said Jenna. "But this is Ukiah."

"We'll see what I can do about that tomorrow. Tell me what happened next."

"We called around. You know, looking for this get-together with Jamie's friends."

"And?"

She sighed. "There was no get-together—at least not one Jamie attended. Few of his friends were willing to admit they had spoken to him that night. He was...being difficult there, too."

"Few were willing to talk, so I assume some were?"

"A couple of the 'newer' friends. Not his long-time friends, not the ones working toward a future."

"The losers, in other words."

"Potheads. Drinkers. Truants."

"Right. What did they have to say?"

Jenna hesitated, then came out with it in a rush. "Jamie *did* go to a get-together that night, but it was hardly innocent movies. In fact, it was more like a wild party than a high school thing."

"Where?"

"We couldn't get that out of anyone—none of his friends went. But there was a big crowd—including some older people that few of the high school kids knew. Do you..."

"What, Jenna? Do I what?"

"Do you suppose someone...*took* him?"

Jim frowned a moment, considering. "In light of the past couple of years, I think it's far more likely he went off with someone. A girl, maybe, and played a little house."

Jenna drew a deep breath, then let it out. "Then you think he's okay?"

"This party sounds like a good place for my people to start. I can have them there late tomorrow, if all goes well, and hopefully, inset into a task force. Do you know of any other missing kids from that party?"

"Jim..."

"Because that will help. More missing people gives me more reason to call for a task force."

"Jim, I—"

"Do you remember meeting Meredeth Andersen a few years back? At our Christmas party?"

"Jim! *Answer* me! Do you think he's okay?" Jenna's voice was filled with anguish, and there was nothing more in the world that Jim wanted to say than yes.

He sucked a breath into the depths of his lungs and bit his lip. "Jenna, honey, listen…"

A small sob filtered across the line.

"He might be, honey, but it's been a week. And he's been totally incommunicado with you and Danny."

"But he might be—"

"Yes, he might be, and I want you to hold onto that for now. He might be communicating with some of these new friends. Meredeth and Bobby will suss all that out."

His sister said nothing.

"We will get to the bottom of it, Jenna," he said, knowing it wasn't a strong enough statement, knowing it wasn't what she wanted—*needed* him to say—but all he could bring himself to promise her. His knees chose that moment to weaken, and he shuffled backward and sank into a chair. "Speaking of which, let me go so I can get started."

"Okay," she said in an enervated, hopeless voice.

"I love you, Jenna."

"Me too," she said and hung up.

CHAPTER 3

HERE'S LUCY!

David Branch's Farm, NY

THE FOOD SLOT dropped open with a bang and a clatter, but Lucy was almost too weak to care. Almost. She craned her head and peered into the light through slitted eyelids. After weeks or months in the box, the daylight filtering into the barn burned her eyes like so much cinnamon oil.

"Hey, Squirt," said a now-familiar voice.

Lucy squeezed her eyes shut for a moment. She couldn't help it. That voice was usually followed by pain—either deafening death metal or electrical shocks. "Hey," she murmured.

"Well, what do you think, Squirt? Are you ready to rejoin the living?"

Her eyes snapped open all the way, and Lucy snaked a hand up to block at least some of the light. "Yes!" The silhouette of a teenager momentarily obscured the light.

"Sure about that, Squirt?"

"Yes. I'm sure. I'm ready."

"Because you know if you screw everything up, you'll be back in the box before you can blink."

"I... I know. I won't screw it up."

"Do you promise?"

"Yes. I..." Lucy had the sense the girl was toying with her—a cat playing with a mouse for a moment or two before eviscerating the little thing.

"Yes, what, Stephanie?"

"That's not my name. I'm Lucy. And, yes, I promise I won't screw it up."

"Lucy, is it? I think I prefer 'Squirt.'"

Lucy hitched one shoulder—at least as much as the confining box allowed. "Lucy is my name, but you can call me Squirt if you like."

"Oh, can I?" The voice dripped with sarcasm and a touch of hostility. "I have *your permission*?"

"You don't need my permission. I'm just saying I don't mind if you want to call me that."

"And if you did mind? What would do then?"

"I suspect you'd do whatever strikes your fancy, and I'd have to live with it."

The silhouette drew away from the opening. "You're not stupid. Let's see how you do." More clatters and clanks preceded the entire section of the box containing the food slot falling away. "Come on out of there, Lucy. Stand and be counted."

A silly grin formed on her lips, and gratitude flooded her mind. She reached above her head to grasp the edges of the opening, pulling herself toward the warm rush of light. Her arms shook with weakness, and she wondered if she'd be stuck hunched over like the bellringer of Notre Dame.

Warm, dry hands grasped her under her arms and pulled her out, then steadied her a few moments while her legs figured out how to support her again. "There. All out of the box," said the girl. "My name is Alex."

Lucy smiled at her. "Hi, Alex. Am I wrong that you've been...uh...teaching me?"

A lopsided grin surfaced on Alex's face. "Teaching, huh?"

"Teaching me the right way to act around here."

"Sure," said Alex. "I've been your guide the way Father was mine."

"Guide, okay." Lucy looked the other girl up and down. "Alex, short for Alexandra?"

The older girl's eyes narrowed a trifle. "Just Alex."

Lucy gave her a slow nod, her gaze flicking to the girl's clothing—all of which had come off the boy's rack. Boys' jeans, a surf shop T-shirt, and a pair of Nikes without socks. "Doesn't..." She shook her head and dropped her gaze to her dirty feet.

"Go ahead," Alex said in a voice that danced on the border between normal and cold. "Ask your questions. It's the only way to learn, and it's far better you ask me and make a blunder than ask Father the same question."

"Okay. It's just that I was wondering if the man... If *Father* doesn't have girls' clothes?"

"Of course he does. The question is, why would I want them?"

"Well, I mean..." Lucy glanced at Alex's face, then closed her mouth. "Sorry if I'm overstepping. I don't mean to get in your business." She didn't understand why, but she felt the charged atmosphere gathering steam around the older girl and knew she'd somehow blundered onto unmarked dangerous ground.

"Around here, Squirt, it pays to mind your own business and let others mind theirs."

"Sure. I get it." Lucy plastered a smile on her face. "You aren't much bigger than me, though, Alex. Maybe 'squirt' is the wrong nickname after all."

Alex's eyes narrowed, and she shook her head once. "No, I don't think so. Look at you, you're a tiny tina."

Lucy couldn't argue that point. She was thirteen—no, she'd turned fourteen at some point in the box—and stood an inch shy of five feet tall. What made her seem even smaller was what her mother called a "fast metabolism." An ache swelled in her throat, and she pinched her eyes shut.

"No, no," said Alex. "Stay in the here and now."

"Right," she croaked past the lump of fire in her throat. "Here. Now." She was far too skinny, and she knew it. She weighed eighty-one pounds fully dressed, and there was nothing she could do to change that. Short, rail-thin, unable to gain weight—she was used to being teased. The kids back at school had called her names: shrimp, short-stack, featherweight, skeleton, things like that. For the most part, she let those comments wash off her back, but it somehow seemed worse coming from a girl who was barely a few inches taller than she was. At the same time, it felt more like a term of endearment than a malicious jab, though she couldn't say why.

She looked around the barn, finding it much like she imagined it would be. Her uncle ran one of the largest dairy farms in New York, and she knew pole barns were places where you put old equipment, old projects that no longer served a purpose. If she had to guess, she'd put the barn she stood in as unused for farming purposes for at least ten years. Old equipment, draped with canvas, supported what looked like pounds of dust and dirt, and the whole place smelled of old motor oil, diesel fuel, and raw wood.

Alex nodded at her once. "So far, so good, Little Luce. You've managed better than old Randall ever has." She thumped a wooden box with the edge of her fist. "He's too stupid to come out." She said the last bit in an over-loud, grating voice that sparked a stream of cursing from the wooden cell.

The older girl gave Lucy a quick grin, then turned and walked over to a bench on which sat several scientific-looking gadgets and a couple of stereo sets. She flicked a few switches on one of the boxes, then pressed a red button, and the boy in the wooden cell she'd thumped screamed. Alex held the button, her grin spreading wider. "You want a turn?"

"To...to press the button?"

"Yes. To shock the ever-loving crap out of Randall. He's the idiot who screams and carries on all the time. You probably heard him on a daily basis." She glanced down at the rectangular piece of equipment and released the button. She tweaked the settings a little, then waved Lucy over. "Take your revenge, Squirt."

"Just press the button?"

"Yeah, I set it up for you."

"I'd like to learn to do that."

Again, Alex's eyes narrowed a skosh. "Why?"

"To help."

"To help me? Or to help Father?"

"Whoever," said Lucy with a shrug. "I just want to do my part."

"Running ECT sessions is *my* part, not yours." She glanced down at the machine and put her finger on a big switch. "If you don't want to take revenge, then we—"

"No. I do." She moved to Alex's side and put her finger on the big red button. "Just press and hold?"

Alex nodded, her face a curious blank, and withdrew her own hand from the switch.

"How long should I hold it?"

"Until you're satisfied."

Lucy gave a one-armed shrug and depressed the button. Behind them, the guy in the box started to thrash and scream, and the sounds of his agony were much more pronounced than they had been before. She glanced at Alex and lifted an eyebrow but didn't release the button.

Alex smiled and jerked her chin toward the big dial in the center of the box. "I turned up the voltage a little bit."

"Is it doing..." Lucy shook her head.

"No, I told you. Ask your questions."

"I was going to ask if it was hurting him, but that much is obvious, and that's not really what I wanted to know. Is this level of current *damaging* him?"

Alex shrugged. "If he doesn't move off the electrodes— those metal discs in the floor of the crates—he might take a burn or too."

"And nothing else?"

"Why? Do you want to cause lasting damage?" Her hand dropped the hilt of a knife hanging from her waist.

Lucy drew a deep breath. "I don't know. On the one hand, this guy is an asshole. He's constantly running his mouth when no one is out here. He screams, he shouts. It's impossible to sleep when he's all wound up."

"Yes."

"And he's always trying to get everyone to break the rules. To rebel, he says."

"Yes. Not very smart, is he?"

Lucy shook her head. Her finger was turning white with the pressure she applied to the button, and behind her, Randall suddenly went silent. Even the thrashing, swimming noises stopped. Lucy pursed her brows at Alex.

"Don't worry. He's playing possum is all." Alex tweaked the big dial in the center of the controls, and the acid-green sine wave drawing itself on the device's monitor got bigger. Randall screamed for all he was worth. "See?" The older girl smiled at Lucy. "I think you might have a talent for torture."

Lucy smiled back, though she couldn't decide if the older girl was kidding or not. She glanced at her finger, now blanched of all blood. She thought she might be feeling heat through the red plastic.

The man-sized door opened, letting in a fresh wash of blinding sunlight and the smell of spring in Western New York—of mud and pollen and lilacs and sunshine. Three boys tromped through the door, all tall, two of them thick with muscle—and they looked like they could be brothers, which Lucy thought impossible given their situation—and one thick with soft fat. They came in laughing at something—or someone—and the muscular two stifled their laughter when they saw Alex, but the fat guy kept right on.

Lucy watched Alex's face go stony, then light up with irritation. "Jonathon?" she said in a soft voice that evoked the gallows or the firing line.

The fat boy didn't react. In fact, he seemed to laugh louder and swat at one of the muscular twins with the back of his hand. "That's a good one, Mack."

"Jonathon?" Alex repeated with something akin to white-hot iron in her voice.

Mack turned on the fat kid—Jonathon, Lucy guessed—and frowned like a man watching a train come off the rails, but the other boy seemed oblivious to the atmosphere. "Straighten up, Jon," he said.

"Why? Your girlfriend doesn't hold *my* reins, even if you let her ride you hard and put you away wet."

A muscle in Alex's jaw twitched, and her lips paled from the pressure with which she squeezed them together. "*Jonathon?*" She hissed the name like a viper ready to strike.

"What, Alex?" Jon's voice was laced with contempt. "What the hell do you want?"

Alex stepped forward, and it was as if everyone else had disappeared from her awareness. Her hand grasped the hilt of her knife hard enough that her knuckles went white. "Watch what you say to me."

"Or what?"

"Let's find out. Go on. Be brave."

Mack lay a restraining hand on Jonathon's arm. "Alex is in charge until Father says different, Jon. You know that."

"Father's not here, is he?" said Jon, whirling to face Mack. "Why the hell do we let this little trollop lord everything over us?"

"Because," said Mack in a matter-of-fact tone, "that's how Father wants it. Do you want to explain all this to him when he gets back?"

"Why not?" asked Jonathon, his bravado ringing false.

"Because he'll kill you," said Lucy.

"Alex is a *girl*, you dink!" snapped Jonathon.

Lucy shook her head, bewildered. She glanced down at her finger, still on the button, and released it. "I meant *Father* will kill you if you break his rules."

"Nah, just look at that idiot, Randall. He ain't dead, and he's done a lot more than put this cross-dressing tomboy in her place."

In a flash, Mack grabbed the fat boy by the shoulders, threw his hip, and pitched the kid over onto his back, then dropped onto his rotund stomach with one knee. "You really are stupid, you know that, Jon?"

Alex leaped across the intervening space, her knife a silver blur as she jerked it from its scabbard and pointed it at Jon's face. "I should cut you." Her voice was icy and calm, the voice of a killer. "Maybe I should cut out your *tongue*." Her gaze traversed the boy's torso. "Or something else so you can never breed and sully the world with your offspring."

Fear tickled Lucy's belly. "I'm sure Jonathon is sorry."

Alex whipped her head around and stared daggers at her. "Is that so?"

"Is-isn't it, Jonathon?"

The fat boy didn't answer, but his gaze flicked to Lucy, and he sneered. Mack reached out, almost casually, and grasped Jon's chin between his thumb and index finger, twisting the boy's head back to meet his gaze. "I think Lucy had better be right. Don't you, Jon?"

The third boy—the other long, tall, and muscular specimen—had backed away as Alex approached and then circled the stack of boxes to come stand near Lucy. She felt his presence like a gravitational mass and was hard-pressed to keep her eyes on Alex. "I didn't mean anything, Alex. I just don't want my first afternoon out of the box to get all messed up."

"Squirt, not every fucking thing in this world is about you."

"Squirt, ha!" laughed Jonathon. "That's a good name for both of you snail trails. Squirt One and Squirt Two."

Alex dropped to one knee, her knife flashing like lightning as it descended to rest across Jon's throat. She hissed, and her lips pulled back from her teeth. Mack lifted a hand toward her knife-hand but stopped short when she flashed a glare at him, then returned to Jon's face. "How about I put my dick in your mouth to prove to you that I'm a boy?"

"I'd pay to see that," said the big guy behind Lucy.

Alex's head whipped around. "Maybe you should be next, Carl. What the hell has gotten into everyone today?"

"Testosterone," muttered Mack.

"Listen, *Alex*," said Jonathon, and Mack dropped his head at the boy's acidic tone. "You show me you have a dick, and I'll apologize. More, I'll be your slave for six months. An anything-goes slave." He didn't seem bothered by the razor-sharp blade pressing against his Adam's apple. "But you can't do that, and we both know why."

"Yeah?" sneered Alex. "And why is that?"

"Because you're a girl, you dumb twat. Don't you look at yourself when you shower?" He pressed himself up, pressing her knife into his flesh, but Mack shoved him back down.

"Are you really this stupid?" Mack asked.

Alex rocked back on her heels and chuckled. "What I do in the shower is none of your business, Jonny." She drew the blade across the boy's throat but lightly. Even so, Jonathon hissed with the pain of the cut she left him with. "Should I cut deeper?" She extended the knife again, this time resting against Jon's pasty flesh a quarter-inch above the angry red line bisecting his throat.

Mack shook his head but didn't move to stop Alex.

"You have a problem, Mack?"

"Not with you, Alex. With this fat tub of shit? Yeah. I hate stupidity. I hate misogyny."

"Oh, big word," said the kid on the floor. "Does that make you feel smart?"

"You don't know when to quit," said Lucy. "Why don't you just shut up before Alex carves you like a turkey?"

His gaze snapped to Lucy's face, his eyes hard with furious hate, his mouth a grim line. "Shut up, twerp. You need to learn your place."

"That's rich, coming from you," said Alex. "Maybe I'll take your tongue and hobble you. You could be everyone's anything-goes slave for the rest of your miserable life."

"Try it, you—"

With a savage grunt, Mack lifted his fist and smashed it down into Jonathon's face. He shouldered Alex aside, shifting his bulk across Jon's torso, and began to rain down fists that struck with the sound and fury of a hammer on hot steel.

"Whoa, whoa, whoa," said Lucy. She hadn't thought about speaking, the words were just there, floating around the ether without so much as asking her permission to pass her lips. A thick, heavy hand fell onto her shoulder, and she glanced back to see Carl shaking his head.

"Shut up, Squirt," snapped Alex. She sheathed the knife but then sent a hard kick into Jon's side.

"Come on," Carl whispered in Lucy's ear. He pulled gently on her shoulder, and she let him pull her back between the boxes, though her gaze never left Jonathon and the beating he was receiving. "Come on," he repeated when they'd cleared the double stack of wooden boxes.

She turned away from Jonathon and resisted the urge to plug her ears. She gazed up at Carl, whose gaze was on the scene across the room. *He's cute in a rough sort of way*, she thought.

His gaze dropped to her face, and a quirky smile settled on his features as if he could read her mind. He lifted a finger to his lips and jerked his head toward the man-sized door next to the wide barn door.

She followed him willingly, and they emerged into the bright afternoon sun. "What's—"

He snapped his finger up to his lips again and pointed across the dooryard to a windbreak of trees. "Over there." He led her to the spot, then sank to the base of one of the trees with a shaky breath. "I hate it when things go like that."

"Do they..."

"What? Do things go like that often? Not so much as you might think. Every once in a while, someone acts out, and either Father or Alex slaps them back into their place. Jonathon will spend some time in his box, and that will be the end of it unless he refuses to learn from his mistakes."

Lucy stood over Carl, fussing at the broken fingernails of one hand with the other. She darted a glance back toward the barn.

"Don't worry. Mack and Alex will take care of everything. When Father returns, he'll hear their side of it and decide Jon's punishment. I have a feeling there will be a lot of physical exercise in fat-boy's future."

"Is Alex in charge like Mack said?"

"You better believe it."

"How did she earn his trust?"

Carl held up his index finger. "Hold on. Sit down, will you? You're giving me a crick in my neck."

She flashed a smile at him and sank to her hunkers. "Good enough?"

Carl shrugged but smiled. It was a nice smile in her opinion. "What you have to understand is that Father is like Anubis. Do you know who that is?"

"Sure, the Egyptian god of the dead. We had a unit on Egyptian mythology in school."

An ugly expression flitted across the boy's face. "It's *not* mythology. It's a religion, and one that makes a hell of a lot more sense than the anemic bullshit we have these days."

She shrugged and looked at him sidelong. "I didn't mean anything by it. That's just what my teachers said. Mythology, I mean."

"Yeah, well, we live in a better world now that Father's freed us from all that bullshit. Use your bean and tell me *why* I say Father is like Anubis."

She cocked her head to the side, thinking. "Anubis weighed people's souls against a feather, right?"

"Yeah, and if your soul was heavier than a feather, he sent you to their version of hell."

"Thoth made those kinds of decisions; Anubis just did the weighing bit."

Carl's eyes narrowed. "Is that right?"

She smiled and held out her hand. "I'm not trying to make you mad, Carl. I loved the unit on Egyptian gods. I learned a lot, and I still remember it."

He lifted his chin but said nothing for a moment. "Your teacher did you a disservice." His voice had lost its angry edge but hadn't regained the warmth he'd shown her before she started flashing her knowledge around.

"Oh?"

"That's right. Thoth wasn't given credit for deciding eternal fates until the New Kingdom, and even then, scholars think Anubis and Thoth were really the same god, or at least closely related."

"The New Kingdom? What's that?"

"Just an era in Egyptian history. It came after Egypt was reunited post-Hyksos around 1500 BC. But never mind that. Anubis is a true son of Ra and was always the god of the dead. Thoth was the moon-god, about as opposite to Ra as you can get. Later, he became the god of the mind. Thoth was something that dribbled from Ra's lips. He's hardly worth mentioning."

Lucy shrugged. "Okay."

"Then tell me why Father is like Anubis."

She shrugged. "He found us, examined our lives, and weighed us against a feather. Those he found wanting, he sent on to hell—the real hell. Those he found worthy, he brought here."

"Very good, but you missed a major point."

"What's that?" she asked with a coy smile.

"Father weighs us against a feather every single day. He isn't above cutting down the chaff."

"Like Randall?" She tilted her head to the side and grinned at him.

"Don't do that," he grumbled.

"Do what?"

"Act like Alex. He won't like it for long."

She arched an eyebrow. "He?"

"You heard me. If you're smart, you'll force your mind to think that way, too. Alex is a guy at his core. Maybe he wasn't always, but Father transformed him."

"Okay."

"I'm serious, Lucy. Don't mess with Alex. It's like playing Russian Roulette with a fully-loaded pistol. He's Father's second-in-command, and he can do whatever he thinks is necessary so long as he's moving us along the path Father has laid out for us." He pumped his shoulders up and down. "Plus, Alex is as crazy as a shithouse rat. Whatever Father did to make him male loosened some screws. Anger issues centered around people thinking he's a girl."

"Okay," said Lucy. "Thanks for telling me."

"Yeah. And listen, Alex *earned* that knife. Know how?"

She shook her head.

"She killed someone at Father's request. She'll do it again, too, at the drop of a hat, so stay off her bad side."

"Didn't anyone tell Jonathon all this?"

"Sure," said Carl, with another shrug, "he's just stupid. And that's another thing: Don't let Father see you acting stupid. Or weak. Or anything but *exactly* as he wants you to act. He'll kill you without a second thought. Or he'll give you to Alex."

Lucy glanced over her shoulder at the barn and shivered. "Thanks for the warnings."

"Any time. Father hates to be disappointed."

"Does he...feel things?"

"Of course. Doesn't everyone?"

She glanced at Carl, studying his face, tracing the ridge of his muscles under his shirt. Before she'd come to the farm, she'd been a shy freshman—a girl who'd never even been kissed—but something fluttered in her belly when she looked at Carl, at his rugged good looks, his dark hair, his muscles.

"What?" he asked.

She shook her head and rose out of her squat. She stepped closer to him, moving to his side, then turned and faced the barn. She sank to the ground next to him, glancing at him from the corner of her eye, then shifted herself closer and closer still, until their hips touched. "Thank you, Carl," she murmured, then reached for his hand.

CHAPTER 4

DUTY CALLS

Hanable's Valley, NY

MEREDETH STRETCHED HER arms above her head and groaned. Her body finally felt human again—no extra parts, no bags dangling from her belly filled with the products of digestion, no lightheadedness when she did too much. It was a heady feeling, to feel normal, and it caused a tidal wave of abstract pleasure to course through her. Kevin and she had been making up for time lost—lots of hiking in the beautiful Western New York countryside, trips to the Finger Lakes, and the plethora of state parks that covered the state. Her muscles felt happy—well-used instead of abused. And the great outdoors were not the only place they'd decided to make up for missing moments.

The sheets felt cool against her bare back, and Kevin's contented sigh was an aria of celebration to her ears. He had a nice bed, she had to give him that. It was night and day better than the superstore crap she'd shelled out for back in Virginia. She made a mental note to correct that issue.

She had to head back in the morning—on a 6:03 am flight from Buffalo to Dulles—and that meant she needed sleep or she'd pay with a tinge of headache. "A girl could get to like being put to bed like that."

"Yeah, a guy could get to like it, too," Kevin murmured, his voice already slightly slurry with oncoming sleep.

"You sure you don't want me to get a car or something? It's after midnight and—"

"No, I'll take you, FBI. It'll give me a few more opportunities to look at you."

"Look, touch, whatever you want, Chief." She chuckled. "But fair warning: touching won't lead to sleep, and I think we might need some after this weekend."

"It was glorious, wasn't it?"

She nodded, rubbing her cheek against a swatch of Kevin's high-stitch Egyptian cotton sheets. "Everything here is."

"It's too bad we can't convince the government that Quantico should move to Hanable's Valley."

"The Bureau would ruin this town, Kev."

"Maybe so, Mere, but we could spend every night together."

She arched an eyebrow but kept her lips shut. It wasn't the first such comment Kevin had made, and though she agreed with her whole heart, she had no idea how to respond. It was an intractable problem: after all she'd done—all she'd sacrificed—for the Bureau, she couldn't just walk away from it.

Kevin's breathing deepened toward the easy pace of sleep, and she let her own eyelids sink, curling to her side and stretching her arm across Kev's chest. She'd almost sunk into unconsciousness when her Bureau phone played McCutchins' ringtone.

With a soft groan, she silenced the ringer and tried to get out of bed with the minimum of jostle, hoping to allow Kevin to keep sleeping. She pulled on her baggy T-shirt and padded across the room, glancing back at the bed every few minutes like a girl sneaking out of the house for the first time.

She thought she'd made it, too, until, as she was pulling the door closed behind her, Kevin said, "Tell McCutchins I hate his ringtone."

"Sorry," she whispered.

"Duty calls. I knew what I was signing up for."

"It still sucks, and I'm still sorry."

"Take your call, FBI. Everything's fine."

She nodded once, then pulled the door to and walked down the hall to the living room. She accepted the call. "What's up, Jim?" she said by way of a greeting.

"Sorry about the hour."

"It's not the latest you've called, Jim, nor the earliest. What's shaking?"

"Uh... This is..."

It wasn't like him to hesitate so, and Meredeth frowned, bunching her eyebrows. "Bobby?"

"What? No, no. Nothing like that. At least as far as I know."

"Then?"

"It's... Meredeth, this is going to be an official thing, I promise you. I'll get that done, but right now, it's personal."

"Okay."

"Jenna just called... My sister? You met her a few years back at Christmas?"

"Sure," said Meredeth, though she didn't know if her memory was providing the right details or not. "From out West."

"That's right. Her son—my namesake—has gone..."

"Kidnapped?"

"He's seventeen going on forty-seven."

"Still?"

"I'm filtered through Jenna's emotion—"

"And your own."

"—so I don't know how much is...is..."

"Just tell me the details, Jim."

"He's had his troubles recently. Adolescent stuff with his father."

"You wouldn't be calling me after midnight for that, Jim."

"No. No, I wouldn't. He's taken it too far. Drugs. Authority issues in and out of school. But we've been working with him. Trying to get him back on the straight and narrow."

"And now he's in serious trouble?"

"Maybe. No one's heard from him in a week."

"Okay," said Meredeth. "No one, or not his parents?"

"Hard to say. He's distanced himself from his older friends. Runs with a new pack of lowlifes."

"Jim..." Meredeth pursed her lips. "Please don't take this the wrong way, but I'm not understanding why you'd call me?"

"It's my gut, Meredeth."

"Your gut?"

"Right. Jamie's in serious trouble. I can *feel* it."

"What do you need me to do?"

"Here's my plan: I want you and Bobby out there in Ukiah. I'll fight for a task force if I can get it, and if so, you'll be in charge."

"And if not?"

"I still need you working the case, Meredeth."

"Of course, Jim. Anything I can do, but my hands will be a little bit tied if the locals don't want to play along, right?"

"Right, but let me worry that knot."

"Are you sure he's not off on a bender?"

"That's what my brain says, but my gut? My *heart*?" A mournful sigh gusted across the line.

"I'm scheduled in Quantico tomorrow. My flight leaves here at six."

"No, fly straight in to Sacramento. When we hang up, I'll call Bobby—"

"Let me handle those details, Jim. We'll get out there soonest and see what we can find out while you work your end in the morning."

"Thank you, Meredeth," said Jim in a voice barely over that of a whisper.

"Not another word, Jim. Of course, Bobby and I are willing to help. And try not to stay up all night worrying and fretting. We're on it, and as soon as we can get out there and get our boots on the ground, we'll start turning over stones. We'll figure this out."

The line fell silent a moment, then Jim sighed. "Let's pray you're right."

"I am, Jim. I always am. Just ask Bobby."

McCutchins issued a weak chuckle.

"Now, let me get off the line and start making this happen. Text me anything new."

"Will do."

"Goodnight, Jim."

"Talk tomorrow."

"Right." Meredeth hung up the phone, then stood there, staring at nothing for a few minutes, her brain awhirl. Both Jim and she knew the statistics, for all their brave talk.

Then again, there were lies, there were damn lies, and then there were statistics.

She shrugged one shoulder and quick-dialed Bobby's cell without much more than a glance at the phone. He picked up on the second ring.

"Bobby's Pizzeria," he twanged.

"We're traveling tomorrow."

"Good evening to you, too, Agent Connelly. Why, my weekend has been fabulous. How was yours?"

"Yaddy. I'm up at Kevin's so you know everything is perfect. Listen—"

"And how is Chief Saunders?"

"Shut up, Bobby. It's serious time." She could almost hear him sliding up out of a slouch. Almost as if he needed to be closer to full attention to answer her tone.

"What's up? That slasher in Dallas?"

"No. This hits closer to home."

"I'm not sure what that means."

"Jim McCutchins just called. His nephew and namesake has gone missing."

"How old?" Bobby asked, all hint of irreverence gone.

"Seventeen, I think. Jim's..."

"*Worried*, I'll bet."

"And more. He knows too much about these things to feel warm and fuzzy."

"How long?"

"About a week."

Bobby puffed out a long breath. "That ain't good, Mere."

"No. No, it isn't, and that's not the worst of it."

"Tell me."

"I will, but first let me tell you what happens tomorrow. You and I are headed to Sacramento at best possible speed. I'll go from Buffalo. I'll have Melanie book rooms and things, but we're doing our own flights tonight. I want you there as early as possible. I'm going to try to switch my first-thing flight to Dulles to SMF instead."

"Check."

"Once there, we'll head over to the local cop shop and get whatever they are willing to share. Then—"

"Do they know we're coming?"

"They will by then. Jim's going to pull for a task force or something."

"Are there other kids missing?"

Meredeth frowned and shook her head. "No idea, yet, Bobby.

"Have there been any kids...*found*?"

"No bodies yet," she said and knocked on the mantle.

"Sounds like a task force will be a tall order."

"Maybe. Maybe not. It's Jim, after all."

"But one missing kid...even if he is the namesake of one of the SACs of the BAU."

"And he's got a history of this." Meredeth suppressed a sigh. "This feels different, though. More..."

"Serious?"

"Yeah. No contact with anyone in his family. Cell seems dead or off, no texts, nothing."

"What was the last thing he did?"

"He snuck out and went to a party. With his *new* friends."

"His stoner friends?"

"Guess so."

"It's a place to start, then."

"Yep. We'll get a list of them from Jim's sister—if she has it—or at least a list of his old friends, who will know the new ones."

"Right."

"Get there as early as you can, Bobby." They said their goodbyes, and Meredeth swapped the phone to her other ear as she listened for the airline's customer service robot to pick up and waste her time until she could get a human to make the changes.

CHAPTER 5

CHAOS THEORY

Ukiah, CA

KAHIN NARROWED HIS eyes at the two newcomers. One of them seemed okay—the kind of person he expected might turn up at his door. He was dressed like a throwback to an 80s punk rock band: skin-tight Lycra pants with long white and red stripes running from ankle to waist, a baggy T-shirt that had been butchered to remove the sleeves, revealing sickly white skin through long, gaping windows, hand-done tattoos, a shaved head (including his eyebrows), a pierced nostril and lip, and one pierced earring—a long, fluttery blue feather that hung from a thin gold chain from a faux diamond stud. His feet were clad in military-surplus jumpboots. A studded belt hung loosely around his waist—not attached to the pants as they had no belt loops—as an accessory.

A poser, in other words, but one who would fit in soon enough.

His friend, on the other hand, didn't belong there, and Kahin had half a mind to kick him to the curb. He wore a pair of dark blue jeans, Nike running shoes—with *socks*—and a collared knit golf shirt. His hair was short off the collar and neatly combed. The guy's gaze darted from left to right, coming to rest on the other occupants of the room, but never long enough for anyone to return his gaze. His hands flitted and fluttered from his jeans' pockets to his waistband to each other, then back again. He bounced a little, his feet seemingly in constant shuffle toward the door, only pulled back by the kid's unwillingness to leave his buddy.

A soft growl burbled in the back of Kahin's throat. The kid was as wrong for his crew as one could get and evidently too stupid to realize it. "Yo!" Kahin called over the cacophony of laughter, shrill jokes, and loud death metal, but the new kid didn't even twitch. The poser turned toward his freaked-out friend, however, and made a comment, which soured the other kid's expression.

The poser's gaze turned and settled on them where he sat with a naked Anya on his lap, and the kid started over in a rolling strut which brought a half-smile to Kahin's lips. Halfway over, the guy jerked his chin upward, staring into his host's gaze with the kind of determination that said all he really wanted to do was ogle Anya. "I'm Rad," the kid said as soon as he was close enough to be heard.

"Kahin." He didn't stir, didn't lift a lame hand to shake. "Welcome to my place."

Rad's gaze flicked to Anya, and he nodded.

"And this is my fiancée, Anya."

"Meetcha," Rad's lips said, though neither Kahin nor Anya could hear him.

"Your friend looks like he's having a rough time," said Anya, her gaze crawling over the kid.

"I told him not to come, but..."

"Loyalty," said Kahin with a nod.

"Sure, but this isn't his scene. He's too uptight about...about..."

"*Everything*," laughed Anya, and Rad smiled his agreement.

"Last of your old friends willing to debase himself?" Kahin's gaze lingered on the polo-shirted kid, who seemed finally aware of his consideration.

"Yeah. My oldest friend." Rad chopped his hand through the air. "But he doesn't get it. Not anymore. He doesn't get *me*."

"That's okay," said Alshaytan. "Plenty of new friends to meet."

"Thanks for letting me crash your party."

With a chuckle, Kahin waved it away. "This ain't no party. We're just hanging out."

"It's always like this," said Anya. "Unless there *is* a party...then this place really jumps."

Rad looked around—a little nervously unless Kahin missed his guess.

"Nothing to worry about, Rad. We're all just people, same as you."

Rad forced a chuckle. "Sure. I'm not worried."

"You might fit in here, Rad, so let me set you on the right path, okay?"

Forcing his gaze back to Kahin's, the kid nodded.

"First, everyone here has my permission to be here. If that changes, that person will no longer be here. Get it?"

Rad nodded.

"Second, anything goes. Want to get high? Sure, go for it. Don't want to share? Don't. Want to get laid"—he slapped Anya's thigh—"then find someone horny." Kahin's smile went a little cold. "Or talk someone around. Want to pound a fifth? Do it, but you'll probably need to bring your own booze for that. There's hardly ever anything around. Hungry? Eat. Tired? Sleep. Want to scream? Scream. Want to fight? Fight."

As Kahin went on, Rad's eyes flicked around at the other folks sitting around, some watching, some laughing, some ignoring them altogether.

"So, no rules?"

Kahin switched his gaze from Rad to the boy who'd accompanied him. "Weren't you listening? I've just told you the rules."

"But you basically said do whatever we want."

"Now you're catching on, honey," said Anya in a singsong. She uncrossed her legs and spread them a little. "Like what you see?"

The boy blushed to the roots of his hair and half-turned away, eliciting a monstrous guffaw from Kahin, while Rad grimaced.

"Don't be such a dumbass, Mick."

Mick turned an affronted gaze on his friend. "Let's go, Ray. I don't like it here."

"Then go," said Rad. "Don't let me hold you up."

Spreading his dirty hands, his nails seeming quite black in the relative gloom, Kahin smiled wide. "No reason to be here if you don't want to be, Mick. It's not for everyone, and there's no shame in that."

"But I..." Mick glanced at Rad and jerked his chin toward the door. "Can I talk to you?"

"Don't be rude. You can talk to me right here. I *like* it here, and I'm going to stay awhile. Mr. Alshaytan is nice—"

"Oh, no!" said Kahin with a laugh. "None of that. Name's Kahin, plain and simple."

Rad nodded to show he'd heard. "*Kahin* is nice enough to let us hang, to do what we want without hiding it."

"But I..."

"*But I, but I,*" mocked Rad. He snaked his hand inside his waistband and withdrew a joint wrapped in cellophane. He quirked an eyebrow at Kahin and Anya. "Want a hit? It's got a little something extra."

Kahin flicked his gaze from Mick to Rad and back, then arched an eyebrow. "I love surprises. Don't you, Mick?"

"I don't do that junk."

"More for us. I think there might be a beer in the fridge. If not, check the pantry. There might be some warm stuff."

"I don't drink, either," mumbled Mick. He cast around a moment, then went and sank onto a stack of cushions that had once lined a couch—but now had more in common with a litter box from the looks of them.

"Great, now he's going to sulk."

"Let him." Anya cast a glance at the boy, then shrugged. "He's no loss."

Rad grimaced but said nothing.

"He's got an attitude," said Kahin. "I'm not sure I like it. Maybe he should go."

Rad's eyes widened. "No, please, Kahin. If you toss him out, I'll have to go with him, and I'd really like to stay." He shot a withering glance at his friend, who seemed oblivious. "He'll just sit over there and stew until he figures out it's not going to work. Then he'll come around and be more...more..."

"Personable?"

"Sure," said Rad with some hesitation.

Kahin lifted a shoulder and flicked the tails of the black turban he had wound around his head. "I've ignored worse." He cast a momentarily suspicious eye on Rad. "But..."

"Yeah?"

"You should think about your loyalties, Rad. Who is holding you back? Who is letting you get closer to your true self?"

"Oh, I know. It's just... We've known each other since we were kids. We grew up two houses down."

"Sure, sure," said Kahin, almost dismissively. "But I'll tell you this, Rad: you're responsible for Mick tonight. Is that fair?"

"I... Um, I don't know what you mean by that."

"What I mean is, if it becomes necessary to, uh, ask your friend to leave, I expect *you* will be the one doing the asking."

"Oh, sure! Absolutely." He twisted the fingers in his left hand with his right. "But it won't come to that. Mick's a big baby...a showboat that's all. He's always been this way. Has to make a production out of it. To try to get his way, you know?"

Again, Kahin shrugged and flicked the tails of his turban. With a sly glance at Anya, he said, "You know, you could avoid any...unpleasantness by telling him to go now."

Rad grimaced and shook his head. "That won't... I mean, that will only piss him off. It'll make it harder. If we let him get bored..."

"I'm just offering advice, Rad. I've been where you're at, and sometimes it's best to cut the string." He glanced at Mick, who sat with his arms folded across his chest, his head bent forward, an expression of revulsion on his mug. "And to tell you the truth, he's starting to offend me a little."

Anya snaked her small hand around Kahin's wrist and tapped her index finger over his arteries. "It will be okay, Kahin," she said.

"Probably," Kahin agreed. When he turned to Rad again, his eyes had seemed to switch from brown to black, and they were as hard as diamonds. "The last guy that offended me is still here. He'll never leave. You get me, Rad? *Never.*"

Rad pulled his chin back, bunched his brows, and glanced at Anya. "What do you mean?"

"It's amazing what a motivated man can do with kitty litter and bleach," said Kahin in an airy tone. "Excuse me a minute." He stood and stretched, his gaze straying to Mick once more, then he turned and trod into the darker, back part of the home.

Rad's wide-eyed gaze fell on Anya, but she only smiled like the Cheshire Cat.

CHAPTER 6

BOOTS ON THE GROUND

Sacramento, CA

MEREDETH STEPPED OFF the gangway in the Sacramento International Airport, a dull throb hammering away behind her eyes. The flight hadn't been a great one despite having enough upgrade points to sit up front with the posh people. There had been weather and frequent altitude changes, which hadn't sat well with her already grumpy innards.

At least she hadn't had to fill the east-to-west coast hours with crime scene photos and ME reports. She'd been able to lean her head back, close her eyes, and relax a little without anyone bothering her. She also hadn't had Bobby's company, and she attributed the relatively minor-impact headache to that fact. The idea brought a wry grin to her face. The only problem with Bobby not being around to suffer her good-natured abuse was that Bobby wasn't around to groan at the jokes.

She stepped out of the flow of foot traffic and pulled out her phone, disabling airplane mode, then waiting with what looked like patience for the device to reconnect to the world and get all the things she missed while flying ready for her. It was going to be a beautiful day if she could believe the scene outside the tall windows—there were no clouds in the sky at all, nothing but a brilliant azure blanket of positivity.

She could almost understand the stereotypes given the beatific scene. Who wanted to be in a rush when Old Ma Nature was kicking back and taking a sun day? Even *she*, Meredeth Lynne Connelly, felt sort of relaxed, despite herself, despite the nature of the trip, despite Jim McCutchins' turmoil.

Her phone rumbled and jittered in her palm, and she tore her eyes away from the cerulean sky. She had three emails from McCutchins waiting for her attention. The first was nothing more than her temporary assignment of duties in the Sacramento area—and to the Bureau's Field Police Training Program. Uh, *oh*, she thought. *Trouble with the task force*. The next email told her not to worry, that the task force was still likely, just that the fastest way in was the FPTP.

Hell, she thought, *it was good enough for Douglas and Richter. We'll make it work*. Even so, she dreaded the idea of days wasted giving seminars to cops who would rather be out on the street working their cases. Plus, every moment she had to spend prepping and giving the lecture was time she couldn't spend looking for Jim's nephew. Added to that was the very real possibility that they'd be formally asked to assist in *another* case.

The third email was a no-nonsense, factual account of everything Jim had told her the previous night. It included a list of Jamie's friends, the address of his high school, and Jenna's contact information. Meredeth nodded to herself and imported the woman's contact into her phone. It ended with a promise of more information as soon as Jim could amass it.

There was also a text from Bobby giving his flight information—he'd be touching down in twenty minutes' time. She replied, telling Van Zandt to meet her at the rental car counters, then shot a quick text to Kevin letting him know she'd arrived safely. She stood there a moment, waiting for Kevin's snappy comeback, but though the text read "delivered," it never updated to "read," which struck her as strange after so many months of almost instant replies from the man.

She frowned at the phone a moment longer, then slid it into her purse, unsatisfied. She shouldered her carry-on and strode down the hall toward the baggage area and the car rental places. The earthy smell of good coffee danced on the air, but try as she might, she couldn't spot its source—she couldn't even spot a source of foul airport coffee, let alone something dark and rich and roasted to within an inch of its ever-loving life. Her left eye gave a little pulse of pique.

Walking past the baggage claim area, Meredeth fixed her most officious gaze on a young man behind the Hertz counter. She strode up to the counter, ignoring the little rat's maze of canvas ribbons someone had laid out.

The man frowned at her with a disapproving twitch of his lips. "Help you, ma'am?"

"I have a reservation. Meredeth Connelly, Federal Bureau of Investigation."

The clerk's eyebrows rose, but he dropped his gaze to the computer without a word. "Conelly?"

"Two Ns."

"And M-E-R-E-D-I-T-H?"

"Here's my card. It'll be easier." She handed over one of her business cards. "The reservation was made by Melanie Rockhart, probably early this morning."

He took the card without looking up, then leaned it against the monitor. "Sure." He tapped away for what felt like at least forty-five minutes before his gaze flicked to the card.

"Whoa. BAU? For real?" He looked up at her, his eyes dancing with excitement. "Like Mandy Patinkin in that show *Criminal Minds*?"

"For real," she said. "Though, to tell you the truth, my job bears about as much in common with that show as Stevie Nicks does with the New York Knicks."

"Who, now?" he asked, some of the excitement draining from his gaze.

"Never mind. You have my reservation?"

"Sure. One subcompact. Let me print the contract."

"Uh, that's not going to work."

"It's policy. I need a physical signature to—"

"I mean the car. We're on a government contract here. We should always have at least a midsized sedan, but an SUV would be best." He looked at her blankly a moment, and Meredeth imagined she could see gears grinding and black smoke puffing from his ears. "We use these vehicles for surveillance, for hauling gear and manpower. You understand?"

The clerk nodded once and dropped his gaze back to his computer screen, his lips pursed, and his brows bunched. "Let me just see..." He again clacked away at his keyboard for what felt like a very long time to Meredeth, then nodded. "Yes, okay."

"All straightened out then?" she asked, arching one eyebrow.

"Yes. Well, no. I don't have any SUVs or sedans available."

"Look, this is a government contract, right? You're required to honor our reservations."

"No, I understand," said the clerk with a tinge of irritation in his voice, "but none of that can make a car appear for your use. I can only rent you what I have available, and that's a Yaris."

"And I've already said that won't work. Get on the horn to whoever you need to and let's get this straightened out. We're here to work a case. We don't have time to mess around."

"We can call the CEO of the company. It won't make a difference."

"I doubt that," said Meredeth as she stepped away from the counter and dialed Melanie's extension.

"*Hello?*"

"Melanie? Meredeth. I'm here in Sacramento trying to pick up our rental car, and the bozo behind the counter is giving me some trouble."

"*Is that so?*"

"You bet."

"*What's he trying to saddle you with?*"

"Toyota Yaris."

"*Well, that's wholly inappropriate, not to mention not what I reserved for you.*"

"I thought as much."

"*Give me ten minutes to get this straightened out, Agent Connelly.*"

"I'm waiting on Van Zandt anyway. Just text me when I should go back to the counter."

"*Will do.*"

With a glance at the clerk, whose gaze rested on her, she turned and walked the length of the room toward the baggage claim for her flight. The belt wasn't moving yet, but she recognized faces from her trip out from Buffalo.

She strolled to within a yard of the tortuous conveyer belt, then stopped. Her phone vibrated in her hand—a text from Van Zandt saying he was on the ground and headed toward baggage claim. She nodded to herself, then glanced over her shoulder at the rental car counter.

The clerk stood straight, his arm cocked, phone pressed to his ear. His face had gone beat red, and his eyes blazed at her across the intervening space. He wasn't speaking—only listening—and Meredeth suspected the person reading him the riot act on the other end of the call wasn't Melanie but rather someone in the car company's hierarchy.

She turned away to hide the grin that wanted to bloom on her lips and caught Bobby walking toward her with a wide grin on his too-tan face. "Good flight?" she asked as he came close enough.

"It was commercial," he said, lifting one shoulder. "Coach, at that."

"Not enough miles to upgrade?"

Bobby shook his head. "I save those miles for when I have to travel with you. Your delicate sensibilities require business class a lot."

She grinned and rolled her eyes a little. Beside her, the baggage belt clanked and began to move. "My delicate sensibilities have arranged for a slight delay with the car."

"Oh?"

"They're trying to fob a Yaris off on us."

Bobby made a face as though he'd smelled a skunk. "That's not going to work."

"Melanie's on it."

Van Zandt glanced toward the rental car counters. "Oh. Mr. Red-face looks upset."

"I'm sure he is. He assured me calling the CEO of the company wouldn't help get us an appropriate car. I'm guessing Melanie called someone at corporate and that someone is currently explaining the man's mistakes."

"Serves him right for trying to pull one over on the F-B-I."

"Worse, still, he's a Criminal Minds groupie."

Bobby frowned and wrinkled the skin on his nose. "Ew." He turned away from the rental counters and watched bags slide down the polished stainless-steel chute and onto the conveyor. "Regular bag?"

"Do I have more than one?"

"Not that I've seen."

"There you go," she said with a grin.

"Still have the blue ribbon on the handle?"

"Of course."

"That's too bad."

Meredeth followed his gaze to her mangled suitcase. The zipper had burst, and some enterprising baggage handler had taped the whole thing shut, wrapping striping tape around and around and around the bag. "That's just awesome."

"I'll grab it. You go find the damage claim forms."

"Right." Her head gave a mighty throb accompanied by the flash of red and blue lights no one else could see. She looked for and found the claims office at the opposite end of the cavernous room, but the door was closed. Affixed to the door was a plastic sign that read: "Hours: Noon to 6 pm. If you need assistance, please call the switchboard." She sighed and flopped a hand at her side. "That's just great," she muttered.

Bobby joined her, her suitcase trundling behind him on squeaking wheels, weaving from side to side like a drunk duck without any input from him to do so. "Closed, huh?"

"Of course," she said with a sour twist to her lips. "Think I should call the switchboard?" She rolled her eyes heavenward.

"It might be faster to make a new suitcase from scratch."

"Too right." She turned and scanned the room, glancing at the monitors above every conveyor belt. "Which one's yours?"

"Eleven," he said, pointing with his chin.

"Might as well stand there as here, right?"

Bobby nodded, glanced at the rental car clerk, then turned and moved toward conveyor eleven. "You should check and make sure everything is in your bag."

"Time enough for that when we get to the hotel," she said. "Besides, I don't think I can get that open without cutting the tape."

CHAPTER 7

OUT IN THE COLD

David Branch's Farm, NY

LUCY STOOD BACK under the eaves of the machine shed, watching the three hulking figures work on the big semi-tractor Mack was so in love with. She wanted to be next to Carl, their arms brushing every now and then. She wanted to be *part of something* that mattered to Father, and she knew the truck mattered to Mack, and Mack mattered to Father. She wasn't sure Father even knew Carl was there as he hardly even looked at him.

The pig—Jonathon—was grunting away in the next bay of the building, working out with Father's meticulously cared-for weights and gym equipment. He was making a lot of noise: savage growls and loud grunts as he pushed the weights around. And to be fair, he appeared to be quite strong. Maybe not as strong as Mack or Carl, and definitely not as strong as Father, but even so, the bar seemed to bend as he pushed it away from his chest.

Butterflies danced in her guts as she contemplated a bold move, perhaps a foolhardy move. She could just walk over there and start helping. She was small, that much was obvious to anyone with eyes, but sometimes small hands were better for working on engines than big, thick, strong hands. Her mom's boyfriend had said as much, and even though the guy was a class-A jerk, she thought he knew what he was talking about, being a mechanic and all, and on the small side himself.

Go on, she told herself. *Father likes boldness.* But she stayed right where she was, frozen in place like the bashful little girl she still felt like deep down inside. *Come on, Luce. What would Alex do? He'd go right over there and start helping.*

Jon let out a snarl to rival the worst junkyard dog going, then slammed the weights back onto the rack, breathing loudly, his face suffused with blood. He never so much as glanced her way despite her open stare.

When she turned her attention back to the truck, Father was standing up straight, his gaze on Jonathon. "Treat my things with respect, Jonathon, or you may lose access to them."

"Sorry, Father," Jon called. "I guess I was pushing it a little, and my arms gave out there at the end."

"Hurting yourself isn't a sign of strength." Father turned his attention back to the truck. "It's better to be in control at all times."

"Yes, Father." Jon snapped his head around to meet Lucy's gaze, and there was something ugly in it. Something mean.

She turned her head away, half-turned her back on the fat boy, hunching her shoulders a little, and heard him chuckle. *I should just go over there and help. Either that or get the hell out of here before Jonathon decides he wants to play.* There was something about the kid that made her wary, something that said he was bad news, and that given half a chance, he'd drag her down to hell if he could. She glanced at the truck and saw Carl looking in her direction. She extended her hand and raised her eyebrows at him.

He gave her a subtle nod, then cleared his throat. "Father, I'm having trouble getting this bolt seated."

"All it takes is patience, Carl."

"Sure, I know, but Lucy's standing over there watching, and she has tiny hands. Maybe she could help us with the tight spaces?"

Father straightened and looked in her direction. His eyes seemed cold like chunks of obsidian, and his face was as empty as the void between the stars. "She won't want to get her hands dirty."

"I don't mind," she said. "I used to help my—"

"This is hard work. It takes strength. Lucy is too frail to be of use."

She closed her eyes as disappointment swept through her. *The man thinks I'm useless,* she thought with more than a little sadness. "I'll try my best."

"It isn't a matter of trying, Lucy," said Mack. "We know you'd try."

"This work requires a lot of physical strength," said Father. "Maybe someday you will be strong enough to contribute, but for now..." His voice trailed away.

She opened her eyes, expecting to find the man watching her for her reaction, but he'd already dismissed her from his mind and was turning some yard-long lumpy chunk of metal, examining it closely in the sunlight. She resisted the urge to heave a sigh and found Carl's gaze.

He gave her a tentative smile and a shrug, then mouthed the word, "Sorry."

She shook her head, then pushed away from the metal wall of the building. If he wouldn't let her help, she needed to be elsewhere, doing something that *would* impress Father. She had to walk past the bay in which Jonathon was working out, and she did it with her head held high, not sparing a second glance for the sweaty fat pig.

When she was as close as she would get to him, Jon lunged up from the bench and pounded a few steps in her direction. She cringed away but was proud she didn't call out.

Jonathon cackled and pointed at her. "So weak," he managed between guffaws.

Lucy felt the heat climbing up from her neck into her cheeks. She wanted to lash out, to curse at him, to hit him—or worse—but what was the use? He was as huge as an elephant, and she was as tiny as a flea by comparison. Everyone knew how battles between elephants and fleas went.

"Jonathon!" Father's whip-crack voice rolled across the distance between them like thunder, and everyone froze, even the fat pig.

Lucy dropped her gaze to her feet. It was bad enough that the man thought she was useless, but now he thought she was too weak to stand up to a thug like Jonathon without his help. She had to do something to change his opinion, but she had no idea what.

"I was just messing around, Father," said Jon in a contrite voice. "I didn't mean anything by it."

"Sometimes I think I kept the wrong brother," said Father in a toneless voice. "Sometimes you make me doubt my decision to save you."

"Don't say that," muttered Jonathon.

"What was that? Did you have something to say?" Again, his voice was toneless but somehow felt more deadly for its lack of emotion.

"No, sir."

"Take it on the arches, Jonathon. You're done with the weights for now."

"But I—"

"Yes?" asked Father, but his voice wasn't devoid of emotion. Instead, his voice contained a hint of acidity Lucy had never heard in it before.

"Sorry, sir."

"Get out of here, Jonathon, before you inspire me to do something you'll regret."

"Yes, sir. Sorry, sir." Jon's voice quavered a little on that last 'sir.' He plodded past Lucy, then broke into a jog down the hill toward the barn.

"That's a good idea!" shouted Father. "Get some miles in. Lose some of that belly."

She watched him run, a snide smile playing along her lips as his belly jiggled one way, his fat ass the other. After a moment, she followed in his footsteps, walking in a stately manner rather than running away like a scared little rabbit.

She wondered what Alex was up to.

CHAPTER 8
HOT FOR TEACHER
Ukiah, CA

IN THE END, the rental car clerk had managed to "find" a Jeep Cherokee, and they'd taken the keys and escaped from Sacramento as fast as Interstate 5 allowed. Bobby drove, one wrist cocked over the steering wheel at the twelve o'clock position, the other in his lap. He'd kept that pose for almost the entire two-and-a-half-hour trip up from Sacramento. At least the scenery was good—especially the portion of the trip they spent on CA-20 as it ran along the edge of Clear Lake.

They entered Ukiah from the north end, picking up US 101 where CA 20 ended. 101 followed a ridge, giving Meredeth a great view of the countryside surrounding the town. It was hill country, not unlike northern Pennsylvania or even the area around Hanable's Valley, New York. The colors were different, more browns than in the Northeast, and it was pretty in its own way she thought.

Bobby took the State Street exit, then continued south for a few blocks until the Jeep's GPS system told him to turn right on Empire. He pointed at the Golden Arches on the corner. "Hungry?"

"For McDonald's? Never."

Once they passed the McDonald's on the right and something called Honey Fluff on the left, they left the commercial buildings behind—with the exception of something called Discovery Inn, which boasted studios and kitchenettes and wasn't averse to long-term stays—and entered a residential district like that found anywhere in the country. Older homes, well-maintained for the most part, lots of cars and wave runners and boats parked in the street. Some of the houses were well kept, with nice landscaping and picket fences, while others had gone to seed, some even growing cars with their weeds. The neighborhood might have been on the lower end of middle class, but it looked nice enough to Meredeth—except for all the cars parked in the street. She hated stuff like that, although at least Empire was wide enough to accommodate on-street parking.

She kept her head on a swivel as Bobby cruised west on Empire, checking out the houses, marking the ones where people cared and the ones where people clearly did not. The farther west they went, the more people seemed to care, and the prettier the lots got, boasting the bright greens of healthy trees and shrubs. And there were fewer cars left on the street.

Empire came to an abrupt end at Despina Drive, across from a wide-open, brilliantly green field that turned out to be the Ukiah High School baseball diamond. Bobby turned left at the navigation system's prompting, then drove four blocks until he could turn west again and enter the Ukiah High School parking lot with its clean landscaping and brilliant red trees. He parked in a spot marked reserved for official vehicles only and killed the engine.

"Are you trying to get towed?" Meredeth asked.

"What? This is an official visit."

"But 'official vehicles' generally means marked or at least hanging government tags. This hunk of junk meets neither criterion."

Bobby slipped one of his business cards out of his pocket and flipped it onto the dash, face-up. "Now it's marked." He opened his door, got out, and stretched with a groan. "California is too big."

"Hey, I offered to split the driving." She got out and performed her own stretching.

"Sure, but that wouldn't make Ukiah closer to Sacramento, now, would it?"

"Has anyone told you how strange you are?"

"Do you count?"

"No, obviously not."

"Then, no. You are the only one who feels compelled to call me strange."

"I have a hard time reconciling that with how weird you are." She pointed at the squat building in front of them. "Want to bet that's administration?"

"Sucker's bet," he said and started toward the entrance. "Do they know we're coming?"

"According to Jim, yes."

"And you have the list of students we need to talk to?"

"Would I let you drive me here if I didn't?"

Bobby see-sawed his hand in the air.

"Remind me to give you scut work to do later. You're getting too big for your britches."

"Yeah, yeah." He opened the glass door and held it for her. "After you."

"Why, thank you. And they say chivalry is dead."

The building smelled like high schools everywhere—part musty old library, part gymnasium locker room, part air freshener factory. A woman in her early forties awaited them from behind the admissions counter. "Can I help you?"

Meredeth fished her ID case out of her bag, then showed her badge and ID to the woman. "I'm Meredeth Connelly with the FBI. This is my partner, Bobby Van Zandt."

The woman's eyes widened a little, but she kept it together and nodded. "What can I do to help the Bureau?"

"We have a list of students we need to speak to. None of them are in any trouble. We just need their help tracking down a missing student."

The woman's face turned grave. "Jamie Wenstrom?"

"That's right."

The woman—Mandy Finster, by her name tag—heaved a sigh. "Such a sad case. Is it official, then? He's been abducted?"

"I'm afraid we don't know that."

"But you're feds. Doesn't that mean it's either a kidnapping for ransom, or he's been spirited away across state lines?"

"Not necessarily," said Bobby.

"In this case, our boss is Jamie's uncle."

"Ah," said Mandy. "I see. Are you here in an official capacity?"

"Yes, we are."

Mandy nodded once. "Please understand that we have policies governing this kind of thing, and I can't just turn you loose to start interviewing our students."

"No, we understand that."

"Very good. Let me introduce you to Ionia McAdams. She's our assistant principal, and she'll be able to assist you further. Some of our students won't be available without parental permission or presence, but some of them will be able to speak with you in Ionia's presence."

"I see."

Mandy reached under the counter and a loud, buzzing click sounded. She jerked her chin toward the half-door at the end of the counter. "Come on back."

Meredeth nodded and led Bobby through the door. Mandy asked another woman to mind the admissions desk for a moment, then took them deeper into the office, leading them down a long corridor that boasted industrial gray carpet tiles and soft yellow walls. Every twenty feet or so, a grouping of three chairs sat to one side of the hall or the other, but they were all vacant.

Mandy approached a door toward the end of the hall and knocked on it, then opened it without waiting for a response. "Ionia, these people are from the FBI. They'd like to speak to some of our students. They work for Jamie Wenstrom's uncle and are investigating Jamie's disappearance.

The woman behind the wide wooden desk was big—not fat, but rather tall and muscular, as if she were a bodybuilder in her spare time. She stood easily and extended her hand to Meredeth. "Ionia McAdams."

"I'm Meredeth Connelly, and this is my partner, Bobby Van Zandt. Would you care to inspect our identification?"

"I'm sure Mandy did that." She cocked an eyebrow at Finster, who nodded. "Fine, fine. Have a seat." She retook her own seat and folded her hands on the desktop blotter. "You understand that there are certain legal issues we—"

"Yes. The kids we need to speak with are probably all minors and would need a parent or guardian with them during questioning—if they were suspects, which they are not."

"Even so," Ionia said, "the Mendocino School District bears a certain responsibility with regard to our students and their families. Some parents will have elected to allow me to serve in their stead as temporary guardians, but others will have stood on their rights and will require parental permission and presence."

"That's fine," said Meredeth.

"We're not here to jam anyone up," added Bobby. "We just want to find out what happened to Jamie."

"And I do, too," said the assistant principal. "Do you have a list of students? Mandy can get started pulling files while we chat a moment."

"Absolutely," said Mandy.

"Can I text it to you?" asked Meredeth.

"Sure."

Ionia wrote a telephone number on a Post-it Note and passed it across the wide expanse of oak separating them. "Here's Mandy's number."

"Thanks," said Meredeth. She passed the slip of dayglo yellow paper to Bobby.

"Jamie's been in some trouble these past couple of years. He's a much better student than his grades and behavioral record suggest." She twitched her wide shoulders up and down. "Problems with authority, if you want my opinion."

"So I understand," said Meredeth. "But you know how families can be. I'd like your assessment of Jamie's behavior."

Ionia released a sigh, then forced a smile to her lips. "It's sad, really. He has the brain power to get himself a world-class education, and had you asked my opinion two years ago, I'd have said he was destined for an Ivy League school. Harvard. Yale. Cornell. Somewhere like that."

"But?"

"But something went wrong. His behavior grew erratic. The polite boy we all knew and liked from his freshman and sophomore years was gone, leaving a sullen, bitter kid in his place. It was such a radical change that I suspected abuse, either at home or elsewhere off school grounds, but both he and his parents assuaged my fears in that regard."

"You suspected mental health issues?" asked Meredeth.

"I did. His moodiness seemed beyond the pale, and his schoolwork suffered. His grades went from A's and B's to D's and F's in a single quarter. I spoke with Mrs. Wenstrom at length, however, and she explained that Jamie had taken up with a bad crowd—a group of students and dropouts I know all too well. Drug addicts. Thieves. You name it."

"Did Jamie stay tight with his old friends?" asked Bobby.

"Sometimes. I know his parents were working hard to get him through this, and he did have good times when he appeared to be his old self, but it never lasted long. Anything, no matter how small, would derail him." She tilted her head to the side. "It was almost as if he were looking for an excuse to act out again."

"And his behavior here at school? Did he get into fights? Cut class? Talk back?"

"All of those things. When he was in a bad mood, he was merciless with his ridicule. In fact, he nearly gave his trigonometry teacher a nervous breakdown. Of course, there were other issues that contributed to Silvia's state of mind, but I'd say Jamie's mockery played a large role. She has a peculiar way of speaking, and many students impersonate her, but Jamie took all that to a whole new level."

"You mentioned his new group of friends were problem students and dropouts. Druggies. Hard stuff or typical high school drug use?"

"I object to the phrase, 'typical high school drug use,' but that group goes far beyond smoking weed in the bathrooms. They shoot up when they can, take pills stolen from their grandparents' medicine cabinets. Just two months ago, I had to suspend one of them for selling cake flour in little packets to members of our freshman cohort. The kids didn't know better, and Matt told them how to turn his 'cocaine' into crack. The recipe included a plastic spoon, Ajax crystals, and other assorted poisons. It was lucky we caught him red-handed before many of the freshmen had had a chance to try out his recipe."

"Can we talk to the boy?"

Ionia shook her head. "His parents have a very liberal attitude—some might be tempted to label them hippies. They withheld consent to have me serve in their stead." She glanced at her open doorway. "But perhaps we can start with Jamie's old friends. Maybe they will have the information you need. Here's Mandy with those files. Let's get you set up in our conference room, and you can review the files while I get the students."

"That sounds perfect," said Meredeth.

She and Bobby followed her across the hall to a long, narrow room, then took up positions on the other side of the table so they were facing the door. Mandy arrayed the files in front of them, then put her hand flat on a stack with blue tags affixed to the manilla folders.

"These students are the cream of the crop. Where Jamie should be." She moved her hand to a second stack, this one with red tags affixed. "But this stack is where you'll find his file." She frowned at her hand. "Do you think he's okay?" she asked in a quiet voice.

"He might be," Meredeth said, "but with each day that passes, the probability he's off somewhere doing his own thing..."

"I understand."

"Come, Mandy," said Ionia from the doorway. "Let's go round up the blue tags."

"Right."

When they'd left, Meredeth reached for the red-tagged files and thumbed through them until she found Jamie

Wenstrom's file. It was thicker than any of the files in the other pile but not quite as thick as some in the red stack. She flipped Jamie's file open and scanned the documents within. "This reads like two files mashed together, one for a perfect student, and one for a major problem child. Two years ago, he went from being near the top of his class with near-perfect attendance to placements in remedial classes. A year ago, he was moved into a program for students with severe emotional disturbances."

Bobby grunted and pulled the stack of blue-tagged files toward him. "Jim did say he got into drugs, right?"

"Yes, but this seems... The incident a year ago that sent him into the special program was a fight in which Jamie attacked three kids in the locker room. He pulled a knife and threatened to, and I quote, 'carve their hearts out and eat them.' Normal high school students don't make threats like that."

"No, I guess not. And starting a fight with such bad odds doesn't make a lot of sense, either, unless..."

"Unless what?"

"Unless Jamie wanted a beating."

Meredeth glanced at him and arched an eyebrow. "What are you thinking? Masochism?"

"No, I was leaning more toward self-punishment."

"That stems from guilt and shame." She flipped through Jamie's file. "There is some mention of self-inflicted burns here, but no cutting, no drinking toxic substances."

"But a lot of fights, right?" asked Bobby. "Fights Jamie lost?"

"There are a lot of fights. I don't know if he won or lost, but his record does show an increase in frequency this year."

"Then maybe Jamie is self-punishing by getting his own ass kicked."

"It's possible. We'll have to ask Ionia and maybe Jenna, herself. And remember that the guilt and shame may stem from something only Jamie gives any credence to. Jim mentioned he was having problems with his father. Perhaps it stems from their relationship."

Bobby nodded. "Sure. He feels he's not good enough. That he doesn't measure up to his father's expectations, that he's not developing into the stand-up guy his father expects."

"Oftentimes self-punishers suffer from borderline or bipolar personality disorders." She flipped to the encounter reports from the school counselor. "The counselor even calls out a potential for borderline personality issues."

"Well, there are all the fights. And didn't Jim say he's been doing better, then falling back?"

"Yes."

"That could tick the self-sabotaging behavior box, right?"

"Sure, and also the mood swings."

"And the separation from his old friends, replacing them with new kids, could be a change of self-identity. Then there's the drug use."

"Okay, I can see the potential there, but we'd need more to firm that up."

"I wonder if he was seeing a therapist."

"We'll have to ask Jenna."

Bobby flipped his pad open and jotted down a note to do just that. "My biggest question is why no one here at school did anything to intervene."

"Well, they did, Bobby. They moved him into the special program."

"Right. I don't know how it was in Georgia, but in Colorado, the kids in those programs were train wrecks in motion. Few, if any, of the kids in my school benefited from those special programs. It was more like a place to put them where they wouldn't interfere with other kids' educations. I mean, we can't expect teachers to fix those kinds of mental health issues, can we?"

"Can't we? Maybe not 'fix' them as you say, but at least take the issues into account and provide the best educational opportunities possible."

"Maybe. But a classroom full of students with varied mental health and emotional disturbances? And one teacher? Do we really still believe in miracles?"

"Sure, teachers get dumped on. They have to deal with these kids five days a week without being able to rely on the student's family situation to back them up, but what's the alternative? Institutionalization? Pack them up and send them to a military academy? Ignore them? Medicate them until they drool?"

"I'm just a Marine, Meredeth. I'm a doer, not a thinker. Point me at a problem and tell me what needs to be done."

"Right, Bobby," she said with a grin. "Tell me something."

"If I can."

"Do you believe this horseshit you spout about yourself?"

"What? I *am* a Marine. I *am* a doer—"

"But you are hardly 'not a thinker.'"

Bobby shrugged. "I solve problems by doing what I'm told, Mere," he said quietly.

"Food for thought: your internal monolog is selling yourself short."

"I appreciate the thought, Mere, but I am who I am."

"Indeed," she said with a nod. "I'm just saying you may not recognize who you *really* are."

The door swung open, and Ionia led a student inside. "Agents Connelly and Van Zandt, meet Darren Rogers. He's known Jamie Wenstrom since first grade."

"Hello, Darren," said Bobby, extending his hand.

The seventeen-year-old shook his hand, then sank into the chair opposite Van Zandt. "Do you know anything?" He blushed. "About Jamie, I mean."

"That's why we're here," said Meredeth. "We're hoping you can help us find him."

Darren's mouth settled into a grim line, and he shrugged with his eyebrows. "At this point, I don't have much hope you can help him."

"Why's that?"

The boy glanced at Ionia, and she offered him a small smile and a nod. "Go on, Darren. You can trust them."

He shrugged, his discomfort evident.

"Look, Darren, we're not here to jam anyone up. We work for Jamie's uncle. We just want to find him and bring him home." Bobby leaned forward and smiled.

"Sure," said Darren. "But he's been home this whole time. It hasn't helped."

"That may be true, but these things are processes, Darren," said Meredeth. "It takes time, and there will be setbacks, but we think Jamie needs to be at home with his family, surrounded by people who care about him. Don't you?"

"I guess."

"Is there something about his home life we need to know?" asked Ionia.

"No, nothing like what you think." Darren drew a deep breath, then heaved it out in a sigh. "It's just that he felt all this pressure to measure up to what his dad wanted from him."

"And that didn't match what Jamie wanted for himself?"

"I don't know. I don't think it's as much that as that he felt like a failure no matter what he did. Good grades, leadership positions on his sports teams. He didn't think any of that really mattered."

"And did his father tell him that?"

Darren shrugged again. "I don't know. I don't think so. Jamie just felt like it wasn't enough, you know, so why try?"

"And all these fights?" Meredeth asked, her hand lying on Jamie's folder.

"He was...angry. A lot."

"With you? Or with other people?"

"Mostly with others, but sometimes with us."

"Us?"

"His *real* friends. The guys he's hung out with since elementary school."

Bobby nodded. "High school is tough, though, right? People's interests start to change, and sometimes old friendships no longer seem to work."

"Nah, it wasn't like that." Darren looked down at his lap. "He'd get mad at us when we called him on his shit."

Meredeth lifted an eyebrow.

"Sorry," said Darren. "But that's what it is."

"Come on, Darren," said Bobby. "Help us out. Help Jamie out."

Darren shrugged.

"Elaborate, Darren," said the assistant principal. "Keep in mind that none of this is going to get Jamie in trouble."

"Drugs, mostly, but also acting like a jerk toward us. Leaving us hanging so he could spend time with those losers." He pointed at the stack of red-tagged files with his thumb.

"And he didn't like it when you confronted him?"

Darren blew out a breath. "Definitely not."

"Did it ever get physical? Between the two of you or any of your crew?"

"No." He cocked his head to the side. "Though there were times I thought it might. He'd get so mad, I thought he'd lose his mind."

"But he didn't?"

Darren shook his head. "He'd just leave, and we wouldn't see him for a week or two."

"I see. Tell me something, Darren. Did you confront him right before he disappeared?" Meredeth leaned forward and met the boy's uncomfortable gaze.

"Well...sort of, I guess."

"When? About what?"

"The night of the party. We were supposed to get together and have a movie marathon. He ditched us for some druggie party."

"Can you tell us about the party?"

"Well, *I* didn't go to it."

"Still. Where was it? Who hosted it?"

"Some older kid. Up on the cul-de-sac by the farms."

"Do you mean Malagar Drive, Darren?" asked Ionia.

"Yeah. Not the big house up on the hill, but the one next door to it."

Ionia nodded. "I know the one."

"One of these?" asked Meredeth, laying her hand on the red-tagged files.

"If he hadn't quit. Well, he'd have graduated by now, but yes, he was a problem student while he was here. I'll have Mandy get his records."

"That's probably not necessary as long as you can give us his name and address."

"I can."

"So, when you confronted him, what happened?"

"Texts," said Darren. "He wouldn't even come talk to us, so it was all texts."

"Would you mind if I read them?" asked Bobby.

Darren slipped his phone out of his back pocket and slid it across the table. "Knock yourself out."

"In the meantime, tell me about these texts," said Meredeth.

Hanging his head, Darren hesitated a moment. "I wasn't exactly at my best. I was so mad at him. We'd had the plan for over a week, and he just blew us off like we were nothing to him."

"And how did the conversation go?"

"Not good. Lots of expletives hurled around, lots of"—he pumped one shoulder up and down—"insults, an ultimatum or two, lots of things said we didn't mean."

"Okay. What happened then?"

"He blocked my number. That was the last I heard from him. Since then, he doesn't even read my messages or return my calls." His gaze was earnest, and he leaned forward. "I don't know where he is. If I did, I'd have told Mrs. Wenstrom when she asked me. Jamie's in trouble, and I don't mean the kind of trouble Ms. McAdams deals out. I'm really worried about him. I think..." He closed his eyes and shook his head. "I have a really bad feeling."

"Is it just a feeling?" asked Bobby, passing Darren's phone back. "I didn't see anything dire in your texts. Just two guys airing out a beef."

"I shouldn't have been so harsh."

"Listen to me, Darren," said Bobby. "Guys have beefs, especially at your age. Your emotions run high. It's okay. The things you said, even though you were angry at Jamie, they showed how much you care about the dude."

"Yeah, I guess. I only hope Jamie sees it that way."

"So, Jamie stood you guys up and went to this party on Malagar Drive. Did you or your crew go over to talk to him directly?"

"Nah," said Darren, once again looking down at his lap. "We figured it was another bender and that we'd be able to talk to him once he'd calmed down."

"Did he give you any indication why he was upset and ditching you?"

"He said something about not acting like his dad," said Bobby.

"Yeah, but that was par for the course. He said stuff like that all the time. Any time we disagreed with what he wanted to do, any time we brought up the drugs, his grades, the fights, whatever, he'd trot out that 'don't be my dad, one is enough' crap."

"Is there anything else you can think of that might help?"

"For instance, has he gone radio silent before?" asked Bobby.

"To his parents, sure, but never with all of us."

Bobby glanced at Meredeth and lifted one eyebrow.

"Thanks, Darren," she said and then nodded at the assistant principal. She held out her business card. "If you think of anything else, please don't hesitate to reach out."

"Or tell me," said Ionia.

"Okay," Darren said with a shrug.

"You can go back to class," said the assistant principal.

He got up and walked to the door, then stopped, his hand on the knob, his gaze resting on the center of the door. "Find him, will you?" he said in a quiet voice.

"We'll do our very best," promised Meredeth.

Without turning, the boy nodded, then opened the door. "Hey, Steve," he said, then turned right and walked away.

Mandy ushered another boy inside. "This is Steve Thendio."

"Come in, Steve," said Ionia. "Have a seat. This is Agent Connelly and her partner, Agent Van Zandt. They'd like to talk to you about Jamie Wenstrom."

"I don't want to say anything." The skinny boy sank into a chair at the end of the table and crossed his arms. "I'm not going to say anything."

"That's your right, Steve, and we're not going to force you, but I do want you to know we're not here to cause Jamie trouble. We're here to help find him." Meredeth leaned back in her chair and flicked a questioning gaze at Ionia.

"Yeah? What if he doesn't want to be found?"

"Come now, Steve," said Ionia. "He's not yet old enough to make that decision. And you know being home with his parents is the best thing for him right now."

"Yeah? You so sure about that?"

"Listen, Steve," said Bobby, "if you know something we don't about his home life, please share. We work for Jamie's uncle, not his mom and dad, and if there's a problem leading to all this, then we should know."

"And his uncle's going to do something about it? He's had two years."

"Maybe he didn't know. He lives on the other side of the country, after all."

"Well..."

"Steve, we're here to help Jamie and his family," said Meredeth. "We're not here to cause him more trouble, just to get him home."

"And what if he doesn't want to go home?"

"If there's a good reason why he shouldn't, tell us," said Ionia, "and we'll deal with it."

Steve chopped his hand through air. "None of this matters, anyway. I don't know where he is."

"Darren told us he stood you up last week?"

"Yeah, so?"

"So, nothing. We're trying to retrace his steps, that's all."

"Yeah, he stood us up and went to that party with all the other horse heads."

"Horse?" asked Bobby. "He was using heroin?"

"Sure thing, Boomer. And anything else he could get his hands on."

A half-grin washed Bobby's features. "I'm hardly a boomer, but call me what you like."

"How serious was Jamie's drug use?" asked Meredeth. A vertical line had appeared between her brows. "Would you say he was addicted to heroin?"

"How should I know? He kept that stuff from us. Almost like he was embarrassed by what he did—at least when he was trying to be better. When he was using, he didn't care what we thought, but when he was clean, he didn't want to talk about it."

"Tell us about the party he went to."

Steve turned his gaze on Meredeth, on his lips a half-sneer, half frown. "Well, I wouldn't know about that, would I? I didn't go to it."

"But you know the host?"

"Everyone in Ukiah knows that asshole."

"Did you know him before he left school?"

"Yeah, when I was a freshman. He was a bully. High most of the time."

Meredeth glanced at Ionia, who nodded. "Did he bully Jamie?"

"He bullied everyone who wasn't on the loser path."

"I see. Why would Jamie want to hang out with him?"

"Well, it was a party, wasn't it? There would be drugs there. Alcohol. Sluts. And who knows? Jamie was on his own trajectory to loser-land."

Meredeth held out her business card. "Please contact us if you hear from Jamie, or if you think of anything new."

"Right," said Steve. He took the card and shoved it in his pocket. "I guess I can go back to class?" He turned his gaze on Ionia McAdams.

"You can, Steve," said the assistant principal.

"Before you go, Steve, can you think of anyone who might be able to give us a better picture of Jamie's activities that night."

"Any of those losers might have been there." He pointed at the stack of red-tagged files. "Talk to Ray Michaels. He was almost certainly there. It's just his scene."

"Very good," said Meredeth. "Thank you for your help, Steve. We'll talk to Ray next."

Ionia nodded and walked to the door to pass the request on to Mandy. Steve got up and met her gaze directly for the first time. "Listen, I've got a feeling Jamie needs help from..." He shrugged and shook his head. "From someone. Maybe you."

"It's why we got up before the sun came out and flew across the country to be here today, Steve," she said in a gentle voice. "We'll do our best to get Jamie where he needs to be. Safe and sound."

"But you can't promise, right? I watch cop shows, I know he might already be..." He snapped his mouth shut and tears glistened in his eyes.

"Don't think that way," said Bobby. "It may be you're right, but until we know, keep hoping for the best."

Steve nodded once, then turned and left with a savage swipe at the tears that threatened to spill down his cheeks.

"His friends are still loyal," Meredeth said.

"Yeah. He must have been a good guy before all this." He waved his hand vaguely.

Meredeth shifted through the red-tags until she found the one belonging to Ray Michaels. It was thicker than Jamie's but still not the thickest. She flipped through his transcripts and frowned. "It seems Ray has never been that worried about his grades. Or minor things like attendance. He failed his freshman year. He had the grades to advance but skipped too much school and was held back due to that. He was labeled a habitual truant and ordered to make up the days on Saturdays but skipped those, too. Hmm. It says here his parents were referred to superior court. Three times."

"Well, I bet that made them happy."

The door swung open, and a kid dressed for full rebellion against society slouched into the room. He wore skin-tight black Lycra pants and an untucked T-shirt embossed with a bloody skull. His head was completely devoid of hair—even his eyebrows had been shaved. A loose studded belt was draped around his waist—just so, with the perfect angle that said he'd spent time in front of a mirror trying different ways of wearing it. He had a pierced nostril and another stud through his lip. He had a rusty nail poked through his ear lobe. He wore slip-on skater shoes with no socks. His skin was as sickly white as Meredeth had ever seen, and his face was splotched with acne.

"Sit, Ray," said Ionia from the doorway.

"I don't want to talk to no cops."

"Good thing we're not cops, then," said Bobby. "Take a seat, kid."

Ray's lips curled with the perfect amount of adolescent disdain. "Whatever." He slipped into the chair recently vacated by Steve. "But I'm not saying anything."

"Listen, Mr. Michaels, we're here about Jamie Wenstrom."

"Goody for you. What's that got to do with me?"

"We understand you attended a party not too long ago."

Ray chuckled. "Every night."

"I'm sure. But I'm thinking about a week ago. A party that Jamie Wenstrom also attended."

"At Tim McMasters's house," said Ionia.

"Well, I didn't go to that one."

"Are you sure?" asked Meredeth. "We're not cops, but we *are* FBI agents, and lying to us is a felony."

"Ohh! A felony! My laws!" Ray threw his head back and laughed at the ceiling. "Lady, if you knew what my life was like, you'd realize that threatening me with prison isn't much of a threat. I'm destined for prison. Just ask Ionia, here."

"That's too bad, Ray," said Bobby. "Boys like you get eaten up in state prisons, but lying to us makes you a guest of the federal prison system. You know, the places they stick all the guys who are too much for the state systems. You'd be property before lights out on your first night."

"Oh, that scares me, Mr. FBI agent!"

"I know it does, kid, for all your bravado." Bobby got up and went down to the end of the table and sat at its head. "There are other options. You're not trapped here in Ukiah."

"Oh, no? Where the hell am I supposed to go?"

"I served in the Marine Corps. I got an education through the GI Bill. The Corps made me who I am. *What* I am."

"Why would I want to join a bunch of gung-ho assholes like you?"

"Because the Marine Corps will teach you discipline, self-reliance, confidence."

"I've got all that, chump."

"Do you, Ray?"

His expression crumpled with anger. "Stop calling me that! My name is Rad."

Meredeth made a show of looking through his file. "Says here you are Ray Michaels. 'Rad' isn't even mentioned."

"I'm the victim of an over-zealous system."

Bobby chuckled. "Dude, you weren't even born when the hippies coined that phrase. Or when punk rockers dressed like you are."

"Punk's okay, but I like grindcore."

"Tell us about the party, Ray," Meredeth said.

"Do that, Ray, and maybe I won't have to search your locker today."

His brow furrowed, and he glared up at Ionia McAdams. "Why are you always hassling me, Ionia? Is it because I turned you down? I told you, I'm not into board of education employees."

"Shall I have Mandy call your parents and inform them that we're searching your locker?"

"No, sweetheart. That won't be necessary, though I want to go on record saying there's nothing in my locker but schoolbooks and gym clothes."

"I'm sure," said Ionia with a shake of her head. "Now, go on and answer their questions."

"Did you attend the party?" asked Meredeth.

"Yeah."

"And did you see Jamie Wenstrom there?"

He shrugged. "Sure. But we didn't speak."

"No?" asked Bobby.

"Nah. Jamie was..." He shook his head. "Jamie was what I call a part-timer."

"What does that mean?" asked Meredeth.

"It means he wasn't serious about his debauchery yet. He kept flip-flopping. Going on the straight and narrow to please his parents, losing it, going off the rails for a while, then he'd be right back in the bosom of the American dream. He couldn't reconcile that it's all bullshit. He kept thinking he was a failure for not finding the path laid out for him of any interest."

"Is that his problem? Boredom?" asked Bobby.

Rad chuckled. "I don't have a friggin' clue what his problem was, man. I'm just telling you he couldn't pick a side."

"And that means?"

"That means he was back and forth. Hanging with us, the so-called losers who realize society is a bunch of horseshit one week, then hanging with those preppy dorks the next. He was trying to straddle that line, man. Trying to fit in on both sides, which made him suspect to everyone."

"Let's get back to the party, shall we?" asked Meredeth.

"Why not, toots? Why not?"

"You didn't speak to Jamie the whole night?"

"No. I was, uh...occupied." He tipped a wink at McAdams.

"Meaning you were high?"

"Yeah, that, too."

"Then what did you mean by occupied?" asked Meredeth.

"A girl, toots. I had a woman's attention and I kept it."

"When was the last time you saw Jamie?"

"At the party."

Meredeth suppressed a sigh. "And what *time* was it?"

"Oh. I took my, uh, date into the back bedroom at about eleven. I think."

"And Jamie was still there?"

"Yeah. Stoned. Watching the boob tube like it was some kind of oracle."

"Did he speak to anyone?"

"At the party? Of course."

"Anyone in particular?"

Rad's eyelid twitched. "No."

"You don't seem so sure of that," said Bobby.

"Well, you know how it is. He talked to people, of course. All the usual people, anyway."

"And no one unusual?"

"No."

"Tell us about the other people at the party. Was there anyone who didn't seem to fit in?"

"Only every single person there. That's the point of those parties. It's for *us*, for the so-called losers of the world. None of us fit in." He hooked his fingers in the air as he said fit in. "We're the outcasts, yeah?"

"What I mean is, was there anyone unusual attending that night? Anyone who *wasn't* an outcast, or someone too weird, even for you?"

"I'm not sure what you mean by that last part, toots. Are you trying to cast dispersions on my lifestyle?"

"Heaven forbid," said Meredeth.

"You've got kind of an attitude, don't you, toots?"

"You have no idea," said Bobby with a grin.

"She your girlfriend, my man?"

"No. She's my partner."

"She's kind of hot for an older chick."

"Thanks," said Meredeth. "I think."

"A friend of mine is older like you, but she's not so uptight."

"Let's get back to the party."

"Yeah, whatever. I don't know what else to tell you."

"What time did Jamie leave?"

"No idea. Like I said, I took my girl into the back. We were, uh, occupied from then on. When I left, Jamie was nowhere to be seen."

"And what time was that?"

Rad cocked his head and looked up at the ceiling. "Five, maybe six."

"And that was Monday morning?" asked Ionia.

"Sure."

"And you came to school that day?"

"Of course, I learned my lesson on skipping without an excuse. You saw to that, didn't you, Ionia? Did I ever show you the scars?"

"The scars?" asked McAdams. "What scars?"

"The ones my daddy laid into my back after the third fine that dickhead judge levied against him. After *you* referred him to court again. They're quite impressive."

Ionia's lips drew into a thin white line.

"Oh, don't worry about it, Ionia. He'd have found some other reason."

"You know we can help you with that, Ray," said the assistant principal. "All you have to do is come to me."

"Sure, sure. I've never heard that before. Besides, what makes you think going into foster care would protect me? Better the devil you know, right?"

"Did you see Jamie that morning in school?"

"Nope. And before you ask, I haven't seen him since. I don't know where he is."

"No? Are you sure about that?"

"I'm sure."

"Would you tell us if you had?" asked Bobby.

"Fuck no."

Meredeth shook her head. "That will be all, Ray."

"Rad, toots. Call me, Rad."

CHAPTER 9

RUNNING WITH THE DEVIL

Ukiah, CA

TIM MCMASTERS'S HOUSE sat on the northwest end of the cul-de-sac at the end of Malagar Drive. The house next door sat above all the rest on the top of a hill and had several layers of fencing between that property that the McMasters' house: one on the property line, and another at the crown of the hill. There was no fence on the opposite side of the property, Meredeth noted.

The McMasters' yard was a mess—runaway ground cover and planting beds that were overgrown and overrun with weeds. What little grass remained was burnt brown by either a lack of water and heat or too much fertilizer. The drive was cracked and crumbling at the edges. The house itself was sided in wood that had seen better days, with a mismatched fence—half iron-rod, half wooden plank—encircling the back. A garbage can lay on its side, its lid thrown open and garbage spilled all over. A single car sat on the drive in front of the closed garage doors—a red Honda on aftermarket wheels, one of them holding a flat tire.

Meredeth eased the Jeep up the incline and parked behind the Honda. "Lovely," she muttered.

"Ten bucks says old Tim lives with his parents, still."

"No bet." She opened her door. "Come on. Let's see what Tim has to say for himself."

They got out and followed the crumbling concrete path to the base of the full flight of cedar stairs that led up to the front porch. Another garbage can sat outside the front door, flies buzzing around it. It was filled with empty beer cans and takeaway containers. A few potted plants were scattered around the porch, all clinging to life by the grace of God.

Meredeth rang the bell, then looked in the big bay windows for signs of life. The house was mostly dark from what she could see despite it being nearly five o'clock. "Maybe they're all at work."

"Could be," said Bobby, though his tone made it clear he didn't think it likely.

They waited another few minutes in silence, then Bobby leaned past Meredeth and pounded on the door. "Tim McMasters!" he boomed. "Come to the door!"

"Wow. Drill sergeant voice and everything."

"I was never a drill instructor."

The door banged open. "What the hell you want?"

"Tim McMasters?" asked Meredeth.

"Who the hell are you?"

"Special Agent Meredeth Connelly. This is my partner, Bobby Van Zandt."

The man sighed. "What do you want?"

"That's something we can only address with Tim McMasters. Is that you?"

"Yeah."

"Can we come in?"

"No. What's this about? You woke me up."

"It's almost five in the afternoon."

"Yeah? What about it?"

"Do you own this property?" asked Bobby.

"It's my parent's house."

Bobby glanced at Meredeth and grinned. "That's fine."

"What's this all about?"

"You threw a party a week ago Sunday, correct?"

"Who told you that?"

"Listen, Tim, we aren't here on a fishing expedition, okay? We're not playing around trying to trap you. This can be fast and easy or slow and hard. It's really your choice, but we will get the information we need, one way or another."

He turned a cold stare on Meredeth but kept his mouth shut.

"Now, why not answer her question?" asked Bobby. "We know about the party already. So, confirm you threw it."

McMasters scoffed. "Well, who else would have? My mom?"

"We aren't in the business of assumption, Tim," said Meredeth. "We are in the business of confirming facts. Is there some reason you don't want to cooperate with a federal investigation?"

"An investigation of what? A party?"

"That's correct. At this moment, we are investigating that party that happened at this address a week ago Sunday. Now, did *you* host that party or not?"

McMasters shook his head. "Yeah, of course I did."

"And did Jamie Wenstrom attend the party?"

"Look, I don't know everyone who showed up, okay? That's how parties around here work. You tell ten friends, but each of them tells five more people, some you don't know, some you do."

"Then you deny knowing Jamie Wenstrom?"

"I didn't say that. I don't know if Jamie came to the party."

"Are you sure about that, Tim?" asked Bobby.

"It's what I just said, isn't it?"

A car pulled into the driveway, then idled up to the house, and the garage door rumbled up.

"Oh, hell," Tim muttered.

"Problem?" asked Meredeth. "I assume that's one of your parents?"

"Mom," grunted McMasters. "Go away."

"We can't do that."

"Tim? What's going on here?" Mrs. McMasters was on the tall side, thin, and very attractive. She gave Meredeth a singular look, then glanced at Bobby. "Police?"

"Hello, Mrs. McMasters. I'm Special Agent Meredeth Connelly, and this is Special Agent Bobby Van Zandt."

"FBI?" She turned a whither gaze on her son. "What have you done now?"

"Nothing, Mom. They made a mistake. They're leaving."

Mrs. McMasters turned her piercing blue-eyed gaze back to Meredeth. "Really? It doesn't look that way to me. Please come in." She swatted Tim on the shoulder. "Get out of their way, Timmy."

She led them into the living room and invited them to take a seat. "Now, what's all this about?"

"I'm going back to bed."

"It's five in the afternoon, Timmy." She said it with the resignation and semi-rebuke of mothers of teenagers everywhere. "Sit down."

"But I—"

"*Sit*, Timmy."

"I'm not a dog, Mom." But even as he said it, Tim was sinking into an armchair, a long-suffering expression painted on his face.

"We're here to ask your son about the party he threw here a week ago Sunday."

Mrs. McMasters swiveled to face her son. "A party, huh?"

Tim wouldn't meet her gaze and said nothing.

"Mr. McMasters and I were out of town. Fort Bragg. We wanted a weekend away."

"I see," said Meredeth.

"And Timmy did not have our permission to throw any parties. I assume there was drinking and drugs involved?"

"I think that's a safe assumption," said Bobby.

Her cold glare pinned Tim to his seat, and he looked as though he'd like nothing more than to disappear. "And what has attracted the attention of the Federal Bureau of Investigation to a stupid party hosted by a very stupid boy?"

"We're investigating the disappearance of a local teenager. Jamie Wenstrom."

"I know the Wenstroms. Jamie attended the party?" She glanced at Meredeth, but then her gaze zipped back to her son.

"That's what we're trying to verify. We have an eyewitness who places him here that night."

"And my idiot son is pretending he doesn't know anything?"

Meredeth shrugged.

"Speak up, Timothy. Do I have it right? You've been standing there lying to the FBI?"

McMasters didn't raise his gaze from the ground at his feet.

"*Speak up, Timothy John McMasters!* You start cooperating this instant, or you go pack your goddamn dirty clothes into that red piece of crap in the drive and go find somewhere else to live."

A moment of silence followed, and Mrs. McMasters sighed. "What am I going to do with you, Timothy? Your father is going to blow a gasket when he hears that not only did you lie to us, not only did you throw a party in *our* house, but you also lied to the FBI. He'll be so proud."

"So what else is new?" snapped Tim.

"Was Jamie at your party?" Mrs. McMasters asked in a cold voice. "You have twenty seconds before I start making arrangements to evict you."

"Evict your own son, how nice."

"Maybe, but do you doubt I will keep my word?"

Tim shook his head. "Jamie was here, okay? Are you happy now?" He raised his face and glared at Meredeth.

"Oh, no you don't, Timothy. Agent Connelly isn't to blame for this. We all know who bears the responsibility."

"Shut up, Mom," he muttered, but they all heard him just the same.

"Show some respect," said Bobby. "This is your *mother*."

"No, duh."

Mrs. McMasters shook her head, then looked at Bobby. "Thank you, but this one has no respect for me or his father. All he wants from us is money, so he doesn't even have to work to buy his drugs and his beer. Do you have other questions you need answering?"

"We do," said Meredeth. "Tim, did you see Jamie talking with anyone in particular?"

Tim lifted both shoulders and let them drop. "There were a lot of people here."

"That's not exactly a productive answer, Timothy."

"Okay, fine. Yes, I saw Jamie talking to the usual suspects. Kids from school."

"From the high school? But you quit."

"Yeah, Mom, I haven't forgotten. The source of your eternal shame, right?"

"Who else attended the party?" asked Meredeth.

"I didn't exactly keep a guest list."

Mrs. McMasters reached across the intervening space and slapped her son. "You ditch that attitude, Timothy. You are in enough trouble as it is. You'd better straighten up and start answering Agent Connelly's questions. Did you miss the part about them being *FBI agents*? Did you miss the part about them investigating poor Jamie Wenstrom's disappearance?"

With one hand on his cheek, Tim heaved a sigh. "That's child abuse, and right in front of a pair of FBI agents."

"What?" asked Bobby. "I didn't see a thing. Did you, Meredeth?"

"Not a thing."

Mrs. McMasters stood abruptly and fished her cell phone out of her pocketbook. She stepped into the kitchen, her phone to her ear. "Where are you?" she asked into the phone. "Oh, nothing, except there's a pair of FBI agents in our living room questioning *your* son about the party he threw the weekend we went to Fort Bragg." She listened a moment, then turned back toward the living room. "You heard me. No, he's being less than cooperative, of course. Why screw up a perfect record? How fast can you get home? I'm afraid I may beat him senseless." She looked at Tim and smiled coldly. "Why sure, dear. He's right here. One moment while I give him the phone."

She strode into the room, her fury evident in every step, holding her phone out. "Oh, Timmy-dear, your father would like a word."

Tim squeezed his eyes shut, but he took the phone and pressed it to his ear. Mr. McMasters' fury was evident to everyone in the room, especially after Tim held the phone away from his ear a little in an effort to escape the shouting.

"Can I get you two something to drink while Tom explains things to Timothy?"

"No, thank you," said Bobby.

"Do you have anything with caffeine?" asked Meredeth.

Mrs. McMasters smiled. "Certainly. We have Coke Zero, or I can brew some coffee if you'd prefer?"

"The Coke is fine."

She nodded once and whirled around to retrace her steps into the kitchen.

Tim's face was a little pale, and he kept his eyes closed. He kept repeating, "Yes, sir," in a surly tone of voice.

By the time Mrs. McMasters returned with a glass full of ice and Coca-Cola, Tim was holding the phone out at arm's length. "He wants to talk to you."

"Fine." She snatched her phone from her son's hand. "Tom? Yes, I still think you need to hurry home. Even after the agents are done with him, I think we need to discuss Timothy's future. That's right." She nodded. "Okay. We'll see you in twenty minutes, then." She disconnected the call and returned to the living room to stand over Tim. "Your father says you've decided to cooperate."

Tim shook his head and rolled his eyes.

"What was that? I didn't hear you."

"Yes! Okay? Yes, I'll cooperate, but I want it noted that I'm cooperating only because you're going to kick me out if I don't."

"Oh, Timmy. No one cares." Mrs. McMasters stepped past him and sank onto the couch. "I'll be right here, dear, making sure you don't forget that you're cooperating."

Tim rolled his eyes again.

"You know, I just had a conversation with one of Tim's friends over at the high school. A boy named Ray," said Bobby. "Now, I'm a Marine, and I admit I'm biased, but I think the Corps might be something to consider. I tried to talk to Ray about it, but..." He pumped his shoulders up and down.

"Do you think military service would help?"

"It helped me."

"I see. Thank you for the suggestion. We'll discuss it as a family later tonight. Judging by Tom's voice, the Marine Corps may be the safest place for Timothy."

Bobby nodded.

"Tim? Did anyone show up to the party that you didn't expect?"

He shrugged his shoulders but said, "A couple of people. That guy that claims to be a Satanist, for one. His girlfriends, too, I guess."

"This is another teenager from the high school?" asked Meredeth.

"No," said Mrs. McMaster through lips that curled with disgust. "He's in his forties. He has some weird name. Carmen. Kamen. Something like that."

"Kahin," said Tim with a long-suffering sigh. "Kahin Alshaytan."

Bobby jotted the name down. "That's Arabic, and not really a name."

"Oh?" asked Mrs. McMasters.

"It means Priest of Satan."

She scoffed and gave her son a glare. "That figures. How could you let someone like that into our home? Do you know what they say he does in that hovel he calls a house?"

"I've been there, Mom. I *know* what he does there."

"Oh, that's just perfect."

"And if you try to stick me in the Marines, that's where I'll be living by tomorrow."

"Oh? Do you think this Satanist will happily support you? Will he give you money for food and gas for your stupid car?"

"He doesn't care about things like that."

"Oh, of course he does, Timothy. He's an *adult*. He's not going to support you."

"He said I could stay with him."

"Oh, you've already spoken to him about it?" Her voice was deceptively mild, but Meredeth thought there was raw magma underneath that tone.

"Not in so many words, but he lets anyone stay over."

"I see. Well, I wish you luck."

"Did Jamie talk to Alshaytan?" asked Bobby.

"I'm not Jamie's keeper."

"Did you *see* them talking?" asked Meredeth.

Tim shrugged.

"That's a yes," she said. "Did they leave together?"

"No. Kahin left earlier."

"Why would a forty-year-old man attend a party of primarily high school students?" Bobby asked.

"You wouldn't understand."

"Try me," said Bobby in an iron voice.

"Kahin's not like everyone else. He goes to parties of all kinds. He's cool, get it? He invites people to his house, to do whatever they want."

"He hosts parties, too?"

"From time to time, but he doesn't need to have a party. He has people there twenty-four seven. There's always something going on."

"And would he have invited Jamie over?" asked Meredeth.

Tim shrugged. "Kahin invites people over who he thinks would like it. People who won't freak out at the sight of someone else having fun."

"And having fun means doing drugs?"

"Not necessarily."

"Sex parties is what I heard," said Mrs. McMasters.

Tim rolled his eyes. "It's not like that, Mom. You wouldn't understand, though, so what's the use of me trying to explain it to you?"

"There's no use, Timothy. I think I'm finally beyond your 'explanations,' your excuses for treating everyone like...like feces."

"Shit, you mean. Say it, Mom."

The door to the garage opened, and Tom McMasters strode into the house. He glanced at Meredeth, then Bobby, then met his wife's gaze for half a second before coming into the living room and smacking Tim in the back of the head. "That's for treating your mother like this." He turned to Bobby and held out his hand. "Tom McMasters."

"Bobby Van Zandt," said Bobby, half-rising to his feet as he shook. "This is my partner, Meredeth Connelly."

Tom nodded to Meredeth, then looked at his wife. "Has the little punk been cooperating?"

"I'm right here, Dad."

"No shit, Timothy."

Tim glanced at his mother and smiled. "See, Mom. It's an easy word to say."

"He has been marginally cooperative," said Mrs. McMasters. "But I'd still like to beat him with a stick."

"Maybe later," said Tom. He turned back to Bobby. "Do you have other questions for Timothy?"

"They were asking about one of the colorful guests Timothy had over while we were gone."

Tom arched an eyebrow at his wife.

"Kahin Alshaytan. Agent Van Zandt translated it from Arabic. Evidently, it means 'priest of Satan.'"

"Good Christ," muttered Tom. "And you thought that jackhole would be a good person to have over? We'll have to fumigate the place."

"It seems this Alshaytan spoke with Jamie Wenstrom."

"Indeed," said Meredeth. "And your house was the last place we can put Jamie."

Tom turned a fierce glare on his son. "Start talking. Right the fuck now."

"Gee, Dad, don't hold back."

Tom's fists clenched. "Did I stutter, Timothy?"

"Kahin invites people to his house. To party. To hang out, whatever."

"Timothy has been to the house, it seems. Agent Van Zandt recommends the Marine Corps for our son."

"It was good enough for me," said Bobby.

"And my father," said Tom without taking his eyes off his son. "What else, Timothy?"

Tim shrugged. "Nothing. They talked for a while, Kahin and Jamie, but I don't know about what."

"And then?"

"And then Kahin left. Jamie hung around a bit, then he left, too."

"Alone?" asked Meredeth.

Tim nodded.

"Did he say where he was going?"

Tim shook his head.

"Where does Alshaytan live?" asked Bobby.

"I don't know the address."

"Timothy, you said you'd been there," said Mrs. McMasters in a toneless voice. "Do you think we're so stupid?"

"Do you want me to answer that?"

The sound of the slap was like a two-by-four breaking, and Tim put a hand to his cheek, looking up at his father teary-eyed. "You want another?" demanded Tom. "You keep on disrespecting the woman who gave you birth, you little twerp, and I'll give you another. And more."

"Child abuse," Tim muttered.

"No," said Bobby. "We've talked about that."

Tom glanced at Bobby and gave him a terse nod. "Now, you little punk, you tell these people Alshartan's address."

"Alshaytan, Dad."

"I hardly care what the asshole's name is, Timothy. Tell them the address so they can get on with their investigation!"

"Fine. It's on Rosemary. You can't miss it."

"Tell them the house number, boy."

"I can't I don't know it. Look for the black front door and follow your nose. You can't miss it."

Tom glanced at Bobby. "Good enough?"

"We'll find it." Bobby glanced at Meredeth, then nodded as she stood. "I think that's all for now. Could we speak to you for a moment, Mr. McMasters?"

"Tom, please." He held his hand toward the front door. "We can chat on the porch."

They stepped outside, leaving Tim and Mrs. McMasters studiously ignoring one another. Out on the porch, Tom raised an eyebrow. "How can I help you?"

"I have concerns, Tom," said Bobby.

"About my son's safety with his mother and me? Don't worry, this is hardly the worst thing he's done to us. But I do thank you for the suggestion about military service. It might be just what Tim needs. The Lord knows nothing else we've tried worked. Addiction counseling, zip. Anger management, zero. Family therapy, nada." He shook his head.

"It must be hard dealing with the drugs," said Meredeth.

"It is, but the rest is almost worse. It's like he's intent on ruining his life. Like he can't get to rock bottom fast enough." He threw up his hands. "And nothing ever changes."

"It will," said Bobby.

"The Marines," Tom said with a little nod. "I think I like that."

"Just promise me that there won't be any fireworks after we leave. No calls to the police."

"Or worse," said Meredeth.

"I appreciate your concern, but as angry as we are, Timothy is our only child, and we do love him."

"Of course," said Bobby.

CHAPTER 10

BESTIES

Ukiah, CA

RAD SAT ON the couch in the front room of Kahin's house with a beer in one hand and a joint in the other. The beer, his third, was mostly gone. The joint dangled unlit between two fingers. He was still suffering the aftereffects of his previous visit to Kahin's stinky house the evening before. The beer was helping, though. What was the expression Anya had used when she pressed the first bottle into his hand an hour before? Hair of the... something or other. Dog? Cat? He couldn't quite remember. Either way, it was having the desired effect—washing away the memories of school, the two FBI assholes, his hangover, everything.

Sitting next to him, with one arm draped over his shoulder, was a mostly naked skinny girl of about twenty-five years old who said her name was Claire but probably wasn't telling the truth. Rad didn't know why he thought this except for the way she had introduced herself, hesitating before she told him her name as if she were thinking it up. It gave him the impression she had plucked it from thin air on the spur of the moment. Not that he cared. She could call herself anything she wanted so long as she kept paying attention to him, so long as she didn't start putting her clothes back on.

"You want another one of those?" she asked in a squeaky voice. Her gaze rested on the beer bottle.

"Sure. I guess." Rad downed the dregs of the beer.

"Coming right up." Claire withdrew her arm from his shoulder, took the bottle from his hand, and stood up. She weaved through the small throng of people sitting around on the floor or lounging in chairs. Kahin's devotees and hangers-on. As she went, Rad enjoyed the view of her ass barely covered by a pink thong and the naked expanse of her back.

He settled on the couch and waited for her to return, ignoring the faint odor of mildew that wafted up and the springs that pushed through flattened seat cushions that had probably lost their resilience before Rad was even in high school.

After a minute, Claire returned from the kitchen, holding two fresh beer bottles. The view, Rad thought with a grin, was even better from the front. Her breasts were large for her frame and bounced a little as she walked, and even though he knew he was staring, he couldn't help himself.

Not that Claire cared. Hell, the sultry smile on her face said she enjoyed the ogling.

Maybe.

She closed the gap between them, stepping over a scantily clad couple lying intertwined on top of the garbage that littered the floor as if they didn't notice the crap strewn all around.

"Here," Claire said, taking a swig of beer and then holding the bottle out to him.

"Thanks." Rad took the bottle and lifted it to his mouth, taking a gulp. He tasted a faint saltiness that might have been from Claire's lips or might also have been his imagination.

Claire drank from the other bottle, then sank down onto his legs, straddling him. She leaned forward, her breasts inches from his chest, and stroked the blue feather hanging from his stud earring. Her hand crept up over his shaved head and then down to his neck, fingers brushing the skin lightly.

"You going to light that?" she asked.

"Light what?" Rad replied, distracted by the view.

"The joint." Claire's finger trailed from Rad's neck, over his shoulder, and down his arm.

"Maybe later." Rad took another sip of beer.

"Or maybe now." Claire reached sideways and grabbed a lighter that was sitting on the arm of the couch. She sparked it up and touched the flame to the joint.

"Guess we're getting high, then."

"We're going to do so much more than that," Claire said, snatching the joint from Rad's fingers and inhaling. "Close your eyes."

Rad did as he was told.

He wasn't sure what was going to happen next, but then he felt Claire's bare breasts push against his chest a second before her mouth was on his. When his lips parted, she exhaled the secondhand smoke. It hit the back of his throat and tickled. Rad resisted the urge to cough and kept his eyes closed, at least until Claire pulled away to take a second hit on the joint.

When he opened them again, Claire was watching him with a devilish grin, her blue eyes wide. "Want to find somewhere more private and up the fun?" she asked.

"Sure." Rad took back the joint. He was about to take a second hit when his eyes drifted to the front door and a familiar figure standing there.

It was his friend, Mick. And, as usual, there was a sour look on his face.

Rad swore under his breath.

"Will you give me a sec?" he said to Claire, putting the beer bottle down and gripping her hips to lift her aside.

Claire resisted. She glanced toward the door, a scowl creasing her face. "What's that loser doing here?"

"He's my friend."

"I'm your friend now," Claire said, leaning forward and kissing Rad's neck. "Forget him. Let's find a dark corner, and I'll show you how friendly I can be."

"I'll just talk to him first, okay? See what he wants. Get rid of him." Rad pushed Claire away with more force this time. "Then we'll find that dark corner."

Claire took back the joint and stood up. "You better not take too long, or I'll have to find someone else."

"One minute. Promise." Rad's eyes lingered on Claire's sinuous body for a moment before he pushed himself off the couch and stepped past her.

Mick shoved the front door closed and met him halfway across the room. "I've been looking for you."

"Now you found me. What do you want?" Rad tried to keep the anger from his voice but failed. Another few minutes and he would have been in a bedroom with Claire. Still could if he could get rid of Mick in short order. "You see that babe that was sitting on my lap? I was just about to get inside that."

Mick rolled his eyes. "Can we talk outside?"

"Why?" Rad looked over his shoulder to see Claire still standing near the couch with her arms folded across her chest. The beer bottle dangled from one hand. The joint was between her fingers in the other. She was watching him with narrowed eyes.

"Why do you think?" Mick's eyes drifted over Rad's shoulder, taking in the filthy room and the mostly naked woman waiting for his friend.

Claire unfolded one arm, put the joint between her lips, then raised her middle finger at Mick.

"Nice. Classy," Mick said, his gaze snapping back to Rad.

"Shut up. Just tell me what you want. I have better things to do."

"I can see that." Mick glanced toward the door. "Outside. Just one minute."

"Fine. One minute and that's all." Rad shoved his friend toward the door and followed behind. But before he could step outside, a voice spoke up behind him.

"Where do you think you're going?"

Rad hesitated and turned around to find Kahin standing in the kitchen doorway. Anya lingered a few steps behind and peered over his shoulder.

"I was just going to step outside and—" Rad started to explain before Kahin cut him off.

"I know where you were going." Kahin beckoned Rad with a curled finger. "Come step into the kitchen with me."

"Just give me—"

"Kitchen." Kahin's attention drifted to Mick. "The dork stays where he is."

Rad turned to his friend. "Let me talk to Kahin, and I'll be right back."

Kahin was still looking at Mick. "As the man said, he'll be right back. You, on the other hand... Act like a statue and stay put." Without waiting for a reply, Kahin turned and walked past his fiancée and back into the kitchen.

Anya lingered in the doorway. "Better do as he says, Rad."

"Shit." Rad grimaced. To Mick, he said, "Just stay there." Then he crossed the room, darting a glance toward Claire, pasting an apologetic smile on his lips as he did so, and followed Anya into the kitchen.

Kahin was leaning against an island covered in empty beer and wine bottles and fast-food wrappers. He fixed Rad with a glowering stare. "You invite that guy around here?"

"No." Rad shook his head. "He just turned up. Said he wanted to talk to me."

"You sure about that?" Kahin turned to Anya. "You believe him, honey?"

"Looks like he's telling the truth to me." Anya sidled around Rad. For once, she was dressed, or at least as clothed as Rad had ever seen her. She was wearing a frayed sports bra and a pair of dirty cutoff jeans that rode so high on her they left nothing to the imagination. Her feet were bare. "He has an honest face."

"I'm telling the truth. I swear," Rad sputtered. "I'll get rid of Mick. I'll tell him not to come back."

"I've got a better idea." Kahin's eyes sparkled. "You should get rid of him for good."

"Not sure I understand," Rad said, even though he had a bad feeling that he did.

"He wants you to *off* your friend," Anya said gleefully. "Put him down in the basement."

"See? She gets it." Kahin nodded. "Take a knife, do him, drag him down the stairs, and put him in the kitty litter."

"Yeah." Anya draped herself over Rad. She pressed against him and whispered in his ear, hot breath tickling his neck. "What *do* you say?"

"Look, I'll make him leave. Okay?" Rad gently pushed Anya away. A knot of dread tightened in his stomach. "I was going to anyway. Claire and I—"

"Sure you wouldn't rather do it our way?" Kahin picked up a steak knife from among the detritus on the island and turned it over in his hand. "How good would it feel to slide this between his ribs?"

"Look at it as a mercy killing," Anya said in a husky voice. "Poor kid's never going to get laid."

"Just stay cool. I'll make sure he doesn't come back," Rad said quickly. He backed up to the kitchen door with his eyes on the knife, then he turned and hurried across the living room, stepping over Kahin's disciples with trash crunching underfoot.

Mick hadn't moved, which was a stupid miscalculation even by *his* standards.

"You have to leave. Right now." Rad steered his friend toward the front door.

"I thought we were going to talk."

"Not now. Not here."

"Then when?" Mick resisted a final push through the front door and outside.

"Who cares? Tomorrow at school. The day after. Any other time but now. You don't want to be here. You don't want to ever show up here again. Understand?"

"Shit, Rad. What the hell has gotten into you?"

"Go home!" Rad screeched, shoving his friend out onto the front path. "I don't want to see you here ever again."

"Hey. You don't want me around... fine." There was hurt in Mick's voice. "I'll find a new friend."

"Yeah. You do that." Rad backtracked and slammed the door. Then he stood there for a moment as the fear and anger drained away. He went to the window and looked out. Mick was slinking down the path toward the street with hunched shoulders. He didn't look back. "It's not safe for you," he murmured.

"Well, that was disappointing." Kahin stood in the kitchen doorway, the knife still in his hand. He looked down at it, then back up to Rad. "Think I need some guidance."

Rad didn't understand what that meant, but before he could ask, Kahin turned on his heels and went back into the kitchen. A moment later, Rad heard the back door open, then slam shut again.

Anya slunk into the doorway and leaned on the frame. "You just made a big mistake there, Rad."

"Where's he going?" Rad asked, ignoring the comment.

"Out to the woods behind the house. It's what Kahin does when he gets upset."

"He goes into the woods?"

Anya nodded. "That's where he communes with Satan."

"Satan... Really?"

Anya nodded a second time. "You better hope he comes back in a better mood. He really wanted you to take care of that kid. Prove yourself. But hey, too late now, right?"

"I guess." Rad wished Mick had never shown up.

"Yeah." Anya made a slight tutting sound. "Big mistake. Maybe not a fatal one, but you'll have to work hard to get back into his good books. I don't think this put you on his blacklist, but sometimes even I can't tell with Kahin."

Rad said nothing. He could feel every set of eyes in the room upon him. Anya waited a moment longer, then disappeared back into the kitchen. When he turned toward the couch, the girl who called herself Claire was gone. Only her empty beer bottle remained, sitting on the floor.

"Shit," he muttered.

CHAPTER 11

A Touch Of Home

Ukiah, CA

THE PHONE RANG three times before Kevin picked up, and when he did, a cacophony of conversations, silverware, glasses, and God only knew what else assaulted Meredeth's ear. "Kevin? Can you hear me?"

"Loud and clear, FBI. What's up?"

"Just calling to chat. Where are you?"

"Give me a second to get outside."

"Where are you? The diner?"

"No, not the diner. I'm up in, uh, Buffalo at an informal meeting for police chiefs out this way."

"Oh. I've never heard you talk about that before."

"It's a new thing. You know, post-Ankou."

"You sound funny, Kevin. What's going on?"

His warm chuckle rattled across the line. "Nothing, FBI. For your part, you sound like you're in the next room."

She wished she could see his face. Something was up, and she was pretty sure he'd lied to her about being in

Buffalo. But that had been way too much noise for the diner, and they both knew it.

"You still there, FBI?"

"Yeah."

"Let me head up to my room. I'll call you back when I get up there. Okay?"

"Yeah, sure. Talk to you in a minute." She disconnected, then slumped lower in her hotel room's only armchair—which was about as comfortable as a block of granite. *Why would he need a hotel room for a meeting an hour from home?* She tried to still her inner detective, tried to turn off her internal lie detector. She didn't like being suspicious of Kevin—something she'd avoided even when Bobby viewed him as a suspect in the Ankou case.

Of course, back then she hadn't been in love with him.

She dropped her phone into her lap and reached for her Coke and her bottle of Excedrin. Her head hadn't been bad that day, but the second she thought Kevin was lying, it felt like her brain had started to swell, to throb, to pulse with every beat of her heat. She swallowed two of Excedrin and washed it down with half the can of Coke. With a sigh, she got up and filled her little ice bag from the ice bucket, then lay on the bed and settled the bag over her eyes and forehead. When the phone rang, she accepted the call before the ringtone cycled a single time. "Kevin?"

"Hey, Mere. Is this better?"

"Yes."

"Good. How's the case going?"

"Okay."

"And Bobby? I take he hasn't killed you with his driving?"

"No."

"Erm, FBI?"

"Yes?"

"What's going on?"

"Nothing."

"Well, I think something's up. See, I'm a detective by nature, and I've picked up on subtle cues that you're upset with me."

"Why would I be upset?"

"I'm not sure, but I'd like to know the answer."

"Why do you think I'm upset?"

"Gee, I don't know, honey. Maybe it's your voice—distant, cold. Maybe it's the one-word answers. I mean, you called me, right?"

"I asked you where you were and you lied to me, Kevin."

He said nothing for a few moments, then, "Yeah, I did."

"Why?"

"It's nothing, Meredeth. I promise you."

"If it's nothing, why can't you tell me?"

"I can tell you, but I'd rather not."

"Why?"

"Because, FBI, I want it to be a surprise. Okay? Can you let me have this one?"

"Does this one involve hookers and a pound of blow?"

Kevin chuckled. "You're the only hooker I want, Meredeth Connelly."

"You say the sweetest things, jerkwad."

"It's a gift. Now that you're calling me names, I'm sensing the Force is settling back into its proper pattern. Am I right?"

"I love you, Kevin."

He was silent a moment, and when he spoke, emotion was evident in his tone. "I love you, too. I think I have almost from the first second I saw you."

"Liar. You thought I was a hoity-toity FBI wank. You thought I was a callous jerk."

"Well, you are, but that didn't stop me from loving you."

"Again with the sweet talk, Kevin? You're going to give me a big head."

"Listen, FBI, where I am doesn't matter. Not yet. But it might. It might matter in a good way. Can I tell you all about it once it's resolved? Can you trust me on this?"

"Oh, Kevin, of course I trust you, but you know how it is. After all, you're a detective at heart."

"I should've known better than to float a story at you."

"You should've."

"Inner lie detector went crazy, eh?"

"You bet, then my suspicious mind kicked in."

"Let me put that beautiful mind of yours to rest. I'm never going to cheat on you. It will never happen, but I promise you that if I ever lose interest, I will tell you, face to face. I'll just have to hope you don't shoot me down like the dog I would be. Okay?"

"Ditto."

"Good."

"Give me a hint?"

"I've probably already said too much, Mere. You'll wake up tomorrow, and that big, beautiful brain of yours will fill in all the blanks. Just promise me that you'll act surprised, even if you figure it out."

"I will try not to think about it, but I don't know if I can turn it off."

"You can't. Any fool knows that. That's why you're the best damn profiler out there."

"You're not biased at all, are you?"

Kevin chuckled. "No, not a bit."

"Give me a hint."

"Let me think a minute. I need to come up with something so devious you won't be able to unravel it."

"Oh, a challenge. I wish I was in the room next door. I'd come over, slip out of my things, and make you tell me."

"Oh, great. Now I wish you were in the room next door even more than before. Rain check until we're in the same state?"

"It's a date. But you'd better be well rested."

"Now this conversation has taken an interesting turn."

"You know what they say: make up sex is the best sex."

"Listen, I'm not going to argue. I'm sorry I made you feel bad, okay? It was stupid."

"In a way, it was sweet. Trying to surprise me an all. Most people give that up after they've known me for a day or two."

"Their loss, FBI. I'm always wanting to surprise you. Your face just lights up when I can pull it off."

"Have your hint yet?"

"No, not yet. Tell me about Jamie Wenstrom."

She gave a little sigh. "It's a real shame. He had everything going for him, then a couple of years back, he just threw it all away."

"Abuse? Drugs?"

"I don't know about the abuse side. We're going to talk to his parents tomorrow after lunch. He's definitely using drugs, however. One of his friends said he's a—and I quote—horse head."

"Heroin? Sheesh, he's still in high school. How can he afford H?"

"No ideas on that. We haven't heard a word about thievery, but maybe Jenna was too embarrassed to tell Jim that."

"Could be. Could it be worse than that, though?"

"Street life? I'm not sure. Ukiah isn't that big a town. I mean, I'm sure there's a stroll somewhere around here, but I don't know that there'd be clientele for seventeen-year-old boys."

"I think there's always a market for debauchery, FBI. What about dealing?"

"None of his friends mentioned that."

"Would they, though? I mean, you and Bobby *are* FBI agents."

"Good point. We'll have to ask point blank and rely on my internal lie detector."

"So what have you learned?"

"He went to a drug party thrown by an obnoxious little twerp who, if my gut is any good at predicting the future, will soon be on his way to Paris Island."

"Oh?"

"Yeah. The twerp still lives with his parents and threw the party without permission. His mom and dad were a little upset, and Bobby pitched the Marine Corps as a potential solution."

"The military has straightened out more than one or two hotheads. Probably a good solution."

"Yeah."

"What did you find out about the party?"

"There's a guy in Ukiah who claims to be a devil worshipper who is in his forties and hangs out with high school druggies. Even his name—Kahin Alshaytan—Bobby says means, 'priest of Satan.'"

"Sounds like a winner."

"Yeah. We're going to track him down in the morning if we can. We have the street he lives on, and evidently, the house will be instantly recognizable."

"Do you think he's for real?"

"As a devil worshipper, you mean?"

"Yeah. Weren't there so many reports of Satanic cults abusing people, that the FBI created a unit to investigate the reports?"

"That's not quite right, Kev. In the early nineties, when I was just getting up to speed with Crimes Against Children, the BAU put out a whitepaper on the subject, and it's been misquoted and misunderstood ever since. What the author of the paper actually said, was that the claims of ritualistic child sexual abuse were probably not Satanic in nature. Many of the victims only 'remember' such abuse while hypnotized—and you remember the whole controversy over recovered-memory therapy. Many of these victims report this that seems to be untrue or are physically impossible. Take, for instance, the claims of being cut up into small pieces and then reassembled. Or the claims that more than doubled the number of murders occurring in the U.S. as ritual sacrifice and the like. And the author went on to say that in none of the cases he reviewed, were any bodies recovered, and in some cases, massive excavations occurred in an effort to find them. In addition, there's never been any physical evidence to support the claim that any murder took place."

"Okay, so no cults, then?"

"There is also no evidence of any well-organized Satanic cult. Most people believe that a criminal conspiracy makes it easier to get away with a crime, but the truth, as you probably already know, is that with each additional conspirator the chances of getting away with it drop considerably. We have tons of evidence to support that. Imagine what it would take to make some of these claims true: local governments run by Satanists, police forces dominated by the same, all while leaving absolutely no evidence behind."

"Yeah, that's unlikely."

"Then consider human nature. What organizations have you ever been a part of where someone didn't get their nose out of joint and quit? None, right?"

"Right."

"People get mad. They become jealous. They resent that the leaders get more out of whatever activity than they do. Now, pretend the group in question is a cult that thrives on child sacrifice. Obviously, the members of any cult like that will view themselves as above the law. They will commit crimes, and they will be caught. Once caught, they will make a deal—trading information on the cult's crimes to lessen their own sentences."

"So all those victims lied?"

"No. They told investigators what they had come to believe happened to them. They were abused, there is very little question in that regard, but there is a plethora of explanations for how their memories might serve up imagined or untrue events as truth."

"Such as?"

"Pathological distortions. Keep in mind that a large portion of these victims had comorbid psychiatric diagnoses—dissociative identity disorder, borderline or histrionic personality disorders, psychosis. The allegations may be errors in processing reality due to these underlying psychiatric conditions. These processing errors become pseudomemories that the victims come to believe are true accounts. Another potential answer is trauma. It's known that severe trauma can distort and confuse memories of events, possibly as a part of an elaborate defense mechanism called splitting. Their minds create black and white—or perhaps good and evil is a better description—manifestations of their victimization to make it more psychologically manageable. Or these traumas may make the victims dissociate, and in a dissociative state, anyone might confuse memories of a movie or film as reality. And keep in mind that molesters use fear to control their victims. Maybe the victims were told of some elaborate conspiracy involving a bunch of innocent people to keep the child quiet. And, they might have drugged their victims, introducing a hypnogogic state to confuse and distort the victim's memory of the crime. And then there are the well-meaning but overzealous interventions by parents, social workers, mental health professionals, doctors, and even law enforcement. Victims have been overtly rewarded for coming up with new details about the alleged cults and rituals they witnessed. In other words, the intervening person may misconstrue or misinterpret what the victim has said. They repeat it, possibly embellishing the story in the process, then get the victim to agree with the new version."

"Yeah, we see that with false confessions."

"Sure, we do. It's the same principle. An authority figure repeats and repeats and repeats the story until the person across the table from them breaks down and stops fighting the inaccuracies and just says, 'sure, whatever you say.'"

"Then you don't think this priest of Satan character is on the level?"

"I believe he's probably mentally ill. He's engaging in magical thinking to explain why the world doesn't measure up to his internal version of reality. He's powerless, probably poor, with very little real influence over the events in his life. As a result, he creates a reality in which he is the central player in the fate of everyone around him, and he *believes* that reality with utter commitment. He's confident that only he knows the real truth. Truth with a capital T. He knows the truth and wants to share it with his flock. Now, it doesn't matter if his flock is only around because he gives them drugs or whatever. To him, they are his disciples. They are his true believers."

"A guy who thinks that way..."

"Yes. He's inherently dangerous, unpredictable."

"Just the sort of guy who might kill a seventeen-year-old boy for some imagined slight."

"For Jim's sake, I really hope not."

"Yeah."

"Anyway, enough gloom and doom."

"Okay."

"So let's hear it, Chief."

"Hear what, FBI?"

"My hint."

"Oh, that."

"Yes, that."

"Would you look at that..."

"At what?"

"Some bird left red feathers all over my room's windowsill."

"Stop stalling, Saunders."

"Who said I'm stalling? That's your hint."

"Red feathers? What am I supposed to get from that?"

"Think about it, FBI. I'm sure you'll figure it out."

"Wow, you have an exaggerated view of my capabilities, Kevin."

"Yeah, no I don't, FBI. Don't sell yourself short."

She shook her head but couldn't keep the soft smile from her lips. "Sometimes, Saunders, you say the sweetest things."

"Yeah, I know. I'm a romantic."

CHAPTER 12

SUBTLETY

David Branch's Farm, NY

LUCY STOOD IN the basement doing laundry. The job always fell to her as "women's work." Not that she was the only female in residence. There was Alex, of course, but no one would dare call Alex a girl, although the truth was blatantly obvious despite the boys' clothing she chose to wear. Besides, Alex was Father's second-in-command and beyond such menial tasks. Michelina was around as well, but she seemed to have perfect timing—she always seemed to be somewhere else when it came time to do the laundry.

"Hey, Squirt," Jonathon said, lumbering down the steps at speed, not pausing at the bottom, coming toward her with a sneer on his face. "I've been looking for you."

"Don't call me that," snapped Lucy, irritated despite her unease. Alex was not around to stick up for her now—nor were Carl and Mack. It was just the two of them alone in the basement, and Lucy wondered if Jonathon had bided his time, if he had planned it that way.

"Why not? What's good for Alex—"

"You're not Alex," Lucy shot back, despite the fear that knotted her stomach. Now was not the time to show weakness. "What do you want?"

"What do you think?"

Lucy shrugged and glanced toward the basement stairs. "You thought coming down here might work off some of that belly flab?"

"Better watch your mouth." Jonathon lunged forward, his hefty bulk descending on her like a charging rhino.

Lucy backpedaled, but there was nowhere to go. She felt the washing machine press into her back. "Get away from me!"

"Or what?" Jonathon loomed over her. She could smell his sweat, pungent and ripe. His eyes were like two small black marbles set into his doughy face. When he spoke, spittle flew from his lips. "I'm getting tired of your sass."

Lucy turned her head away to avoid the worst of the spit shower. "Touch me, and Alex will kill you."

"Alex isn't here. The freak is out in the barn. Everyone else is working on the truck. House is empty. It's just you and me."

Lucy tried to squirm around him, but Jonathon pressed forward, and she found herself wedged between the washing machine and his belly. "If I don't finish this laundry, Father won't be happy."

"That's not my problem." Jonathon put an arm on each side of her and gripped the edges of the washing machine.

"Well, it should be. Because if it doesn't get done, Father will want to know why. So will Alex. And I *will* tell them."

"You think I'm afraid of them?"

"Yeah, I do."

"Better find some respect, Squirt...be careful what you say"—he traced her jawline with a fat, dirty finger—"stop running your mouth off or else. Someone like you could disappear real easy."

"Someone like me?" Lucy pushed back against Jonathon, found enough room to duck under his arm, and released herself. She retreated a few steps and then turned to face him. "What's that supposed to mean?"

"A pipsqueak, runt of the litter. You're nothing but a scared little girl trying to sound big. So go ahead, run to Father. It won't work out how you think. He doesn't like kids who can't take care of themselves. He hates weakness. Alex figured it out. That's why she got where she is."

"Really?" Lucy watched Jonathon with a wary eye, waiting for him to pounce again. This time, though, she stood a good chance of reaching the stairs before he caught her. Jonathon might be muscular, but he was also carrying a lot of unnecessary weight, and she, the opposite. She had quickness on her side. "I figured it was because she's more of a man than you'll ever be."

Jonathon's face flushed about as close to purple as Lucy had ever seen. His breath came in quick gasps. "You're one to talk. A skinny little girl who's no use to anyone. He'll see through you in a flash, and then you'll be gone. You won't be the first."

"He's already seen through you." Lucy's fear was giving way to a strange sense of bravado. Jonathon was a bully, and bullies didn't like it when you stood up to them. "That's why he treats Mack and Carl so much better than he does you."

"That's not true."

"Sure it is. He spends time with them. Overlooks their mistakes where he won't overlook yours. He treats them with respect and treats you like a rat that scurried over his shoe. Why is that, Jonathon?"

"Shut up." The corner of Jonathon's eye twitched. He clenched his fists. "You don't know nothing."

"I know enough." A sense of empowerment washed over Lucy. Her words were as good as a dagger in Jonathon's heart. Better still, at that moment, she wasn't afraid of him. He wouldn't lay a finger on her. Because despite his belligerence and posturing, Jonathon knew she was right. *He* was the weak link, not her. And if he did anything to harm Father's latest project, there would be hell to pay. "You'll never be as good as Carl or Mack, let alone Alex. They're all better than you and always will be."

"I told you to close your stupid little mouth, bitch!" Jonathon took a step toward her with a raised fist but then appeared to change his mind. He glared at her through slitted eyes. "Alex is nothing but Father's circus freak. A girl too stupid to know she ain't a boy. And Mack can't think straight. All he wants to do is get in her pants. As for Carl..."

"What about him?" Lucy felt a hot flush come to her cheeks at the mention of his name. She wondered if Jonathon had noticed.

But Jonathon was oblivious as usual. "Carl's nothing but a doe-eyed puppy following Mack around wherever he goes. He worships Mack like he's some kind of hero. It's pathetic."

"I think *you're* the pathetic one," Lucy said, putting her hands on her hips. "Blaming everyone else for your own inadequacies."

Jonathon sputtered but said nothing.

"What's the matter? Don't have anything left to say?" Lucy took a step toward him. "You really are pathetic." She threw her head back and laughed, the sound echoing back at her in the enclosed space.

Jonathon opened his mouth, then shut it again. He observed her for a moment longer, his flabby body quivering with rage. Then he turned and stomped back up the stairs.

Lucy watched him go with a sly grin, then she turned her attention back to the laundry.

CHAPTER 13

DIG DUG DOG

Ukiah, CA

RAD WAS IN the back bedroom of the dilapidated house on Rosemary Lane getting high when Kahin burst in like he owned the place. *Which*, Rad thought through his dope-induced haze, *the guy kinda does.* It was the day after Mick showed up, and Kahin got the idea to kill him. Or rather, for Rad to do it. That was never going to happen, and Rad had said as much, pushing his naïve and somewhat lame friend out the door with instructions never to come back. After that, Kahin have been absent the rest of the night and still had not returned from the woods when Rad left around midnight to go home.

In the time since, he'd thought long and hard about whether he wanted to go back to the disgusting house on Rosemary Lane, but in the end, the lure of complete freedom was too strong. There were girls, drugs, and free alcohol. Not to mention Claire, who he was still hoping to hook up with despite her own vanishing act the previous evening. Which was why he was lying there in his undies, head propped on a pillow that smelled of other people's sweat, and sucking in the last of a not-so-great joint scored from some fat guy in the living room when Kahin slammed the bedroom door back on its hinges.

"There's my boy." Kahin stepped into the room. His dreadlocks fell around his shoulders like greasy strands of rope. He was shirtless and sweaty. When he approached the bed, Rad could smell his stink even before Kahin sat down on the edge and slapped Rad's bare leg just above the knee. "I've been looking for you."

"Why?" A tug of dread coiled in Rad's stomach despite the mind-altering drugs flowing through his system. Maybe it had been a mistake to come back here, after all.

Kahin stared him in the eye and pressed his lips together into a thin line before speaking. "When you first came here, I told you the rules, right?"

"Yeah. Sure you did." Rad nodded. "You were sitting right out there with Anya on your lap."

"That's right." Kahin tilted his head. "Which is why I don't understand what happened last night. I mean, you knew the rules. They aren't hard to follow."

"I didn't break—"

"Yeah, you did. You broke rule number one. Screw all the girls you want around here. Smoke all the dope and knock back all the liquor you can stomach. But when I ask you to do something... when I ask you to repay the hospitality I've extended... I expect you to man up and do it."

"That wasn't one of the rules," Rad said, instantly regretting the words, which tumbled out before his brain had time to engage. That was what too much pot did.

"Yes, it was. First rule. If you don't have my permission to be here, you will no longer be here." Kahin leaned close enough that Rad could smell his fetid breath. "But maybe you weren't listening good enough. Maybe you were too busy ogling my fiancée to fully comprehend the rules."

"This is about Mick. Right?" Rad thought Kahin's logic on rule number one was a bit off. Maybe his host was high, too.

"Hallelujah. He sees the light. Your friend Mick wasn't welcome here. I asked you to make sure he wouldn't be here anymore. You didn't do that."

"But I made him go away. He won't come back. I told him to never come back." Rad resisted the urge to draw his legs up. He felt uncomfortable. Exposed.

"But you didn't kill him!" Kahin roared, leaning over and pressing his face close to Rad's. "You didn't do that for me."

"I'm sorry." Rad scrambled and pushed himself up, so his back was pressed against the wall. "Please don't hurt me."

"Hurt... You thought I came in here to..." The anger fell away from Kahin's face like a discarded mask. He threw his head back and laughed, the sound shrill and unhinged.

"Holy crap, kid. Relax. I was messing with you. You really thought I was still mad over last night?"

Rad nodded.

Kahin waved a dismissive hand. "Water under the bridge."

Rad breathed a sigh of relief, which might have been premature.

"If...you do something for me now." Kahin fixed Rad with an unblinking stare. "Think you can do that?"

"I don't know. What is it?" Rad couldn't imagine it would be anything good.

"Remember what I said about the last guy who offended me?" Kahin asked. "How I said he never left."

Rad had a vague recollection of some such statement, but he'd smoked a lot of pot and drank more than his fair share of alcohol in the meantime. Things had gotten fuzzy. He nodded anyway.

"Well, I wasn't joking about that. He's down in the basement. Now it's time for him to go."

"You kept a guy captive in the basement?" Rad asked, his dope-soaked brain latching on to the most obvious scenario. "You want me to bring him up and kick him out?"

The look on Kahin's face was a mixture of bemusement and disbelief. "Hell, kid. You really are out of it, huh?"

"Little bit."

"Then try to focus. This is some important shit. Do this for me, and I'll forget about last night. Even-Steven. With me so far?"

"Uh-hunh." Rad nodded.

"Good. I don't have some random dude captive in the basement. I have a dead body. I'm done with it. I want it gone. Keeping corpses around too long isn't hygienic."

Rad thought this was funny, considering the state of Kahin's house, but he didn't laugh. Instead, he asked, "What do you want me to do with him?"

"What normally happens to people who have expired?"

"They get buried?" Rad thought expired was a weird turn of phrase.

"Exactly. I would like to give our friend in the basement a dignified burial. There's a nice little plot of land out by the back fence near the woods and a shovel in the garage. Go dig a hole and put him in it."

Rad didn't move while he contemplated this gruesome request.

"Confused about something?" Kahin asked, raising an eyebrow.

Rad shook his head.

"That are you waiting for?"

"Nothing."

"So get going." Kahin reached around his back and drew out a knife. The same knife he'd wanted Rad to kill Mick with the previous evening. His eyes looked like a pair of black coals, hard and emotionless. "Unless you'd prefer I slit your throat right now and bury the pair of you in a shallow grave together?"

"Nuh-no nuh-need for that." Rad was overcome by a sudden conviction that Kahin actually wanted to slit his throat. That he was hoping it would play out like that. The guy was giving off weird vibes. Then again, it could be the pot making him paranoid. Either way, Rad didn't want to be on the receiving end of Kahin's knife. He swung his legs off the bed and reached for his pants, which lay discarded on the floor.

"Don't bother with those." Kahin stood up and went to the door. He held it open for Rad. "Better to wash the dirt and crap off your body than have to burn your clothes. Trust me."

Rad wasn't sure he wanted to bury a body in nothing but his skivvies, but for once, Kahin was making sense. He dropped the trousers back on the floor and stepped through the door into the short hallway beyond. Anya was standing there, like always, as if she and Kahin were tethered by an invisible leash.

There was a smirk on her face.

She watched Rad make his way toward the basement door before calling out to him. "Hey. Wrong way. Hole first, body second."

"Right." Rad tried to focus through the pot haze. He changed direction and went to the garage door in the kitchen. The shovel was leaning against the wall next to the door as if it were waiting for him. He grabbed it and hurried through the kitchen to the back door. When he stepped outside, the chill night air raised goosebumps on his arms and legs. The dewy wet grass felt springy under his bare feet, and he realized he had put no shoes on either. Probably for the best.

Rad crossed to the fence, which leaned in places and was missing several slats. He chose a spot where the fence was still winning its fight with gravity and far enough from trees that roots would not be a problem.

Then he started to dig.

Rad had never buried a corpse before, although he'd heard the expression six feet under. That felt like a lot of hole. Especially since the hard-packed soil wasn't exactly cooperating with the shovel. Would three feet be enough? Rad didn't know, but it sounded reasonable. Even that shallow depth took him over an hour to excavate, and by the time he was done, the goosebumps were gone, and he was dripping sweat.

He stepped back to admire his work. The hole looked nothing like the neat oblong trenches they used to bury people in cemeteries. There were no straight edges or neat sidewalls. It looked more like something had crash-landed and made a deep furrow in the backyard. But Rad figured it would do.

Rad dropped the shovel and padded back to the house, leaving muddy footprints on the tile floor when he walked through the kitchen, stopping at the fridge to grab a bottle of water. He was beyond thirsty and had a raging dehydration headache, but all he found were a couple of beers and a half-empty gallon of milk that smelled when he opened the cap. Plucking an empty bottle from the trash on the island countertop, Rad went to the sink. He rinsed the bottle twice, then filled it to the brim. He slurped the water down in a single pull, then refilled it a second and went looking for his hosts.

Kahin was nowhere in sight. Neither was Anya. The house was strangely empty for once. Maybe that was why Kahin had decided it was time to bury the body. It also meant Rad wasn't going to get any help in moving the corpse from the basement to the backyard. Worse, his high was wearing off, which made the task all the more unpleasant.

Rad descended into the basement and fumbled in the darkness to find the light switch. He looked around. At first, he didn't see a body and wondered if Kahin was playing a practical joke. He could imagine the man sitting upstairs and laughing his ass off at Rad's expense. That was fine. Digging the hole had been bad, but dragging a corpse upstairs was in another league.

A wash of relief surged through Rad. He turned to go back upstairs... and stopped in his tracks. There was a body, after all. It was laying atop a plastic tarp in the space under the basement stairs. It was mostly covered by gray pellets that Rad knew were kitty litter, not only because Kahin had mentioned it, but because of the plastic tubs stacked nearby.

Rad approached the corpse and looked down at it. He resisted the urge to vomit. The face was gone. All that remained was a bloodied crater of pulp and bone. Had Kahin shot the guy in the face point-blank? It certainly looked that way. Rad briefly thought about turning around and going back upstairs, telling Kahin to bury the body. But he was a little too fond of living to carry out that plan.

He still had that woman's card—the FBI agent. Maybe he should call her, tell her about the body, then get the hell out of there before the cops showed up. He spent a few minutes running various scenarios through his mind, but none of them ended up with Rad happy. The only thing that seemed to point in that direction was keeping Kahin happy.

"Just get it done," Rad muttered to himself.

He stood there a while longer, gathering his nerves, then bent down and grabbed the corners of the tarp because he didn't want to touch the body. Even semi-buzzed, that grossed him out.

He tugged. He tugged hard, and the tarp moved a few inches. He tried to drag it across the floor to the stairs, but with one end of the tarp lifted, the corpse shifted and started to slide off. Flies buzzed into the air, angry at being disturbed. An odor of putrescence wafted up— rotting meat and worse.

Rad gagged and swallowed hard. He shifted his stance and tried to drag the tarp at a lower angle, but it didn't help. The body soon tumbled off along with the kitty litter. The sudden shift in weight caused Rad to stumble backward, almost falling. He flailed and managed to regain his balance.

With no other choice, he gripped the corpse's arms and hauled it up out of the kitty litter, struggling to get it over his shoulder in a fireman's carry. The body was heavy and limp—true dead weight. It smelled even worse now he was closer to it. Pungent and sickly sweet. The odor burned his nostrils, and again, Rad felt bile rising in his throat.

He staggered toward the stairs with the dead weight over his shoulder, and his leg muscles screaming. He labored upward, worried the whole time that the corpse would shift and topple him back into the basement.

He looked around when he reached the top to make sure no one was there. The last thing Rad wanted was a witness to his crime. Satisfied, he plodded through the kitchen with one hand gripping the corpse to make sure it wouldn't slide from his shoulder. In the backyard, he almost slipped more than once on the slick grass but kept his feet long enough to drop the corpse into its shallow grave.

Thirty minutes later, the pile of dirt he'd excavated was back in the hole, although now it didn't lie flat thanks to the added mass of the body underneath. Rad didn't care. He'd done his part. He patted the earth down as best he could with the shovel, stomped it down, and then trudged back to the house, tired and filthy.

When he entered the kitchen, Anya was there. She grinned and went to him. Slipping her fingers into the elastic band of his undies, she slid them down and waited for him to step out of them.

"Can't leave these lying around. Cops get a hold of them, and we're done for," she said, her gaze taking in his dirt-streaked nudity. "Go take a shower, then meet Kahin something stronger than pot to take the edge off."

"Sure." Rad couldn't argue with that. Anything to dull the memory of what he'd just done. He started toward the bathroom.

Anya watched him for a moment, then called his name.

Rad turned back to look at her.

She smiled, her eyes glittering. "You did good, kid. Real good."

CHAPTER 14

LIAR

Ukiah, CA

BOBBY AND MEREDETH left the hotel before seven the next morning, grabbing coffee from the hotel's breakfast spread, and made their way around the Ukiah Municipal Airport with its single runway

Rosemary Lane was a short little residential street at the edge of mountains on the west side of Ukiah. A ton of cars were parked at the edge of the tree-shaded lane, but most of the homes were well-kept, though small and on small lots. The neighborhood may not have been dotted with high-dollar properties, but the people who lived there cared.

Most of them. But not the people who lived in the second house from the end; the mess that was 1408 Rosemary Lane. Bobby pulled up in front of the house and killed the Jeep's engine, then leaned forward to take a look at the age-yellowed white paint and the peeling black trim. "Well, ain't that pretty."

"Not really, no."

"Check out the front door."

"I saw. Let's go see if anyone's awake."

"What's all the crap on the door?"

"We'll see when we get up there."

They got out and were immediately assaulted by the stench of ammonia and decay and mold. The scent overpowered Meredeth's olfactory nerve, seeming to burn all the way down to her lungs, and her stomach roiled with the urge to evacuate her coffee into the overgrown grass and weeds next to the front walk.

"I can't wait to smell the inside," said Bobby.

"Yeah," Meredeth all but gasped. "Whew. I wish I had some VapoRub."

"You always say that."

"Yeah, and I mean it every time. I have four jars. Want to know where?"

"Back at the hotel?"

"Worse. Back in Virginia. I always remember to buy some when I get home after a trip, and I always lay it out so I'll remember to pack it."

"Yet you never do."

"Yet I never do. It's some kind of mental block."

"You look a little green. Headache?"

"Not until I smelled this place."

"Hop back in. There's a Walmart back by the hotel."

"They won't be open yet."

"Then we'll find that CVS I saw last night on the way to the hotel. Or maybe a RiteAid or something."

"Nah. We're due to talk to the Investigative Bureau at the Mendocino County Sheriff's Department at nine. Let's just go ring the bell and muscle through the nausea."

"You sure?"

"Yeah, I'm sure." She turned and climbed the three steps up from the street level to the front walk and then went on to the black front door. "Oh, this is cute." The door was layered in thick black paint with a skull affixed to the top left corner, overrun with black plastic Halloween spiders. In the upper right hung a "BEWARE OF DOG" sign like those that could be purchased at any hardware store. Below the sign, someone had used white stick-on letters to spell out "ARE YOU THREATENING ME?" Meredeth scoffed. "Do you believe this guy?"

"What a nutcase."

Above the peephole was an upended crucifix, and below it, someone had taped pirate flags to either side of a handmade sign stuck in the center that read "Evil will always triumph over good." The door was marked with the remains of other stickers either peeled off or degraded beyond readability. But the star of the show was the giant hand-written sign that read: "No gang members allowed. No one representing the so-called government of this land—which was stolen by terrorists two hundred and some odd years ago—has permission to enter this domicile. That includes cops, social workers, deputies, feebs, drug-addicted enforcement agents, IRS criminals, Department of Homeland Silliness, or anyone else. If you don't know whether this applies to you or not, *it does*. Turn around. I will not be presumed guilty until proven innocent. If you can make laws in a land you stole, so can I. So be it. Punishment for disregarding this notice is death."

Meredeth pointed to the Arabic that had been chipped in the paint beneath the sign. "What's that say, Bobby?"

"No idea. I can't really read the language, though I have enough verbally to make my way. I'll send it to the language guys in Quantico." He pulled out his phone and snapped a picture, then shot it to the east coast in a quick email.

Meredeth shrugged and rapped on the door, spotted the doorbell and pressed the button, but instead of a door chime, a sickly buzz sounded. "Ah, ha." She rapped on the door a second time and was rewarded with the sound of running footsteps pounding closer. The door opened, and two things happened at the same time: first, a horrid stench at least ten times as powerful as what they'd been smelling washed over her, and second, a skinny male came charging out, pulling a T-shirt over his head as he did so, and running blind—right into Meredeth.

She staggered back, fighting for balance, and before she recovered, Bobby had the guy shoved up against the wall next to the front door, Van Zandt's Glock pressed into the base of his skull. "Don't move," Bobby said. "I don't want to shoot you, but I will."

"Don't do that. Please." The voice was familiar, even shaking as it was. "I didn't do anything. I'm...I'm late for school."

"Ray?" asked Meredeth. "Ray Michaels?"

"Yuh-yes?"

Meredeth waved Bobby off high alert, and he grimaced, shaking his head, but put his Glock away and stepped away from the kid. "What are you doing here, Ray?" she asked. She pointed to the scars crisscrossing his back, and Bobby nodded, his mouth set in a grim line.

"I... Uh, I fell asleep after Anya and I... I didn't mean to, I just did, and Anya didn't wake me up. Now, I'm late, and I can't be late. I have to get to school."

"Slow down, Ray."

"Rad," he said sullenly.

"Rad, then. Why are you here?"

"I came over last night to help...to help with a project, and—"

"What kind of project?" asked Bobby.

"What? Oh. Nothing big. Home improvement, I suppose. I just helped clean out the basement."

Meredeth pulled his shirt down over his head. "You can turn around, Rad."

He did so, his eyes still a little round, a little wide. "Can I go? I've got to go."

"I know, Rad. I'll give you a note for Ms. McAdams saying you were helping us out."

"Um, no offense, but leave that last part out."

"Fine, I'll say we were questioning you, again. Good enough?"

"Yeah. Yeah, I suppose that works."

"Who is Anya?"

"Just a girl."

"A girl you slept with?"

"A gentleman would never say, so, yeah. I slept with her last night. She's one of Kahin's girlfriends, or whatever, but he didn't mind. He has others. I think he chilled with Claire."

Bobby pulled his pad out and jotted down the names. "Last names?"

"Um... I don't exactly know their last names. It's not that kind of place."

"You partied here last night?" asked Meredeth. "Got high? Drank, what?"

"Me?" Rad squeaked. "No, nothing like that. I just helped clean up the—"

"Basement. Yeah, we heard that the first time," said Bobby.

"So grumpy," muttered Rad.

"Rad, look me in the eye," said Meredeth and waited until he met her gaze. "What was it? Weed? Booze? Horse?"

"Nothing," he repeated. "We were just hanging out."

"What if we pack you into our backseat and run you over to the hospital for a tox screen?"

His eyes widened, and beads of sweat appeared on his upper lip. "No. I refuse."

"Then we'll call your parents."

"Good luck with that," he said.

Meredeth glanced at Bobby and nodded. He stepped forward and grabbed Rad by the elbow, then pulled him down toward the street.

"Aw, man!" snapped Rad. "I've got to get to school!"

Bobby ignored him, pulling him down to the sidewalk. "So, go," he said in a bland voice, then turned and climbed back up the three steps and returned to Meredeth's side.

She had her eyes on Rad, and when he glanced her way, she lifted her arm and pointed north, toward the intersection of Rosemary Lane and Canyon Drive, toward Ukiah High School. Without another word, Rad sprinted toward the end of the street.

"You believe him?" asked Bobby.

"Not at all. He came over to get high, to get laid." She jerked her chin at the open door and the mess beyond. "And why bother cleaning out the basement?"

"Because, Officer, one must start somewhere." A tall man stepped out of the shadows. He had what Meredeth first took as a sheet wrapped around his middle, wearing it like some kind of wrap-around skirt, but on closer inspection, the fit was too good for a makeshift getup. He followed her gaze and looked down at himself, his greasy, untamed dreadlocks swinging forward like a heavy curtain. "You can get anything on Etsy."

"My name is Special Agent Connelly, and this is my partner, Special Agent Van Zandt."

"Ah, the FBI. What have I said or done to warrant this intrusion?"

"We're here to speak with Kahin Alshaytan. Is that you?" said Bobby.

"I don't believe I'm required to say."

"Well, you are wrong about that. Let's see some identification."

The man again looked down at his skirt and patted around his waist. "No pockets, no ID."

"Go get it." Bobby's voice was hard, commanding.

"Let me take your picture, first," Meredeth said. She lifted her phone and snapped a picture without giving the man a chance to reply. "There. Now, go get your ID as Agent Van Zandt requested."

"It didn't sound much like a request."

"A euphemism. You're required to produce identification when requested by a law enforcement officer."

"Am I?"

"You are. Go on."

The man sighed, then smiled. "I'm Kahin. This is my house."

"We still need that ID," said Bobby, his face set and hard.

Kahin sighed. "Oh, all right, but you can't come in."

"Got something to hide?"

"Not at all, but you read my notice on the door, I'm sure.

"Yes," said Meredeth. "We'll wait right here."

"See that you do. You do not have my permission to enter."

"Sure. We got it. Go."

He turned and disappeared into the artificial gloaming inside. Meredeth lifted her eyebrow at Bobby and tried not to breathe through her nose. Bobby rolled his eyes and shook his head.

Kahin was gone for ten minutes, and when he returned, he wore a sour expression. "I guess you'll have to arrest me. I can't find the damn thing."

"Is Kahin Alshaytan your real name?"

"Yes. Oh, it wasn't the name my mother gave me when she pushed me out, but I've taken care of that. All nice and legal, too."

"Then we'll find your records under this name?"

He lifted his arms out to his sides, palms up. "I'm sure I have no idea how any of that works."

"I'm sure," said Bobby. "Let me make it simple. Is your identification under Kahin Alshaytan or the name your mother gave you when she pushed you out?"

"Which was what, by the way?" asked Meredeth.

"My ID reads Kahin Alshaytan. I told you, I had my name legally changed," he said, narrowing his eyes at Bobby a little.

"And your birth name?" asked Bobby.

Alshaytan sighed. "I don't see why that matters."

"It matters because Agent Connelly asked you for it."

Kahin sighed and dropped his chin to his chest for a moment. "Agents, let me apologize. We've gotten off on the wrong foot, and that's no doubt my fault." He lifted his gaze and settled it on Meredeth's face. He flicked his fingers at the open door. "The sign. I wrote that at a low point of my life, and sometimes I forget the state of mind I was in at the time. Would you like to come in? I only want to help your investigation into...into... What did you say you wanted from me, again?"

"That's well and good, Mister Alshaytan, but we still need—"

"Fair enough," said Meredeth. She glanced at the interior of the house—which was the last place she had an interest in going. "Perhaps we can speak out here?"

Kahin looked around, then grinned. "The smell, right?"

Meredeth nodded. "And the low light."

"I see. Sure, we can talk here."

"Is there anyone else in the home?"

"Not a soul," said Kahin, but he scoffed the second he finished. "Sorry. That was a lie." He smiled bashfully. "Old habits die hard."

"Then there are others in the house?"

He shrugged. "Yes. My mother's in her bedroom. Anya, Claire, and Steph are around here somewhere, most likely." He glanced over his shoulder. "And there may be others in the bedrooms. I didn't look."

"Fair enough. What are Anya, Claire, and Steph's last names?"

"They are my fiancées."

"And their full names," asked Bobby.

Kahin lifted his hands, palms out. "Sorry, sorry. Anya Seneca, Claire Mastrantonio, Steph Andrews." He gave Bobby a meek grin. "Old habits die hard."

"As you've said," Bobby said.

"I really am trying to help. Please bear with me."

"Do you find people in your house you didn't know were sleeping here?"

"It's not like that," said Kahin. "In the mornings, sure, I don't know what goes on after I fall asleep. And my guests are welcome to stay as long as they want. I don't impose limits on them."

Bobby cast a meaningful glance at the garbage and worse that littered the floor of the room behind Kahin. "Really?"

"Ah, sarcasm," Alshaytan said with a smile. "I'm going to like you, Agent Van Zandt."

Bobby returned his rock-hard gaze to Kahin. "Is that so?"

"I think so, yes."

"How many guests do you accommodate on an average school night? How many *underage* guests like Ray Michaels?"

"Ray? Who's that?" A genuine look of confusion washed over Alshaytan's face.

"Sorry, Rad."

"Oh, Rad!" Kahin chuckled. "He does come over quite often. He's a good kid, just misunderstood."

"Aren't they all?" asked Bobby with a subtle roll of his eyes.

"Teenagers, yes," said Kahin, then he chuckled. "That's part of my mission here in Ukiah. I provide a judgment-free place for everyone, including people still trapped in that gladiator school."

"You mean the high school?" asked Meredeth.

"Indeed. High schools are places of conformity, state-sanctioned bullying, even torture. But I don't want to give you the wrong idea. I only allow seniors, or people old enough to make adult decisions for themselves. I never ask someone who's say, sixteen or younger. They have to muddle through on their own until they become seniors."

"Yeah, and why's that?" asked Bobby.

"Well, you said it yourself. Teenagers are volatile, labile, and overly emotional. And immature. There's only so much I can stand."

"I see," said Meredeth. "And do you invite seventeen-year-old girls over?"

"No, ma'am."

"Why is that?"

Again, he raised his hands, palms up. "I can't be everywhere at once. I'm afraid an unscrupulous guest might take advantage of them or worse."

"Very noble of you," said Bobby.

"Joke all you want, Agent Van Zandt, but that's the honest reason I don't invite—or admit—high school girls. Well, unless they are eighteen."

"What, eighteen-year-olds can't be taken advantage of, can't be raped?" asked Meredeth.

"No one gets raped here, Agent Connelly. Anya and the girls would never allow that, and neither would I."

Meredeth scoffed.

"No, I mean that, Agent Connelly. We work hard to provide a safe, judgment-free place—with an emphasis on safe. If a young woman chooses to spend her time here, we will ensure her safety. Partly, by imposing restrictions on who can be here. I try to keep people I don't like or trust from casting a shadow on my step."

"Why?" asked Meredeth. "I mean, why go to all this trouble to provide a...a drug den? Do you deal? Are your guests your customers?"

"A drug den?" Kahin laughed loudly. "Do I deal?" More laugher. "No, Agent Connelly, I'm not a drug dealer. If people bring an illicit substance into my home and consume it, well that's on them, isn't it?"

"Maybe, maybe not. Especially not for the underage people you bring over."

"My lawyer assured me otherwise."

"You may want to consult a criminal lawyer," said Bobby.

"Oh, that's what my lawyer specializes in."

"Why would you need a criminal lawyer?" asked Meredeth. "Are you a criminal?"

"Nope, not at all. I mean, I had my run-ins with the law when I was younger, but I've left all that behind. The fact of the matter is, I'm *different* than most citizens of Ukiah. I push the wrong buttons. I give off the wrong vibes. I don't fit in, and I never have. Even as a child I made people nervous, though I didn't at the time understand why. People fear me. They fear the one I serve."

"Satan?" asked Bobby.

Kahin turned his head slowly and met his gaze head-on, then nodded once, solemnly. "As 'accepting' as our society claims to be, there are still things that earn instant hostility. Islam, Satanism, hell, any religion that is not mainstream Christian or Judaism. Oh, I suppose Buddhism has gained some traction—there are multiple Buddhist temples here in Ukiah."

"I'm not sure I agree with that."

Kahin shrugged. "I bet you're not a Satanist, are you?"

"No," Bobby said, shaking his head. "I don't believe in Satan."

"That's okay, Agent. He doesn't require your belief."

"Do you use your position as host to recruit these young people?" asked Meredeth.

"Recruit them? To what?" asked Kahin, shaking his head.

"To your cult."

He threw back his head and laughed. "There are no Satanic cults, Agent Connelly. It's just like Christianity. Are Methodists in a cult? How about practicing Catholics? Lutherans? I have no need to recruit. I'm here as an example. It's true that some of my guests become interested in what gives me my foundations, what allows me to accept whatever it is that makes them happy. To those that seek it out, I provide guidance to coming into Satan's embrace."

"People like Jamie Wenstrom?"

"Who?"

"He's a senior at Ukiah High School. Rad knows him. So does Tim McMasters."

"Who?"

"Is this one of those old habits?" asked Bobby. "Or do you really expect us to believe you don't know those two?"

Kahin shrugged. "I'm not saying I don't know those people. I'm saying I don't recognize their names. You see, in my circles, people often choose a new name for themselves—like Rad has."

"I see. Tim McMasters hosted a party you and Jamie Wenstrom attended together. You were seen conversing with Jamie for some time."

"It's entirely possible, but he probably used another name, or I've just forgotten."

"Then he wasn't someone you invited over."

"Since he made so little impression on me, I sincerely doubt I'd have invited him."

"He's tall for his age—six feet four inches."

"Oh, yes, the tall kid. Sad story. Parents can do so much damage to a young man's sense of self, his sense of worth."

"Then he did make an impression?" asked Meredeth.

"Sure, I guess. And I probably invited him, but I don't think he ever took me up on the invitation."

"No?"

Kahin shook his head. "Not that I recall."

"Babe?" A shadowy figure moved into the living room beyond him. She was nude.

"Company, Anya."

"Oh." The woman disappeared into the back of the house, then reappeared a moment later wearing a housedress that hung from her like a tent without poles. "You remember Jamie. He came over the night of that party, but he didn't stay long."

Kahin cocked his head and looked up at the ceiling. "Hmm. Did I talk to him?"

"You did, Kahin," said the woman.

"Are you Anya Seneca?" asked Meredeth.

"Yes." The woman stayed in the background, clothed by shadows.

"How was Jamie's state of mind?"

"Fine, considering."

"Considering what?" asked Bobby.

"His parents were giving him a lot of flack about his grades, his plans for college—which he isn't even interested in. Stuff like that. You could see it weighed on him, but he wanted to forget it all, to have some fun." She shrugged. "He didn't stay all that long, as I recall."

"An hour? Two?"

"Time gets fuzzy here, but I'd say he left within the hour of his arrival."

"I see." Meredeth cocked her head to the side and peered into the gloomy interior. "Could you step forward into the light? I'd like to take your picture."

"For what?"

"It's standard investigative technique. It helps me keep your face and name together."

"Do I have a choice?"

"I can't compel your cooperation unless we arrest you."

"Then I decline."

Meredeth shrugged, making it seem like it didn't matter. "As you will. Did Jamie say where he was going when he left?"

Anya shook her head, her blonde hair dancing, showing darker roots beneath. "I don't think he said anything. He was here one minute, hanging out here in the living room, then the next time I looked in from the kitchen, he was gone."

"He wasn't one of the people you discovered in one of the bedrooms the next morning?"

"As Anya said, he left."

"And he didn't come back on Monday?"

Kahin shook his head. "If he did, I didn't see him."

"You don't care who's in your house?" asked Bobby with a note of incredulity in his voice.

"No. It's open to anyone who needs or wants to be here."

"Sounds like an expensive policy."

"Not really," said Kahin. "We don't provide anything but the roof and the walls. If they're hungry, they go grab food from a take-out place. Thirsty? The same. Everything here is strictly B-Y-O."

"Even the drugs?" asked Bobby.

"If one of my guests wants to do drugs, they can do so under my roof, but they provide their own good time."

"I see."

"How many high school students would you say hang out here on a given night?"

"Very few," said Anya. "Kahin is pretty selective."

"And my other guests sometimes feel overwhelmed if I invite too many kids."

"On average, how many guests do you have?"

Kahin repeated his hands-out, palms-up shrug. "I really have no idea. People come and go. And I do have long-time friends who come over when they please. I don't care much for formality."

"Ten? Twenty? More?" asked Meredeth.

Again, Kahin shrugged. "I think maybe the maximum is less than twenty. Some nights it's much less. Five, six. Something like that."

"And of those, how many might be high school students?"

"Two or three," said Anya, "at the most, if any."

"I see. And do you allow these teenagers to consume alcohol, to do drugs?"

"I provide them with nothing, and neither does anyone else. But if they've swiped a six-pack from their father's stash or whatever, I don't kick them out. It's a—"

"Judgment-free zone. Yeah, we heard that," said Bobby.

Kahin flashed a wild smile. "It *is* true, after all. It isn't my role to parent them, nor to enforce their parents' rules."

"What about society's laws?" asked Bobby. "What about contributing to the delinquency of a minor?"

"I've never been charged with such, and I've lived here all my adult life."

"That doesn't mean you're not guilty of the crime."

Again, he shrugged. "Maybe I technically am, but I want to reiterate: I do not provide anyone with alcohol or drugs. All I do is open my home and provide a safe place for my guests to hang out and do what they want. When I throw a party, when I'm supplying drinks, I only serve people with proper identification, and I generally do not allow high school kids in that night."

Meredeth peered past him at Anya. "Did you speak to Jamie that night?"

The woman shrugged inside her voluminous house coat. "Yeah, sure. He looked so lost. I saw him waiting for someone to answer the door, and when this place is rocking, that rarely happens."

"You let him in?"

"No, not really. I told him to go inside, is all. I was up on the roof, taking a time out."

"I see."

"He was a nice kid."

"Was?" asked Meredeth pointedly.

"Yeah. That night he was nice to me. Very polite, very proper. His mother would be proud."

"But he didn't stay long?"

"No. To tell you the truth, I think he *wanted* to be cool with everything here, that he wanted to be comfortable with everything, that is, but he wasn't. It was too much for him, and he wasn't ready yet."

"I see." She turned her gaze on Kahin. "Is that the impression you got, too?"

"Well, as I said, I don't really remember him being here. I may have spoken with him, or I may have ignored him."

"You talked to him, baby," Anya said quietly. "Remember? You liked him. When I told you he left, you said it was a shame, but maybe he'd be back."

Kahin sighed and shrugged. "It's possible, and Anya's memory is far better than mine."

"What time did he leave?" asked Bobby. "And did he drive?"

"He was on foot," said Anya. "But he may have parked up the street."

"And the time?"

"It was around two in the morning when he left, I think."

Meredeth nodded. "And he didn't mention where he was going."

Anya shook her head. "He may have said something to one of the other guests, but I kind of doubt it. He seemed shy to me."

"What's a phone number for each of you?" asked Bobby.

"Did you just ask my fiancée for her phone number? How bold."

"Ha-ha," said Bobby in a flat tone.

"Relax, Agent Van Zandt. I'm just teasing you. Anyway, we share a number. If you like, I'll write it down for you."

Bobby shrugged and tore a sheet of paper from the back of his notepad. "Sure." He handed over his pen and the paper, and Kahin scrawled something on it and handed both back. "Very good."

"Is that all, then?" asked Kahin. "My belly's empty."

"Sure," said Meredeth. "For now. We'll call to arrange another meeting as other questions come up."

"That would be fine. We can meet you somewhere."

Meredeth nodded, then backed up a few steps and looked up at the roof. When she dropped her gaze, Meredeth looked at Anya. "How'd you get up there?"

Anya laughed. "Everyone asks that. Kahin has a ladder."

Meredeth nodded. "Very good. Thank you for your time."

"No problem, Agent Connelly," said Kahin. "Please call if we can provide any other help. I really hate to hear that a fine young man has gone missing."

"Why would you say that? We didn't mention he was missing."

"I believe you did, but even if you didn't, Ukiah's got a small-town mentality. I'm sure we read about it in the paper or something."

"No, babe. Rad told us. Remember? It was three or four nights ago. He was upset about it."

"Oh, yes," said Kahin. "Well, however I heard it, I just want to help find him."

Meredeth nodded. "We'll be in touch."

"Good," said Kahin, placing his hand on the open door.

Bobby nodded once, then turned and walked to the steps leading to the road. Meredeth watched Kahin and Anya for a moment longer, then turned away. The door snicked shut before she was halfway across the front lawn.

CHAPTER 15

PUPPY LOVE

David Branch's Farm, NY

Jonathon found Carl, Mack, and their father working on the semi-tractor. He ambled toward them slowly, scuffing his feet through the dirt and gravel, and observed them under hooded eyes. As usual, he was excluded. No one had asked if he wanted to lend a hand. He felt a flicker of resentment at that, at being excluded consistently from the project. It was always the same, and he was getting tired of it. Lucy's words echoed in his head, her claim that Father liked Carl and Mack better than him. He didn't want to believe it was true, but the signs were plain to see. The way they chatted among themselves and didn't even notice his approach.

"Hey," he said, gathering all the nonchalance he could muster. "You want some help with that engine?"

Father looked up and wiped a bead of sweat from his brow. He picked up an oily cloth sitting on the front right fender and wiped his hands on it. "Think we're good here."

"You sure?"

"Pretty much. Won't be room for four big men all crowding around the same engine." Father put the oily rag back down and turned his attention back to the engine.

"What about if I stand right there?" Jonathon asked, motioning to the fender. Carl was standing on the left side. Mack and Father were both facing the truck from the front, leaning inside the engine compartment with wrenches in their hands. That left plenty of space on the other side of the truck.

"No." Father glanced up at him. "I said we're good here."

Jonathon didn't move. He was unwilling to slink away with his tail between his legs but didn't know what else to do.

Father grimaced and straightened up. "If you really want to help, how about you go work on the utility tractor in the barn. The plugs need changing, and maybe the fuel filter. That should keep you busy for a while." He turned his attention back to the truck.

"Fine. I'll work on the tractor."

Only Mack acknowledged him. He cast Jonathon a sideways glance and sniggered.

Jonathon ignored the slight and made for the barn as the other three continued to work. As he stepped in through the wide double doors, he heard them chatting, and a fresh wave of resentment flowed over him. He didn't want to be excluded from Father's coterie. It wasn't fair. He worked hard just like everyone else, didn't he? But Jonathon didn't dare go back and challenge Father. That would be foolhardy. Still, there was no reason he couldn't still be included. Father had told him to work on the tractor but hadn't specifically said where he had to do it. It was nothing but semantics, Jonathon knew. A thin interpretation. But still...

He went to the tractor and released the parking brake to push it out of the barn. It was smaller than the old rusting agricultural tractor sitting farther back, but it was still a heavy vehicle. Father had never used it, but Jonathon knew it was the perfect size for the rotary tiller parked behind it. The fields around the house were overgrown, gone to seed. Father sometimes leased the fields farther away from the house and barn to surrounding farms. Though even that wasn't a regular occurrence anymore.

Jonathon gripped the steering wheel and put his back into it, digging his feet into the compacted earth of the equipment shed floor and pushing with a grunt until the tractor inched forward. It would have been easier, he thought, to get the keys from the house. But that would require walking back past Father, who might get the wrong idea and think he was slinking off to avoid work. And anyway, the tractor probably wouldn't even start. He wasn't sure why Father had even told him to work on it—no one had used it in the time Jonathon had been part of the family. He doubted anyone had used it before that, either—not since Father had taken over the place.

Jonathon pushed the tractor out through the big roll-up doors and wrestled it close enough to the truck that he could be part of the conversation.

No one paid any heed.

He stomped back to the barn and collected the necessary tools, then returned to the tractor. Carl was pontificating, as always. Sucking up to Father and saying he was studying the early Christian church and how they equated personal cleanliness with luxury, materialism, and pagan beliefs. The debauched lifestyle of the Roman baths offended the church, he said. They called it the 'monstrous sensualities' of Rome. True believers were beyond such hedonism, not to mention vanity. He speculated that the modern penchant for frequent bathing was directly linked to the proliferation of so many illnesses. As if taking a shower caused you to get sick or somehow made the germs spread easier, instead of the opposite.

To Jonathon, it sounded like pretentious bullshit, but Father was eating it up. Hanging on every word. Unable to think of anything better to say and equally unable to resist a cheap dig at Carl, he peered up over the tractor with a sneer. "Explains why you quit showering every day. Trying to lead a healthy lifestyle, are you?"

Father put down his wrench, raised himself to his full height, and glared at Jonathon. "That's enough of that."

"I was just pointing out..." Jonathon started, but his words faltered under Father's disapproving stare. He changed tack. "Sorry."

Father grunted and turned his attention back to the truck.

Carl glowered at him over the engine.

"It was only a joke," Jonathon said to Carl. He hadn't come outside to pick a fight. He just wanted to be included. But things had a habit of getting out of hand, at least for him. "I didn't mean nothing."

"Sure, you didn't," Carl replied before reaching into the engine with a wrench. He took up where he'd left off, talking about Pope Gregory the Great, who tolerated infrequent bathing so long as it didn't become a time-wasting luxury.

Jonathon listened to this and resisted the urge to snicker. He decided to take a softer approach. One that might earn him a spot in Father's good graces. "Hey, maybe you could lend me one of those books on religion you've been reading. Sounds interesting."

Father paused a moment, his head bent low in the engine, then he pushed himself up and turned to Jonathon. "What is it with you?"

"What?" Jonathon was glad the tractor was between him and Father. "You seemed interested in the topic. I just wanted to—"

"So read something different. Don't just copy Carl." Father shook his head. "Try to have an original thought, for once."

"I have original thoughts," Jonathon replied. The insinuation that he wasn't capable of independent thinking stung as surely as if Father had whipped him.

"Then act like it." Father sighed. He glanced between the three men. "It's important that you all develop your own interests. Don't just steal ideas from your siblings. That's not the way of things around here. You hear me?"

Mack nodded.

Carl looked up with a smug grin. A grin that would have gotten a swift rebuke from Father if that same look were on Jonathon's face.

"That's better." Father turned back to the truck.

Jonathon swallowed his rage. He glanced at Carl, then Mack, but neither one of them engaged. Gritting his teeth, he turned his attention back to the tractor. Better to keep his trap shut for the rest of the day. At least that way, Father wouldn't humiliate him further.

CHAPTER 16

SCHOOL TIME

Ukiah, CA

BOBBY THREW THE Jeep into park but left the engine running so they could benefit from the air conditioning. He'd driven across town and pulled into the Mendocino County Sheriff's Office off Low Gap Road—just up the road from the high school—and had chosen a spot next to a garish pink Camaro that was equipped as a police car and festooned with lavender ribbon graphics. The clock on the dash said they had some time before they were due inside. "What do you think?"

"I think that's one ugly car."

"No, I mean about Kahin Alshaytan and his girlfriend."

"They're both liars, for one thing."

"Yeah, I think so, too. Alshaytan definitely remembered Jamie for all his protests."

"Yes. And I'm not a hundred percent sure of her, but I think Anya is lying about how long he stayed."

"What's your gut say?"

"What does *your* gut tell you, Bobby?"

"I'm not sure Jamie ever left that house."

"Is he alive, then? Trapped in a back room or the basement?"

Bobby sighed, set his mouth in a grim line, and shook his head. "I don't know."

"Gut?"

Bobby grimaced. "I believe he's dead."

Meredeth lifted her chin, then let it drop.

"You agree?"

"Unfortunately. We need to dig into this Kahin Alshaytan. Find his records, see what's what."

"Agreed. Why did you want their pictures?"

"Michelina," she said, pulling out her phone. She opened the Bureau's email app, typed Dana Jensen in the 'to' field, then attached the image. In the subject line, she typed, "An old friend?" In the message area, she added, "Hi, Dana. You asked me to look up your old friend Carl if we could find him while we were out in California. I think we did. Here's the photo. Is this the guy?" She hit send, then dropped her phone to her lap. "I'm asking her if this guy is really Carl."

"Ah. Do you think Jamie was purposefully targeted then?"

"Maybe." She leaned her head back against the headrest and sighed. "I hope not, or Jim will spend the rest of his life feeling guilty about it."

"And I bet his best profiler will, too."

"I don't know about that, but I probably will."

"Ha," said Bobby.

"Ha," she replied.

"Do you still want me upfront for the class?"

"Yes. I'll chip in where I'm needed."

"All right, but you owe me lunch."

"Put it on my tab, Van Zandt."

"No credit, no checks."

"Since when?"

"Since I want you to buy me lunch."

"Whatever, Boomer."

Bobby chuckled at that. "I guess to this generation, everyone older than them is a baby boomer."

"I guess."

"How do we get inside that house? Rad mentioned cleaning up the basement. I want to get down there, see what's what."

"He wasn't lying about that."

"No?"

"No. Did clean down there. I wonder if he cleaned blood off the concrete slab."

"Could be. We'll still raise it with luminol even if he did. I doubt they went to the lengths necessary to make it truly clean."

"Given the state of the house, I bet luminol will make the whole place shine as bright as the sun."

"You're probably right. That place is going to be a nightmare for the CSI team."

"I'm sensing full hazmat suits in their future—and ours."

"Yeah. How could... I mean, why would anyone *choose* to live in horrible conditions like that?"

"Did you catch a whiff of him? I doubt he's bathed in months."

"That's gross."

"He probably can't smell himself in that olfactory overload zone."

"Why would any woman want to put up with that, let alone *three*."

"I bet he catches them young and stupid, then uses his charm and confidence to rope them into his 'religion.'"

"About that... Did you buy it?"

"No, not really. Oh, I think he *believes* what he says, but I don't for one minute think he's part of any organized religion—Satanic or not."

"Then why say he is?"

"Credibility. Without something behind him, he's a crackpot. With a 'religion' in his pocket, then he's a persecuted believer, and anyone against him is denying him his constitutional right to choose whatever religion he wants. Even so, we should find out if he has any non-profits set up."

"Right. And we should see who owns that house. If it's his mother, maybe we can convince her to let us in."

"Good idea."

At quarter to nine, they got out of the car and headed inside. Bobby brought his laptop to run the presentation.

They strolled into the lobby and approached the window set into the wall and showed their identification.

"You're here to give the talk to the Investigative Division?" asked the young guy behind the window.

"That's right," said Bobby. "We'd like to get into the room early to set up." He lifted his laptop bag.

"Sure thing. Just let me page Detective Saville."

They waited a few minutes, then a heavy-set man in a cheap suit came bustling out of the electronically-locked door leading to the staff areas of the building. He eyed them both for half a second, then raised his hand and approached Bobby. "Agent Connelly?"

"That's her," said Bobby. "I'm Bobby Van Zandt."

Saville had the good graces to look sheepish. "What's that thing they say about assumptions?" He shook his head and held his hand out to Meredeth. "My apologies."

"No problem. I'm used to it," she said with a small smile.

"Well, I should know better, but my lizard brain sometimes takes over, and I turn into a pig. You two ready to set up?"

"Sure," said Bobby.

"Good. Follow me back. We've got the roll call room set up for you so we can fit as many deputies and detectives in as possible. I hope that's not a problem."

"Not at all," said Meredeth. "Bobby likes a full house."

"Oh... I assumed you'd be the one giving the talk?"

Meredeth shook her head. "Bobby will handle that. I'll be there to field questions or to weigh in where necessary."

"Very good," said Saville. "Good grief, where are my manners? I'm Al. Al Saville, Detective Sergeant, Investigative Division."

"How many detectives in your squad?" asked Meredeth.

"A baker's dozen."

She nodded once. "And are you on the Jamie Wenstrom case?"

He cocked his head for a moment. "Why are you asking about that case? It's nothing more than a local matter."

"Our boss is Jim McCutchins," she said.

Al shook his head. "I'm not following you."

"James Wenstrom was named after his uncle, James McCutchins."

A revelatory expression dawned on Saville's face. "Ah. I was wondering why a small department in Northern California suddenly rated an in-service put on by the BAU. So, you're *really* here looking into the disappearance of your boss' nephew."

It hadn't been enunciated as a question, but Meredeth chose to take it as one. "We're here to do both. Jim thinks there's more to his nephew's disappearance than a runaway situation. I have to tell you, we've been here less than twenty-four hours, and it certainly looks like Jim is correct."

"Is that so? Care to share what you've turned up?"

"Of course. And I'd like your help on a few things."

Saville said nothing for a few moments, then pointed at a door on the left. "Through here is our roll call room. You can plug your laptop in at the podium."

Bobby nodded, and then with a glance at Meredeth, he stepped past them and went inside. Once the door closed behind him, Saville turned to Meredeth, and he didn't look happy.

"I can't say I'm happy about the subterfuge."

"There's been no subterfuge, Al. We're here to support the Mendocino County Sheriff's Office with a field training day, and you'll get the best we have to offer. What we've done so far is to interview some of Jamie's friends and discover who hosted the party, which is the last public event where Jamie was seen. From the host of that party—Tim McMasters—we learned a local character named Kahin Alshaytan attended the party and was seen talking with Jamie for an extended period of time. We interviewed Alshaytan this morning and learned that Jamie was invited to Alshaytan's house. He accepted the invitation, and Alshaytan and one of his women admit he came by. Now, I'm ninety-nine percent sure they lied to us about numerous things, and we're going to follow that up. Which brings me to my request for assistance. We'd like to pull this Alshaytan's rap sheet, and we're going to run the property records on the house to see who actually owns the place. I'd also like to know your thoughts on Alshaytan and his little community."

Al blew out a breath. "I'd heard about you through the grapevine, Agent Connelly—"

"Meredeth, please.

"Okay, Meredeth, then. I've heard about your tactics, but more importantly, I've heard about how good you are."

"Thank you."

He waved that away. "I'd also heard you could be hard to work with."

She shrugged. "It's true. I tend to get hyper-focused and lose patience."

Saville sniffed but nodded. "I've got a little of that as well."

"So what do you say, Al? Will you help us?"

"Of course. Despite what Jenna and Daniel Wenstrom may have told your boss, we are taking Jamie's disappearance seriously. You have to bear in mind, however, that Jamie is a troubled kid. He's run away from home before. He does drugs, and he's on our radar for multiple misdemeanors in and around Ukiah, including a serious allegation of assault."

"Okay. That's good information. Have you done his cell phone?"

"Of course. It went dead a week ago."

"A week ago, as in last Tuesday, or was it perhaps early Monday morning."

"Last Tuesday. We have localization data from his cellular provider that has him moving around Ukiah most of Monday, then taking a trip north to the National Forest.

It goes dead up there, but frankly, cell coverage in the park is spotty."

"You're talking about the Mendocino National Forest?"

"Yes, that's it."

Meredeth nodded once, a speculative look in her eye. "And his usage data? Did you pull that as well as his tower pings?"

"Yes. Lots of calls and texts, mainly from his mother's cell phone, but no connections, and nothing outgoing."

"Hmm. What's your theory? Is he a runaway or is he a victim of foul play?"

"I don't mind telling you that when Mrs. Wenstrom first reported him missing, I figured he'd just run away again and that he'd be back as soon as he ran out of cash."

"But now?"

"Well, after seeing that cell data... It's weird, right?"

Meredeth nodded. "I'd say so."

"Yeah, I agree."

"Then you'll pull Alshaytan's sheet?"

"Sure, why not."

"Could you also pull anything you have on Anya Seneca, Claire Mastrantonio, and Steph Andrews?"

"Easy as pie."

"Good, I appreciate it."

"Let me get that started before the talk starts. Though, I've got to tell you, Alshaytan doesn't own that house. It belongs to his mother: Roberta Black."

"You don't happen to know Alshaytan's birth name?"

"Yes, I do. That guy's been a problem around here for more than two decades. About ten years ago, he changed his name from Benjamin Black to this nonsense he goes by now."

"Please pull the sheet for Benjamin Black, as well."

"I would have, anyway."

Meredeth nodded, then turned and entered the roll call room. She took a seat against the back wall and flashed a smile and a nod at Bobby. "He's going to help."

"Good," said Bobby.

Meredeth's phone beeped, and she glanced down at it. "Email from Michelina," she said. She scanned it quickly, then looked up at Bobby. "No help there. She says Kahin might be Carl, but she can't be sure. She says he's about the right size, though if he is Carl, he's lost most of the muscle mass he'd amassed under Ankou's guidance. She also says his eyes look—and I quote—not right."

"So we can't know for certain until we get more information."

"That's right."

"Well, shoot."

"We'll see what we can find out through his records. Oh, his birthname was Benjamin Black, and his mother owns that hovel."

"Well, that's good news."

"You bet. We'll try to get her alone and get her permission to search the place."

CHAPTER 17

HOUSE CALLS

Ukiah, CA

MEREDETH PRESSED HER phone against her ear as she got off the elevator and walked up the hall toward her room. It had been a long day of sitting in the back of that tiny roll call room, fielding questions for Bobby and listening to the lesson she'd written and delivered hundreds of times. It would have been mind-numbing if she didn't understand the need for it, didn't understand where these deputies were in their careers, didn't understand the sparsity of their education and training.

Even so, the day had worn on her nerves, and she had a headache of epic proportions. Be that as it may, she owed Jim an update, and she wanted nothing more than to pass along where they were with the case so she could get Kevin on the phone.

Jim picked up on the third ring, which given the time difference, she didn't begrudge him. "Connelly?"

"Yes, boss."

"What do you have for me?"

"We've made some progress. The field op training went well, though. Lots of questions, lots of well-thought-out questions."

"Good, good. Jenna called."

"Yeah, I figured she might. The training ran over, and it was dinner time, so I called and rescheduled for tomorrow."

"Get over there first thing."

"Right."

"She's a nervous wreck, Connelly, so play nice."

"Of course, Jim. She's not suspect, not even close."

"Speaking of which..."

"Right. Here's what we've learned. We interviewed some of Jamie's friends at the school, one of which gave us a lead on the party he went to last Sunday. It was hosted by a dropout by the name of Tim McMasters. We learned that Jamie also spent a long time talking to a man in his forties who seems to see himself as the savior of Ukiah's youth. He invites vulnerable teenagers to his house, where he provides—and I quote—a judgment-free zone. Also, no rules. He's changed his name to Kahin Alshaytan, which means 'priest of Satan' according to Bobby. If you ask me, there are psychiatric issues with Mr. Alshaytan." She slid her keycard into the reader mounted to her hotel room door as she finished up, then pushed through it and closed it behind her.

"You interviewed him already?"

She set the security bar, then turned and walked to the room proper and lay her purse on the little round table near the window. "We did. This morning before the Sheriff's Office."

"And?"

"He's lying. Pretending to want to help while trying to minimize his contact with Jamie. He first claimed not to know Jamie, then said he might but not by that name. Then one of his three girlfriends joined the conversation and refreshed his memory. Even so, though, they both say Jamie came by but didn't stay long. There's something there, and we're working on a potential avenue of search for the home. I've enlisted the help of Al Saville, the detective sergeant with MCSO's Investigative Division. By the way, despite what Jenna has said, Al assures me they are now taking the disappearance seriously. He did admit that in the beginning he thought Jamie'd just run off, but once he pulled his cell phone data, he changed his mind." She stepped out of her shoes and sat on the edge of the bed, arching her feet and spreading her toes, fighting the urge to sigh with relief.

"Why?"

"Jamie's cell phone stayed active on Monday. It showed him tooling around Ukiah for most of the day, then he went north into the Mendocino National Forest, where the signal went dead."

"Shit," muttered Jim. "Wait a minute..."

"That's right, boss. The cell data ends in a National Park." She lay back on the bed and let the muscles in her back relax.

"That puts it in federal jurisdiction."

"Yes, but with the NPS's Criminal Investigations Unit."

"Sure, but you know people there, right?"

Jim sighed. "Yes. I'll make some calls and get them to request your help formally."

"Good, then we assert jurisdiction and formally ask Al Saville to be our liaison with local law enforcement. We can build the task force, after all."

"Good work, Meredeth."

"It's Al Saville's work. I just get the glory."

"Tell me about this Alshaytan character."

"He's a piece of work. Doesn't bathe, and doesn't clean his house, but he's smart. He has a criminal lawyer on retainer and has already asked the hack about his liability in hosting this party house. The only thing we might have him on right now is contributing to the delinquency of minors. If we can get one of them to talk to us. I do have one in mind, a friend of Jamie's named Ray Michaels."

"Get him on board."

"I'll try, boss, but he doesn't trust me. Or any adult, it seems."

"Then arrest him on something. Arrest him, scare him with real time, and flip him."

"I'll try. Al is pulling together all of Alshaytan's criminal history for us, including mental health records. We were going to pull the property records, but Saville is familiar with the house—he says the mother owns it. We're going to take a run at her tomorrow as well if we can arrange to speak with her alone."

"Good. Tell Jenna everything. She deserves to be in the loop."

"Okay, boss, whatever you want."

"Good."

"And call me tomorrow night. Earlier if the situation warrants it."

"Will do."

"And, Connelly? Meredeth?"

"Yes, Jim?"

"What's your gut say?"

"We don't know anything for sure, Jim."

"Maybe not, but I don't like that cell phone data. It sounds like..."

"Yes," she said softly, "but there's still hope, Jim. There's hope right up to the point where we find a body."

He sighed and it was a heart-wrenching sound. "Yeah. Goodnight, Meredeth."

"Goodnight, Jim." She wanted to add something like, "keep your hopes up," or something equally inane. Jim knew the stats as well as she did. He had years of experience in the field and knew what the cell phone data meant as well as anyone. She clicked the disconnect button, then got changed into her hotel-room-lounging outfit—her big T-shirt and little else.

She hit Kevin's contact and pulled back the covers. Her head still ached, but it wasn't bad enough that she wanted to crawl into a hole and puke in isolation. She lay in the bed and flung one arm over her eyes, holding the phone to her ear with the other.

"Hey, beautiful."

"Hello, sexy."

"Oh, it's one of those calls, is it?"

"Well, maybe later. Right now, I'm beat."

"Then put on that humongous T-shirt, order some dinner from room service, then kick back and relax."

"Already ate with Bobby, and already under the covers, T-shirt on."

"Good girl."

"What are you up to tonight?"

"Nothing. Just got back to the room. I had dinner with...some people."

"Oh, my man of mystery. Where'd you eat?"

"At a place with food."

"Ha. Very amusing, this secret-keeping side of you."

"You haven't figured it out, yet?"

"What? Based on the red feathers? No."

"Well, I must say I'm surprised by that."

"Yeah, well, I've been busy with other things."

"How's the case going? Making any headway?"

"Some. We've figured an angle for a task force at any rate."

"Oh, yeah?"

"Yeah. Jamie's cell phone went dead last week in a National Forest."

"Ah. Are the local cops going to be pissed?"

"I'm not sure, but we're planning on including them in the task force."

"Yeah, that could help matters."

"I met the detective in charge of the case. He admitted they didn't take it too seriously until they ran those cell records."

"Well, shame on him."

"Yeah," she shrugged. We also have a possible angle to arrest the guy we think is behind it—not for Jamie, but at least to get him off the street so we can investigate without worrying about him manipulating the witnesses."

"Good. Get the asshole off the street."

"He hasn't bathed in what I'm guessing is months. And he has *three* girlfriends."

"Maybe they have olfactory nerve issues."

"I didn't get the impression they were much cleaner than he was."

"Why would someone choose to live like that?"

"No idea. Mental health issues, maybe. Oh, he's in his forties and lives with his mother in the same house as his three girlfriends."

"God almighty. Is everyone out there crazy?"

"Everyone at that house, maybe. There is a layer of garbage on the floor, and by the horrid odor, pet and human waste under there somewhere, too."

"Yech."

"Yeah, let's talk about something else."

"Okay by me. Are you wearing your bra?"

"Why, Chief Saunders!"

"Can we convert this call to video?"

"That depends," she purred.

"On what?"

"On what *you're* wearing..."

CHAPTER 18

MOTHER'S LITTLE HELPER

Ukiah, CA

KAHIN'S FURY THRUMMED through the house like a living, ravaging thing. He roved through the house like a whirling dervish, sitting down momentarily only to shoot up the next minute and go for another tour. He ranted nonsense at whoever would listen. He was off in la-la land, lost in his paranoia, talking all kinds of crap about his mother.

Rad was sitting on the couch in the living room, trying to keep a low profile and have fun again despite the heinous task he'd been forced to perform the night before weighing on his mind. But it was impossible to ignore the delusional ranting of his host, even though the guy was in a different room.

Rad kind of understood Kahin's newfound paranoia. After all, there was a corpse buried in the backyard. And the fact that Rad had been the motive force behind that burial had kept him up most of the night, staring at the ceiling as he lay in bed listening for the sound of cops kicking in the front door. A part of him wished he'd foregone Kahin's house that night and had instead gone home to the eleven-hundred-square-foot block house he shared with his parents. Although his parents were also assholes who probably wouldn't notice him gone for a week if he was hauled off to jail. That was how bad his home life had gotten. His father, who wasn't averse to doling out a swift backhander just for the sake of it, had made it clear that Rad was nothing but a waste of space. His alcoholic mother had checked out years ago and didn't show any signs of ever wanting to check back in. They were nothing but a waste of human flesh, and he'd wasted enough breath speaking to them, wasted enough time trying to please them

A part of him wished that as he'd fled Kahin's digs that morning and run into that FBI agent woman, he'd come clean. He could have asked her for help, could have told her what was going on in the house, what Kahin had made him do. If he'd done that, maybe things could have been different for him, and he wouldn't be afraid of being caught. But he hadn't, and now he was an accessory to murder. Given the state of his home life, he had nowhere to turn for help. Nowhere but Kahin's house to go to for solace.

It was no wonder Rad's nerves were shredded.

But the rabbit hole Kahin had fallen down didn't appear to be related to the guy he'd shot in the face and made Rad stick in the ground. No. Kahin was ranting about his mother, who either suffered from wicked agoraphobia or was so afraid of her son that she wouldn't leave the master bedroom within which she had been ensconced ever since Rad first stepped foot inside the Rosemary Lane house.

"Hey. Don't worry about Kahin. Pay attention to me," said a sultry feminine voice as a hand brushed his cheek.

"Kind of hard to ignore him, don't you think?" Rad turned toward the owner of the voice. The girl who said her name was Claire. That was one good thing about coming back to the house. She had decided to give him a second chance and was back on the couch with her bare legs draped over his. Later, after more weed and booze, that bedroom visit might become a reality. But not if Kahin kept up his semi-coherent rant and spoiled the mood.

The kitchen door burst open, and Kahin stomped into the room, sending several of his disciples who were lounging on the floor scuttling away like cockroaches, and Rad's hopes for a raunchy evening with Claire fell.

"Fuckin' woman," Kahin growled in a voice that sounded like it had risen from the depths of hell. "Wants to get me sanitized and tranquilized. Says I'm not right in the head. Like she's some freaking pillar of sanity."

"Sanitized and tranquilized," said a scrawny guy with limp blond hair and pallid skin who was lounging in a sagging chair near the front door. He drew the ends of each word out in a slurred drawl, then giggled as if he'd said something funny. "Sounds like a nice place to be."

"Shut up, Wade." Kahin spun on the guy, anger glinting in his eyes. "Bet your mother ain't trying to have you put in the loony bin."

"Nah, man. Haven't seen my Ma since I was sixteen," Wade replied, with a dopey grin on his face.

Kahin had already moved on. "I don't believe this. How can she betray me like this? After all I've done for her!"

"What exactly have you done for me, Son?" asked a voice from the archway leading to the bedrooms.

Rad's gaze shifted toward a stocky woman who looked like she was in her early sixties. She was standing there with her arms folded. Her hair, which must once have been jet black, was now turning a wiry silver. She wore a pink housecoat that did little to hide what lay underneath.

"What are you doing out here?" Kahin asked. "Why don't you go back to your cave? WE DON'T WANT YOU OUT HERE!"

"This is still my house, Benjy. Or did you forget that?"

"And who keeps the power on? Who makes sure there's water in the taps?" Kahin took a step toward his mother. "It's me. If I weren't here, you'd be sitting in the dark with no way to flush the toilet. And my name is Kahin! K-A-H-I-N!"

"If you weren't here, this place wouldn't look like a drug den." Kahin's mother stepped farther into the room. "As for the toilet... None of your houseguests appear to bother using it, given the way it smells around here. As for your name, *I named you*. I know what your name is, and it's not that Arabic nonsense!"

"Get back in your room, Mom!"

"Just cool your jets." Kahin's mother reached out to take his hand. "I never said you should be committed. All I said was that living like this ain't right. You need to find a new path. You need friends who care about *you*, not these losers who are only taking advantage of your generous nature. You deserve—"

Kahin snatched his hand away as if his mother's touch would burn him. "I like living like this. And my friends *do* care about me."

"Why would you—"

"I like it!" Kahin screamed the words. His face was beet red. He raised a hand and brought it down across his mother's face in a resounding slap. "Don't embarrass me in front of my friends ever again. You hear me?"

Rad jumped up. "Hey, take it easy."

Kahin half turned toward him, surprised by the sudden intervention.

"Look. There's a new joint over on Hammond," Rad said, hoping that removing Kahin from the situation would calm him down before he did something really bad. "Let's go over there and grab a couple of burgers. Maybe get a milkshake. I'll buy. What do you think?"

"Yeah, honey. What do you think?" Anya was standing in the kitchen doorway with the usual smirk on her face and her boobs out for all to see. "You want to go on a fast-food date with the kid and share a milkshake?"

"I'm not hungry," Kahin muttered, staring at Rad through slit eyelids.

"Sorry, kid. He's not hungry." Anya shrugged.

Rad got the impression that she was enjoying this. Soaking up the drama like water to a sponge.

Kahin's eyes flicked back to his mother. "I thought I told you to get back in your room."

"You didn't have to slap me," she said, tears glistening at the corners of her eyes. "I'm worried about you."

"It's a bit late for that. Maybe you should've been worried when I was growing up and there was no food to eat. Maybe you should've been worried when the cops dragged me out of school because they said I beat on some kid I'd never even seen just because of how I looked. Where were you then?"

"I did my best."

"Yeah? YEAH? It wasn't good enough!" Kahin's anger had reached a fever pitch. He raised his hand again, but this time there was no open palm. It was clenched into a hard fist. Before he could land the blow, a guy with a paunchy belly and tattoos covering both arms stepped between them and grabbed Kahin's wrist.

"That's enough," said the guy, with narrowed eyes. "You don't hit women. Especially not your own mother."

Kahin lunged forward and shoved him hard. "Who the hell are you to tell me what I can and can't do in my own house? Come in here and smoke my weed? Lie around and enjoy my generosity? What are you, Mother's little helper?"

"This is getting out of control, is all." Some of the fight had dropped from the guy's voice. He pushed his hands into his pockets and looked at the floor.

"Out of control? I'll show you out of control." Kahin lunged toward Rad and gripped him by the arm before he had time to react.

Rad flinched, expecting a closed fist to land in his face. Or worse, the knife to make another appearance. But instead, Kahin dragged him off in a vice-like grip and didn't let go until they were in the kitchen. Anya slid through the door and closed it behind her, shutting out everyone else.

Kahin was shaking. He clenched and unclenched his fists, beady eyes locked on Rad. "You kill him. You hear me? You kill that mother—"

"He was just trying to help," Rad said in a small voice. "He was just trying to chill you out, to avoid any...any unpleasantness that might lead to the cops paying us a visit."

"He disrespected me in front of everyone. He didn't follow the rules." Kahin went to a drawer next to the sink and opened it. He pulled out the knife, then pressed it into Rad's hand. "Kill him for me. *Now.*"

Rad looked down at the knife. He didn't want to kill anyone. But he didn't want Kahin to be mad at him, either. Especially now that he'd seen the true force of his temper. He didn't know how to respond, but it didn't matter. When Rad looked back up, Kahin was already on his way out of the room, striding toward the back of the house and the bedrooms.

But Anya was still there.

She walked over to Rad with the feline grace of a house cat, looking for affection. Or maybe, Rad thought, a hungry leopard looking for its next meal.

"You do as Kahin says and kill that asshole. Do it for me, and I'll make it worth your while," she said, pressing her bare skin against him. "You want to sleep with Claire?"

Rad nodded on autopilot even though he was numb.

"It won't happen." Anya rubbed herself on him. Her mouth brushed his neck. "She's a flirt, but she doesn't put out. At least not for scrawny kids like you. Me, on the other hand... I like men who take charge. You kill that shithead out there, make him pay for his disrespect, and I'll give you a night you'll never forget until the day you die." She grinned. "I might even make Claire join us."

CHAPTER 19

MORNING READING

Ukiah, CA

MEREDETH SLID INTO the booth and lay the file folders Al had handed to her as they entered the restaurant on the table in front of her. "His sheet must be long to have this much paper."

Al nodded as he slid in across from her, then around into the bottom of the U-shaped booth, as Bobby slid in behind him. "Like I said yesterday, we know him well." He took a menu from the little silver clip holding them at the edge of the table and opened it.

Meredeth also took a menu but didn't open it. "Before we order, Al, I have something you deserve to know."

"Yeah? What's that?"

"You know how Jamie's cell phone data dies out in the Mendocino National Forrest?"

"Yeah. That means it's federal. That's what you're dancing around, right?"

"Well...yes. But we're building a task force. FBI, National Park Services Criminal Investigations Unit, and the Mendocino County Sheriff's Office."

Al gave a little one-shoulder shrug. "It's nice of you to include us."

"You found the data, and you know the story on Alshaytan. It only makes sense. There will be a formal request coming from Washington for you to serve as our liaison office."

"Be happy to. Look, Agent Connelly—"

"Meredeth."

"Right. Look, Meredeth, I don't care much who gets credit. I want to close out this MP case, hopefully by bringing Jamie home to his mom and dad."

Meredeth nodded, glancing at Bobby.

"But you know how unlikely that is," said Bobby.

Al sighed and closed the menu, dropping it on the table. "There's always hope."

"There is," said Meredeth. "But..."

"Right. But. Look, I'm not a naïve dreamer. I've been doing this a long time—started out at L.A.P.D. in the nineties. I know the drill."

"Okay, enough said then."

"Are you going to speak with the Wenstroms?"

"Right after we finished here."

"Okay if I tag along? I don't want them thinking I just abandoned the case."

"We'd be happy to have you along," said Bobby.

"And we'll make sure everyone knows you didn't ditch the case."

"Good," said Al as he picked up the menu. "Now, let's order before I wither away and die of starvation." He raised his hand without looking and signaled the waitress. "I recommend the flapjacks, any kind of eggs, the quiche, any of the baked goods, and the Belgian waffles, but stay away from anything with sausage."

"Oh?"

"You've heard of Montezuma's Revenge?"

"Sure."

"The sausages here are the original version of that malady."

"I see."

"I heard that, Al," said the waitress as she approached. "Don't listen to the weak stomach here. Ain't nothing wrong with our sausage."

"Not if you're already dead," murmured Al.

"Watch it, Saville, or I'll spit in your coffee."

"That's no way to talk in front of two FBI agents, Melody. If you murder me with your spit, they'll probably be the pair that investigates."

Melody rolled her eyes. "Al, kiss my lily white—"

"I'll have three eggs, Melody. Sunny-side-up. A rasher of bacon. Rye toast. Grape jelly, too, damn you. A cup of that swill you call coffee—sans spit, if you please. Oh, and breakfast potatoes." Al closed his menu and squinted up at her. "And no damn onions. You know I hate them, and you leave them in on purpose. Don't think I don't know that."

"Right, right." She flashed Meredeth a smile. "Mistakes happen, Al."

"Yeah, and I might mistakenly have your car towed again."

"That was you? Oh, you little prick! I owe you for that."

"Hey, I made sure they released it without charging you, didn't I?"

"You think you're so tough hiding behind that badge. Take it off and see what happens!"

"Now, Melody, don't get your feathers all ruffled up." He sat back in the booth. "Besides, I don't put out on the first date."

"As if!" She turned her attention to Bobby. "Now, you, on the other hand..."

"Hey, leave me out of this."

"Too bad. You look...*yummy*."

"Um, I'll have the flapjacks."

"What kind of meat?"

"Bacon."

"The sausage is fine."

"Sure, I know."

Al blew a raspberry. "It's death in casing."

"Shut up, Al," she said without looking at him. "What else, darling?"

"Uh... Wheat toast with butter. Hashbrowns?"

"Sure."

"Good. And I'd like some orange juice with my coffee."

"You got it, sexy." She turned to Meredeth. "And for you?"

"Quiche, I guess. Toast, any kind of bread. Coffee. No meat or potatoes, please."

"You sure, hon? The quiche comes with both."

"I'd never finish all that food, and I hate to waste it."

"Hear that, Al?"

"What are you trying to say, Melody?"

"Maybe you should consider not making such a pig of yourself. There are people starving in San Diego, you know."

Al lifted a finger and spun it near his temple. "Uh, sure thing, Melody, but I'll eat all my food."

"You know I can see you, right?"

"I do. I do, indeed."

"I'm spitting in your coffee."

"Good, I like the extra flavor."

She rolled her eyes, then smiled at Meredeth. "I'll be right back with the coffee."

"Oh, can I have a large Coke, too?" asked Meredeth.

"Sure, hon. Coming right up." She turned and walked behind the lunch counter and called their orders in to the kitchen.

"She's all right is Melody," said Al in a stage whisper. "But don't tell her I said so."

"Did you really tow her car?"

"Maybe. I can't recall. I wasn't even in town that day. The devil made me do it."

They laughed a bit, then Meredeth opened the top file in front of her, then unfolded the rap sheet and scanned it. "He beat up his own mother?"

Al nodded. "More than once. She had him committed when he was younger, and their relationship has been strained ever since."

"Committed?"

"Yep. It's in there. He's a paranoid schizophrenic with psychotic features." Al shrugged. "At least, that's what the headshrinkers said back then. To tell you the truth, he seems better now, but maybe he's masking his behavior. He's gotten good at insulating himself from things."

"Uh-hunh," said Meredeth, scanning further. "Shoplifting... multiple beefs... indecent exposure. What's that about?"

"You've met him, right?" asked Al. When she nodded, he continued. "Well, he's not much on hygiene, as you no doubt noticed. He also doesn't care much about...well, urinating in front of others."

"Ah," said Meredeth. "What's with the bathing thing?"

"He's always been like that, I guess. He used to get grief for it. People called him 'turd man' to his face. That was before the commitment, however. Since then, nobody calls him on his crap. Too scared he'll go full psycho on them, I guess."

Meredeth kept reading, then put her finger on a recent entry and looked at Al. "And this murder investigation?"

"I'd hardly call it that. Five years back, we got an anonymous report that Alshaytan was telling people he'd killed someone and put the body in the basement. A drug dealer by the name of Victor Vanderheugan. The only problem was there was no body in his basement—the house was only half the train wreck it is today. We ran the house with luminol—inconclusive. We took Alshaytan in a swabbed him for residue—negative. We interviewed the neighbors and his house guests—no one heard gunshots."

"No body, no evidence," said Bobby.

"That's right. We put out an APB on Vanderheugan, but we never got anything from that either. But still, the guy was a drug dealer. He dealt major weight up and down the coast and was rumored to be affiliated with the Costas Cartel out of Mexico City."

"And their dealers don't last long."

"That's right. We figured he was either in hiding, or the cartel had taken him out. See, Alshaytan has an honesty problem. He doesn't have a moral compass, and he sees nothing wrong with making up stories that make him look powerful, a badass, you see. We figure that's half the reason he hangs out with high school kids—they're easily impressed and don't have the sense to see through his bullshit."

"So you think that's what it was? He told a tall tale to someone who believed him, but he never did the crime?" asked Bobby.

Al wagged his head from side to side. "Probably, but with no body, no evidence..."

"Right, you were stuck either way."

"Yeah. The case is still open but cold, and to this day, no one's found Vanderheugan. Alive or dead."

Meredeth nodded. "Which lends credence to the cartel theory."

Al made a finger gun and shot her with it. "Bingo."

Melody came out from behind the counter carrying a tray with three mugs, a glass of orange juice, and a big glass of Coca-Cola. She stopped ten paces away, picked up one of the steaming mugs, and pretended to spit in it. "This one belongs to Al."

"Like I said, flavor. Bring it here."

CHAPTER 20

WHEN THE CAT'S AWAY

David Branch's Farm, NY

at night, Carl knocked on Lucy's bedroom door, and she was surprised to see him because no one ever came to her room that late except Alex, who sometimes dropped by to check up on her, but Alex was away with Father on one of his trips. Lucy hated it when both Alex and Father were away. Not only was she constantly worried that Jonathon would try something in Father's absence—he had eased up on her a little since their talk in the basement, although not by much—but she always ended up going to bed hungry. Mealtimes, when they had to fend for themselves, turned into a free for all with only one rule. Grab what you could get while it was there and defend what you could grab or someone would take it from you. It was definitely a wolfpack mentality, and she was as far from the alpha as she could get.

So, because Lucy was the smallest of the siblings, her bigger siblings took advantage of her—especially Jonathon, who ate like a pig at the best of times—and she ended up missing out more often than not and went to bed with an empty, grumbling, and gurgling stomach. Even when she managed to snag a tasty morsel, Jonathon would snatch it out of her hand with a gleeful cry and stuff it into his mouth. Neither of the other boys would interfere in this because Father said that everyone had to learn resilience, that everyone had to fend for themselves because once they left the farm, no one would help them.

So when Carl eased the door open and showed her a plate of food, she all but jumped off the bed and ran to him to give him a giant hug. It wasn't much. Some bread and cheese and homemade pickles, but in her eyes, he'd brought her a feast of royal proportions, a feast that would kill the monster in her belly with extreme prejudice.

"Sorry, there's not more. I saved what I could, but I had to be sneaky and hide it," he said, sitting on the bed next to her while she dove in with her fingers, not even caring if she made a mess. Father and Alex had been gone for two days already and wouldn't be back for another three. That was a long time to survive on whatever scraps she could scavenge in the dinnertime melee.

"S'okay," she said with a mouthful of bread topped by a sliver of cheese. "Didn't think I'd get anything."

"Yeah, well…"

"Why did you do this?" she asked when most of the food was gone, and her hunger had diminished.

Carl shrugged, and she thought he might have blushed a little. "Seemed right, that's all. That Jonathon is a pig. I saw him take your plate, but I couldn't say anything then." He stood as if to leave, but she grabbed his hand and pulled him back onto the bed.

"You can stay awhile if you want to. I don't mind."

"I don't know," he said, glancing toward the door as if he expected Jonathon or Mack to appear at any moment and tease him for being so soppy. Or maybe he was afraid they would tell Father what he'd done, and then he might end up on the receiving end of a tongue lashing. Or worse, the box. But, after a moment of looking at her, he relaxed. "You've really started to fit in around here."

"Thanks." Lucy wasn't sure she wanted to "fit in" with the likes of Jonathon, but it was better than the alternative. And there was Carl to consider. She considered him a hotty.

"I'm happy about that. I enjoy talking to you. Jonathon has all the intellect of a cockroach and the personality to match. Mack's okay, but..."

"But what?"

"I don't know. All he talks about these days is getting out on the road in a truck. Cruising the highways. Living free and easy."

"I thought the two of you were best friends," Lucy said.

"We were. I mean, we still are sometimes. But he's got all these ideas. He thinks he'll ace his final test and then be out of here."

"You worried he'll leave you behind?"

"Nah. Nothing like that." Carl shook his head. "I'll pass my test soon enough; I'm not sticking around to take orders from Alex and watch Jonathon stomp around having tantrums. They won't see me for the dust of my passage, and that's the truth."

"What's the big deal, then?"

"Those ideas of his. Don't misunderstand me, he ain't wrong to dream of a life where no one tells him what to do, and he can go where he pleases—"

"Free and easy."

"Yeah. But it's the other stuff. When I was younger, I idolized Mack. Put him on a pedestal. It was like having a big brother and best buddy all rolled into one, even though we aren't that far apart in age. But now I want better. Mack's not being smart. He hasn't thought it through. This life on the road of his, it's going to get him in trouble. It's risky. Too much paperwork and too many regulations. Too many cops looking to keep truckers in line. He'd be better to find something less obvious that won't draw attention to him. This trucking thing... All it would take is to get pulled over at the wrong time or travel the same route once too often looking for victims. Sooner or later, someone will catch on to his game."

"You can't stop him from following his plan, even if you don't agree with it. Better to focus on your own future. You won't be here forever, like you said." She picked at a stray thread hanging from the hem of her T-shirt. "I was reading about the Aztecs. They had these ritual sacrifices, and they didn't care where the victims came from. Warriors captured in battle. Women. Even children. No rhyme or reason to it. That's the way to be. Unpredictable. Nothing to tie you to your victims." What Lucy didn't say to Carl was that there was more. Her encounter with Jonathon in the basement had planted the germ of an idea in her head. It had been *easy* to manipulate him once she'd made him angry. Emotions were a powerful weapon. She wondered what would happen if anger like that was directed and controlled. And not just anger... There were all sorts of emotions to play with. Love. Lust. Even religion.

"You done eating that?" Carl asked, nodding toward the plate.

Lucy looked down. There was nothing but crumbs left. She wet her finger and slid it around the plate to catch the last remnants of food, licked it, then nodded. "I'm done."

Carl picked up the plate. "Aztecs, huh?"

"I know you are interested in them, so I thought I'd see what they were about."

"I'm finished with the Aztecs. They got consumed by their own bloodlust. Want to know what I'm interested in now?"

"Sure."

"Druids. You know, like the Celts. Now those people knew how to live. Hell, half their rituals amounted to little more than an excuse to indulge in orgies." He wagged his eyebrows at her playfully.

"You like orgies?"

Carl worked his shoulders and looked toward the far corner of the room. "I've never had one."

Lucy smiled and pulled his face back around to face hers with two fingers planted on his chin. "You ever been with a girl at all?"

"I... Well..." Her question had left Carl's cheeks burning, flushed red with hot blood.

When she reached out and touched his hand, he didn't pull away. "I really am grateful you brought me that food."

"I know." He nodded.

"I'd like to repay you. What do you say?" She was interested to see how far lust could take her.

"Repay me. Like how?"

Lucy smiled and pushed the plate aside. Her eyes flicked to the open bedroom door. "Why don't you go shut that, and I'll show you."

CHAPTER 21

LIKE BEING BURIED ALIVE

Ukiah, CA

JENNA AND DANNY Wenstrom lived in a fancy house up on one of the hills to the west of Ukiah—more of a compound than a house, really, with a brick wall and a wrought-iron gate. The house itself was Spanish-style, with red roof tiles and sweeping arches. It had one of the most beautiful pools Meredeth had ever seen and a gorgeous view from all four sides.

Jenna answered the door when Meredeth rang the bell and stepped forward to embrace her. "Thank you," she whispered in Meredeth's ear. "No matter what happens, thank you for coming."

"It's no problem, Jenna. Of course, we came to help."

Jenna stepped back and wiped her eyes. She extended her hand to Bobby. "Agent Van Zandt."

"Jenna, I'm so sorry we meet again under these circumstances."

"Yes," she said. She turned her attention to Al Saville and gave him the barest of nods. "Detective."

"Mrs. Wenstrom, allow me to express my deepest regrets for the cause behind this meeting. Also, let me apologize for giving you the impression we didn't care about Jamie's disappearance. I'll admit right now, in front of God and everybody, that my initial assumption that he was just off blowing off steam was wrong."

"Thank you." Jenna stepped back and beckoned them inside. "Danny is in the den. We'll join him there. Can I get anyone coffee?"

"No, thank you, Jenna," said Meredeth. "We've just had a big breakfast with multiple cups each. I'm afraid we may be wired." She gave Jenna a grin. "But we do have some news."

"Let's save it until we're with Danny." Jenna turned and led them through a beautifully decorated formal living room, up three steps, then down a short hall. She rapped on a closed door with one knuckle, then pushed through the door. "Danny? Meredeth Connelly, Bobby Van Zandt, and Al Saville are here."

Danny Wenstrom was seated on a brown leather couch, staring at nothing through red-rimmed eyes. He gave a sigh as they entered, then glanced at Meredeth and nodded hello. "Agent Connelly," he said. "Thank you so much for coming out."

"Of course, Danny," said Meredeth.

He forced himself to his feet and extended his hand, first to Meredeth, then to Bobby, then he sat down again. If Al Saville noticed the snub, he didn't react. "I'm glad Jim could spare you two. He speaks very highly of you both."

"We are happy to help," said Bobby.

"That's good of you to say. I know this case isn't really your cup of tea."

"That doesn't matter," said Meredeth. "We're here to get this sorted out, to bring you relief from the interminable suffering you're feeling now."

"Yes," said Danny in a voice that shook. He cleared his throat harshly. "I'm just sitting here, wondering how the hell we came to this point. You know, what did I do to drive my son away? I just wanted what was best for him. You know?"

"We do," said Meredeth as Jenna sank next to her husband and took his hand.

"You can't blame yourself, Mr. Wenstrom," said Al Saville. "Kids these days...it's like they have so many choices they can't bring themselves to pick one. It was the same with my boy."

"Was it?" asked Danny in a voice devoid of emotion—or interest.

"Yes, it was. Scott had his problems, too."

"Did he disappear?"

Saville hung his head. "I've already apologized to your wife, Mr. Wenstrom, but please accept my apology for slow-rolling things at the beginning. I thought he was just off somewhere and would be home as soon as he ran out of money."

"And what changed your mind?" demanded Danny in a harsh voice. "The arrival of the best damn criminal profilers our country has to offer?"

"No, sir," said Saville. "It was when get got Jamie's cell phone data back."

"Oh?"

"Let's get to that in due course," said Meredeth, taking an armchair opposite the couch. "Bobby and I poked around on Monday and early yesterday. We were able to track Jamie's movements last Sunday."

Both Jenna and Danny pinned her with their gazes.

"He attended a party at Tim McMasters's house."

"Dammit!" muttered Danny.

"While he was there, he spent a while speaking with a man named Kahin Alshaytan. We understand Alshaytan invited Jamie back to his house, and Jamie accepted the invitation."

"He knows better than to..." Danny squeezed his eyes shut. "Did he... Did Alshaytan...kill my son the way he did that drug dealer?"

"We're investigating that, Danny," said Bobby. "Right now, we can't say one way or another, but we do know he was at Alshaytan's house at around two in the morning Monday. Detective Saville tracked Jamie's cell phone, and it was active after Alshaytan claims your son left."

Danny glanced at Saville.

"And," said Al, "we have evidence his phone traveled around Ukiah most of Monday, then headed north to the Mendocino National Forrest."

"And then?" Jenna asked in a weak voice.

"And then the phone was turned off or destroyed," said Meredeth.

"Mendocino National Forest," muttered Danny. "Federal land." He looked a question at Meredeth.

"Yes, Danny. We've taken jurisdiction and have formed a task force with the National Park Service Criminal Investigations Division and Mendocino County Sheriff's Office. Detective Saville will serve as our local liaison officer."

"I...see."

"What does all this mean, Meredeth?" asked Jenna.

"We're giving Alshaytan a hard look. We'll be tasking the NPS CID with finding the cell phone if they can. They will also perform a hard-target search for Jamie up in the forest." She paused, squeezed her lips into thin white lines, then went on. "I need to tell you that their search will include dogs—both tracking dogs and...and cadaver dogs."

A single sob escaped Jenna, and she covered her mouth with a hand that shook.

"I know how that sounds, but you can't read anything into it. It's standard procedure for a search like this."

Jenna nodded, and Danny put his arm around her shoulders. "I suppose it's better to hear it from you than the news," he said.

Meredeth nodded. "That's why I told you. I didn't want you ambushed by those reports. For what it's worth, I don't think those searches will turn up anything."

"No?" asked Danny.

She shook her head. "I believe someone drove his phone up there as misdirection. In case the inevitable investigation got too close to home."

"Then you think this Alshaytan—"

"Danny, we just don't yet. It could be that Jamie really did run away, or that he's staying with Alshaytan and everyone's covering for him."

"Can't you search the place? Can't you just—"

"We're working on that," said Bobby. "We have a possible way in, but it relies on certain conditions we're not yet able to guarantee."

Danny nodded, his gaze turning bleak. "He's dead, isn't he?"

Meredeth had barely heard him; his voice had been so quiet. "We're not there, yet, Danny. Give us a day or two."

"But the statistic on this kind of thing..."

"They are just statistics, and you know what they say about those."

"What?" asked Jenna.

"There are lies, there are damn lies, and then there are statistics." Meredeth smiled as she always did when she trotted out that joke, but neither Wenstrom returned it. "Look, each case is idiosyncratic. Yes, statistics can inform our investigation, but in isolation, they are meaningless. Give us a few days, then I promise I'll come back and tell you my honest opinion—*if* we haven't already found him."

"Okay," said Danny in a lifeless, enervated voice.

"Do you know what this feels like?" asked Jenna. "It's like...it's like being buried alive, bit by bit. It's like drowning, but instead of water, you're drowning in uncertainty, in your deepest, darkest fears, in a horror show of waiting and thinking and assuming the worst and hoping and loving and...and..." She ran down like a windup toy at the end of its spring.

Meredeth got up and crossed the room to sit by her side. She put her arm around the woman and pulled her close. "Jenna. I don't...I never had children, so I can't say I understand, not fully, but I've been doing this a long time." She paused for a moment as that scene from Hanable's Valley flashed before her eyes, the small, black-rimmed hole in Brad Besson's blood-soaked pillow, splattered gray matter on the wall. She shook her head to clear away the images. "And in my time investigating all those murders, I've seen my share of pain, I've had countless meetings like this, and some have resulted in the worst possible news for the victims' families, but *not all of them.* Now, I don't want to leave you with false hope, but I don't want you to give up, either. As hard as it is, please don't draw conclusions yet. Let me find out for you. Let me find out *for sure*. Until then, please just do your best to keep your minds open." She switched her gaze to Danny, looking him in the eye. "Can you do that?"

Danny closed his eyes a moment and sighed. "We can try."

"Good. I also want you to know that Detective Saville did not, at any time, give up on Jamie. I'm sure the news that we took over the case wasn't good for him, but do you know what? The first thing he did was offer to help."

Danny glanced at the man and nodded.

"And nothing Detective Saville did or didn't do last Monday would have made any difference. Plus, pulling the cell phone data was an inspired move, a move that puts us much farther ahead today than we would be otherwise. Did he make a mistake? Maybe. But he's apologized, and in my opinion, he's a good man who means well."

Saville nodded. "I wish I could do things differently, but I can't roll back time. Having said that, I requested the cell phone data right away because, even though I thought Jamie was just off sowing his wild oats, I wanted to let you know exactly where he was. Unfortunately, these kinds of requests take time. We had to get a court order, then the cell company had to take their time pulling the data."

"I...we understand," said Danny. "I can't say no hard feelings, because, Al, I do harbor some, but only because of how you upset Jenna."

"I understand," said Saville. "And I'm very sorry I added to your pain. Both of you."

Jenna looked at Meredeth, her gaze flicking back and forth between Meredeth's eyes. "Hurry, please, Meredeth. I don't know how much longer I can stand not knowing."

CHAPTER 22

CORPOREAL PUNISHMENT

David Branch's Farm, NY

EARLY IN THE evening, Lucy stumbled to Carl's room and found him lying on the bed with his eyes closed. But not for long. When she staggered in, slamming the bedroom door back on its hinges, he sat bolt upright.

"What's going on?" It took a second for him to focus his mind and eyes on the bloody and battered girl who stood at the end of his bed. "How did all that happen?"

"How do you think it happened?" Lucy mumbled through a fat lip.

"Did Father do this to you?"

Lucy shook her head. "Father would never do this. It's not his way."

"Then who?" Carl was off the bed now. He stood up and approached Lucy, giving her a more detailed once over. He winced, taking in her eye that was swollen shut. The other wasn't quite there yet, but it wouldn't be long. A thin crust of blood had dried on her upper lip. The right side of her face was swollen, too. Like someone had landed more than a couple of decent punches there. Her clothes were soiled and dirty, and she was limping. "Holy Mother... Father needs to see this."

"No. He'll find out soon enough. And then he'll make me say what happened. I don't want to get anyone in trouble."

"The way you look, what's been done to you, you can't let that ride." Carl pushed a strand of blood-matted hair away from her face. His eyes were wide with concern. "Tell me who did this, or I'll go question everyone on the farm. Shouldn't be hard to find the culprit. Not if you gave half as good as you got."

He turned toward the door, but Lucy stopped him with a hand on his shoulder. "If I tell you, you have to promise not to go to Father."

"Why would I agree to—"

"He already thinks I'm weak. I have to handle this myself." Lucy coughed—hacked like she had pneumonia—and it turned into an uncontrollable spasm, ejecting bloody spittle. "We have to handle this how Father would expect."

"Fair enough." Carl steered Lucy to the bed and sat her down. "But first, we clean you up. Take care of those injuries."

"No. I want him to see what he did to me—how he messed me up—when we exact retribution."

"Him?" Carl's eyes narrowed. "Mack wouldn't do this. That only leaves one person."

Lucy nodded mutely.

"*Jonathon.*"

Lucy looked up into Carl's eyes. Her bottom lip trembled. A tear weaved down her cheek, leaving a trail through the dried blood. "He did more than... He..."

"What did he do?" Carl asked in a low voice. "Tell me, Lucy, and right now."

"He..." She gulped back a sob. Took a stuttering breath. "He made me go out into the woods behind the barn. He wanted to perform a druidic ritual. He begged me to help, told me it would get him in Father's good graces because you'd gotten into Druids but were too afraid to do as they did. He wanted to prove that he was better than you." Lucy stopped and took a deep breath. "He wanted to do a Celtic ritual he read about and... and..."

"Go on," Carl said with narrowed eyes.

"I didn't want to, but he forced me. He said the ritual required a sex offering. He said that since I'm the only 'real woman' on the farm—I guess Michelina and Patricia don't count—no one else could do it."

"And did you?" Carl's face had turned to stone. He was talking through clenched teeth.

Lucy nodded. "Not willingly. He forced me...he *raped me*... I couldn't fight back, he's so much bigger than me. Stronger. He was on me before I knew what was happening. At least his claim that it would take long wasn't true. Once he got me on the ground, it was over in about a minute, but that didn't stop him from wailing on me, even though I didn't fight him. He said I deserved it, said it was a lesson not to be so standoffish. Then he..." She coughed a bit more, then hung her head. "Afterward, he said that if I told anyone what had happened, he'd kill me."

Carl stood over Lucy in stunned silence. After a moment, he shook off the fugue, the shock. "Why would he do this?"

"Because of you." Lucy took Carl's hand. "He hates that you're better than him. He hates that you have me. The whole time...you know, when he was doing that stuff to me, he was ranting about how it would make him just like you."

"That doesn't make sense."

"Really?" Lucy gripped Carl's hand tighter. "He's always talking about you. Complaining that you make him look dumb by all the stuff you say at breakfast and all the books you read. He's been jealous of you from the start. He thinks you manipulated your way into Father's heart."

"This is crazy. Why would he—"

"You don't believe me?" Lucy withdrew her hand.

"You say Jonathon raped you, I believe it." Carl clenched his fists. His voice trembled when he spoke, but his eyes were hard, dark. "I'm going to make sure he never does anything like that ever again."

"Deal with him as Father would expect," Lucy said. "You have to do it right. I don't want you to get in trouble."

Carl didn't answer. The rage that he'd contained until that point spilled over. He turned and bolted from the room, leaving Lucy perched on the edge of the bed. A moment later, she heard his voice, guttural and full of menace. He called Jonathon's name. A door slammed. Then another.

Lucy stayed where she sat a while longer, listening to Carl tearing through the house, then she stood and went to his nightstand and opened it. She reached in and found what she was looking for, then she hurried from the bedroom.

She found Carl in the kitchen at the back door, looking out through the peephole. He yanked it open, and there was Jonathon in the dooryard with a bucket of soapy water in one hand and a sponge in the other.

When he saw Carl, his eyebrows raised an alarm. "What's going on?"

"You know damn well what." Carl lunged out the door and was on him before Jonathon could even react.

He fell backward and hit the ground hard; the bucket flew from his hand and spilled water across the flagstones.

"Get off me," he screeched, even as Carl's fist flattened his nose. He flailed and bucked but couldn't displace Carl, who, with his knees in Jonathon's armpits and his butt on the other boy's torso, was raining down blows like a madman, slamming one fist into his face, followed by the other. Jonathan's head snapped back and forth with each successive impact. Drops of blood flew with each jolt of his head. He wailed and tried to cover his face with his hands, but Carl slapped them away.

"What's going on?" Alex appeared, breathless. He watched the ruckus with a flat expression mimicking disinterest, though his nostrils flared with each titanic blow Carl dished out.

Lucy turned to him. "Jonathon raped me. Took me out behind the barn and raped me."

"That's not—" Alex furrowed his brow and snapped his mouth closed. "Are you sure about that? You don't want to go making accusations before you have time to think them through."

"Not an accusation." Lucy turned her attention back to the beating. For a moment, she thought Alex was going to intervene, but he just folded his arms and watched the beating.

Jonathon was still struggling, but his attempts to defend himself had become feeble. He pawed the air as if he couldn't quite get his bearings. His protests had dropped to nothing but incoherent and barely audible mumbles. His face was a bloody mess. One eye was swollen closed, the other had rolled lazily upward as if he couldn't quite focus.

Carl was still whaling on him, but his blows had become less frequent, and his breath was labored. With one last punch, Carl leaned back and looked over his shoulder. "Lend me your knife, Alex."

"You sure about that?" Alex asked, sensing what Carl was about to do. "What will Father say when he and Mack come home?"

"Nothing," said Lucy. "Not when he finds out that Jonathon raped me."

Alex hesitated. She met Carl's gaze. "Fair enough. Guess you better finish it, then."

"I already brought your old hunting knife," Lucy said, pulling a folding blade from her pocket. The one Carl always kept in his nightstand. "Thought you might want it."

Jonathon mumbled something that sounded like a plea. He tried to squirm out from under Carl, but there was no fight left in him.

Even if Carl doesn't use the knife, Lucy thought, *Jonathon might not survive until Father got home anyway.*

But Carl took the knife, flinging the sheath away as if it and not Jonathon, disgusted him. He glowered down at Jonathon's battered and bleeding face. "Since you're so interested in religious studies, I'm going finish you off just like the Aztecs would have."

"Cut out his beating heart," Lucy said under her breath.

"Damn right." Carl gripped the knife in both hands, lowered the blade, and pressed the point against Jonathon's flabby stomach. Then, with an unholy screech, he rammed it deep and went to work.

CHAPTER 23

SQUEALER

Ukiah, CA

OVER LUNCH, THEY discussed possible methods
for getting Roberta Black out of the house and away from
Kahin and his friends. The best solution they could think
of wasn't all that great: they could have someone in the
county offices call her about a "problem" with her house
and tell her she had to come down to straighten it out. The
issue with the plan was that Kahin would probably come
with her.

"Why don't we take another run at Ray Michaels," Bobby
suggested. "He's a kid. He should be easy to sway to our
side."

"Two problems with that, Bobby," said Al. "One, if he's a
minor, we either need someone from the school to sit in,
or we have to involve his trainwreck parents. Second, as
easy as it may be for us to bring him around to our side, it's
just as easy for Kahin. We'd need to convince him to stay
away from the Rosemary Lane house, and from what

you've already said, he's pretty dedicated to spending time there."

"We already spoke to him in the presence of Ionia McAdams," said Meredeth. "At any rate, I'm not sure he's still seventeen."

Al shrugged. "Hey, I'm up for whatever you want to try, just playing devil's advocate here."

"What if we look at this another way?" mused Meredeth. "What if, instead of getting Ms. Black out of the house, we get *everyone* out of the house."

"Code Enforcement?" asked Bobby.

Meredeth nodded. "The place has to be a health hazard."

"We can try that," said Al. "I've got a golfing buddy in the unit."

"What do we do once we have them all out?"

"We can put a tail on Kahin and his fiancées, another on Roberta Black. We can pull her over on the way to wherever they are headed."

"What, and just hope she takes a separate car from her son?"

"Yes."

Al steepled his fingers in front of his mouth. "Here's another issue. If Alshaytan is getting unstable, he may refuse to leave, refuse to let *anyone* leave, and then we'll have a hostage situation and a barricaded home to infiltrate. It could make the situation worse."

"I agree," said Bobby. "It's better that he doesn't see us coming. It's best if we can get enough out of Rad to give us just cause for making entry."

"But can we do that?" asked Al. "Won't the kid be loyal?"

"Maybe, but I'm betting Meredeth can get it out of him."

"It might be better coming from you, Bobby," said Meredeth. "The whole father-figure thing."

"I think I blew that the other day, trying to talk him into the Marine Corps. Besides, you heard the comment he made about his father giving him scars."

"I remember that incident," said Al. "Kid ended up in the hospital but wouldn't say a bad word about his father."

"Everyone knows boys love their mothers best," said Bobby. "Put on your maternal hat, Mere."

"What maternal hat? I'm pretty sure I don't have a maternal instinct in my repertoire."

Al pursed his lips. "What if we brought Jenna Wenstrom down to the high school? What if *she* asks Ray for his help?"

"That could work," said Meredeth. "But once we've got him on our side, then what?"

"Then we get him to come clean about someone in the house giving him beer or dope or worse. We get him to tell us what's going on behind that black front door. Then, armed with that information, Al can try for a no-knock warrant, and we can stage an early morning raid."

"I like it," said Meredeth. "We won't need to risk asking Roberta Black for permission and having her warn Kahin."

"It's a good plan. The only hiccup is whether Jenna Wenstrom can play the part given her state of mind." Al dropped his hands to the table, then leaned back in his chair.

"Her state of mind is exactly what she needs to show," said Meredeth, her gaze far away, unfocused. "She needs to play on his sympathy, to show him what this is doing to her and Danny, to ask him to help her find out what happened to Jamie."

"I see," said Al. "Tug on his heartstrings."

"Exactly."

"You should call Jenna," said Bobby. "Talk to her woman to woman."

"Yeah, I guess you're right, but not from here. Give me the keys to the Jeep and stay here until I text you."

Bobby pulled the keys from his pocket and slid them across the table. She grabbed them and pushed away from the table, nodded to the two men, then turned on her heel and walked out to the car. She got in on the driver's side and started the engine and cranked up the air conditioning. She considered running the plan by Jim McCutchins but discarded the idea—better to ask forgiveness than permission.

She dialed Jenna's cell and waited as it rang three times. She was in the middle of trying to find another number when Jenna picked up.

"Huh-hello, Meredeth," said Jenna in a voice filled with foreboding. "Have you—"

"We haven't found him, Jenna. Not yet. But we do have a plan, and we could use your help executing it."

"Me? What can I do?"

"We want to take another run at Ray Michaels. We want to convince him to help by giving us information that could lead to charges of contributing to the delinquency of a minor. That—"

"But that's a nothing charge!"

"Yes, it is, Jenna, but all we want it for is to support a warrant. The plan is to stage a pre-dawn raid on Alshaytan's house."

"Oh, I see. Why do you need me."

"To Ray, Bobby and I are just cops—not to be trusted. But you, you are a mother from his community, and what's more, you are Jamie's mom. You can ask him for help and that will sledgehammer through his defenses...especially if you show him how badly this situation is affecting your family."

The line went silent for a few breaths. "You'll bring him by the house?"

"No, if we did that, we'd have to bring his parents into it, and who knows what would happen then? No, we'll come get you and take you to the high school with us. Ionia McAdams will facilitate the interview in lieu of the Michaels. We've already interviewed Ray that way."

"Oh," said Jenna. "Let me talk to Danny. I'll call you back in a few minutes."

"No problem, Jenna. Our only time constraint is that we want to get him while school is still in session, and we'd like to do it today."

"What... What if I can't do it, Meredeth? What if it's too much?"

"Jenna, the last thing I want is to add to your suffering, but the simple answer is: the more emotion you show Ray, the more likely he will cave. Your motherhood is the key, your love for Jamie, your compassion toward Ray."

"I...see. Call you back."

"Right. I'll be here."

Meredeth hung up and sat staring out the front window. They hadn't even considered that Jenna might not *want* to face one of her son's friends, that she might find going to the high school and seeing all those kids painful, torturous. She set her mind to work on an alternative plan. *Can I pretend at maternal instincts? Some kind of good cop-bad cop thing, with Bobby or Al playing bad cop?* The idea made her nervous. She and Bobby had played the routine on numerous suspects, but none of those had relied on her pretending to mother the suspect.

Her phone chimed, and she glanced down at the Caller ID: Jenna Wenstrom. She accepted the call. "Hello, Jenna," she said in a soft voice. "Listen, I didn't think how this plan might affect you. We can—"

"Give me thirty minutes to get my face on. I'll wear heavy mascara so that crying with leave black streaks across my face, and I *will* cry. A lot."

"Are you sure?"

"It's the best plan, right? Thirty minutes." She hung up without another word, and Meredeth's head gave her a solid thump right behind her eyes.

"Oh, I know, you bastard, I know," she muttered. She texted Bobby, then leaned forward and rested her head on the top of the steering wheel. "This had better work."

Bobby opened the passenger door. "You okay?"

"Yes. Asking Jenna to go through the pain has given me one of my headaches. That's all."

"Want me to drive?"

"Yeah, that's for the best I think." Meredeth got out and crossed around the front of the vehicle, then slid into the back passenger seat. "You take shotgun, Al. That way Jenna and I will be in the back for the ride back to the high school. Bobby, you should call Ionia and let her know we're on our way back and what the plan is."

"Ten-four."

Meredeth lay her head back and pinched the bridge of her nose. Spots of colors danced on her eyelids—blue, red, blue, red, blue, red.

"Here, Mere," said Bobby.

She cracked open an eyelid. He was holding a Coke in a to-go cup, and two bottles of medicine: her Sumatriptan and Excedrin. "I don't want the Sumatriptan."

"Take it, Mere. We need you at your best."

She took the drink and wedged it between her thighs, then reached for the pill bottles. "Yeah, okay, but there's no guarantee the Sumatriptan will do much of anything."

"But it might."

"Tell him, Bobby," she said as the Jeep got rolling.

"Al, you're not seeing or hearing any of this."

"Migraines?" he asked.

"Yes."

"Mostly controlled," said Meredeth, "but if the Bureau were to hear of it..."

"Say no more," said Al. "We all get headaches from time to time. I see no reason to speak of this to anyone."

"Thank you."

"We're all cops here," he said.

Meredeth popped two Excedrin and one of the tiny Sumatriptan pills into her mouth and washed it all down with a giant sip of her cola. "Done and done, Mother hen."

"Good. We're almost to the Wenstrom's. Get your game face on."

"I'll have you know this *is* my game face."

"Yeah. Don't you forget it."

"Tell me when we hit the driveway. Until then, shut it, Van Zandt."

"Ma'am, yes, ma'am!"

She let her mind drift, clearing away her worries, her concerns, her thoughts as much as that was possible, and just listened to her body breathe. It was a relaxation technique many swore by, and one Meredeth tried off and on with limited success. She pictured herself walking barefoot down a red clay road shrouded over by magnificent oaks and laurels, a cool breeze rustling the leaves and kissing her cheeks. She imagined the sound of animals in the woods to either side, but they were as peaceful as she felt. The clay felt cool beneath her feet, as cool as air-conditioned tile. She imagined the road opening onto a wide clearing in which a brook babbled ceaselessly, its gentle susurrations pleasant and soft. Warm Georgia sun shone down on her, and she turned her face to the sky in welcome. When she tired of that, she opened her eyes. Ten feet in front of her, a Northern Cardinal hung in the air, hovering like a hummingbird.

It was beautiful, bright red for the most part, but with orange, dark red, and black strategically placed for camouflage. The black around the bird's red beak and eyes seemed so deep, so rich, that she found herself staring at it, even as the bird stared at her.

"I'll be damned," she muttered. "Red feathers. He's in Virginia? Why?"

"Did you say something, Mere?"

She opened her eyes and found Bobby looking at her in the rearview mirror. "What do you about Kevin's trip? Why is he in Virginia?"

"What are you talking about?"

"Red feathers. That was my clue. Red feathers on his windowsill. Cardinal feathers, Bobby. *Northern* Cardinal feathers."

"And?"

"It's the Virginia state bird, doofus. Kevin is in Virginia. Now, tell me why."

Bobby turned his eyes back to the road. "There's the driveway." He pointed ahead of them.

"Great. Why is Kevin in Virginia?"

"I don't know that he is, and even if I did, it wouldn't be my place to tell you why."

"What a weasel answer," she grumbled. "The second we're done with Jenna, get prepared to tell me what I want to know."

"You're in trouble, Van Zandt," said Al. "Who's Kevin?"

"Kevin Saunders, Chief of the Hanable's Valley Police Department and Meredeth's beaux." Bobby brought the Jeep to a stop in the U-shaped drive near the front doors of the Wenstrom house. "I'll go to the door. Everyone sit tight." He was out of the Jeep before anyone could reply, let alone protest, and when he was halfway to the door, Jenna came out and closed it behind her.

Her face was set in an expression that Meredeth had seen on several occasions—on death row. Meredeth's head pulsed. "This had better work," she murmured.

"Amen," said Al.

Meredeth slid across the back seat until she was wedged behind the driver's seat, and Bobby opened the passenger side rear door for Jenna. "Hello," said Meredeth as the woman climbed in. "If, at any time, this gets to be too much, just tell me, and we'll stop."

"He's my son, Meredeth. It can't be too much. I will endure any pain you can imagine if it means finding Jamie."

Bobby closed the door after she got settled, then ran around the front of the Jeep to jump into the driver's seat. "All set?" he asked.

"Yes," said Jenna.

"Okay. Ionia McAdams will have Ray in the conference room waiting for us."

"Good. I want to get on with it."

Bobby nodded and pulled out of the drive, then took them down the side of the hill and wove through the streets of Ukiah to get back to Low Gap Road. He passed the county buildings on the left, then pulled into the Ukiah High School parking lot and found a space near the administration building.

They all climbed out and headed inside. Mandy Finster nodded to them and pressed the button under the counter. Bobby opened the door to the inner office, holding it for the rest of them.

Inside, Mandy left her post momentarily—just long enough to give Jenna hug and murmur something in her ear. Jenna smiled a little and patted her on the back. "Ionia is in the conference room with Ray," Mandy said. "You can go on back."

"Thanks, Mandy," said Meredeth.

In the conference room, Ray Michaels sat with his back to the door, his feet splayed out under the table, slouched so low he could rest his head on the back of the chair. His eyes were closed, and he pretended to snore.

"Up and at 'em, Marine," said Bobby.

Rad cracked open one eye, scorn dominating his expression, his mouth open with some wisecrack, but when he took in Jenna Wenstrom standing there, he swallowed whatever he'd planned on saying and sat up straight. "Mrs. Wenstrom. I didn't... I mean, what are..." He shook his head, then offered up a weak smile. "Hello."

"Hello, Ray," said Jenna. She circled around the table and sat down opposite him.

Rad turned his head to give Bobby a stern look. "Dirty pool," he mouthed.

Bobby only shrugged and pointed at Jenna.

"Any news on Jamie?" Rad asked hopefully.

"No, nothing new," said Jenna. "Ray, I'm here to ask for your help finding him."

"Me? What can I do?"

"I understand from Agent Connelly that you are..." A pained expression crossed her face. "That you are friends with Kahin Alshaytan."

Rad glanced around at Meredeth and gave her an impenetrable look. "I am," he said, turning back to Jenna. "But he's not involved in Jamie's disappearance. Jamie's never even been to Kahin's place. Kahin told me so himself."

"He lied to you," said Meredeth. "Both he and Anya admitted Jamie came over."

A momentary look of horror washed over Rad's face, but he buried it quickly. "No, I don't believe you."

"Ray," said Jenna. "Look at me, Ray." She waited until he did so. "Jamie met Kahin Alshaytan at Tim McMasters' party a week ago Sunday. He—"

"Mrs. Wenstrom, I know. I was at that party. Kahin talked to a lot of people that night, including me. But he and Anya left alone, and a long time before Jamie left."

Jenna nodded, and a tear overflowed her left eye and streaked down her cheek, leaving a black line of mascara in its wake. "Be that as it may, Jamie did go to the house on Rosemary Lane. He spent the night there, and the next day, he ran around Ukiah—at least someone did, carrying Jamie's cell phone. Then, late afternoon, his phone went dead in Mendocino National Forest."

"See? There you go. Even if he did hang out with Kahin, he left and went up north. That's where you will find him."

More tears streaked down Jenna's cheeks. "I don't think so, Ray, and neither do Agent Connelly, Agent Van Zandt, nor Detective Saville. I don't think Jamie ever left Kahin's house."

"No?"

She shook her head. "It breaks my heart to think it, but no, I don't believe he did. I think Alshaytan took Jamie's cell phone for a ride and threw it away in the forest after killing it."

"Mrs. Wenstrom, please don't cry."

"How can I not, Ray? My baby is missing, and with each passing day, it becomes harder to keep the faith, harder to believe he's still..." She choked on the word, then fiddled with her purse, looking for a Kleenex. "You'd tell me, wouldn't you, Ray? You'd tell me if you knew something?"

"Yes, absolutely. But I haven't seen Jamie since McMasters threw that party."

"But you've been inside that house. You talked to Alshaytan."

"Yes, I have. There's nothing wrong with that, is there?"

"I don't know, Ray. Is there? Is there something wrong in that house?"

"I..." He shook his head. "Kahin's all stressed out because of his mom. She wants to get him back on his meds, but he doesn't need that. Kahin's *fine* if people would just leave him alone."

"Is his mother in danger?" asked Jenna, looking at Ray a little wide-eyed.

"I..." He shook his head. "What's this got to do with Jamie?"

"Agents Connelly and Van Zandt need to get inside the house, Ray. They need to search the place to see if Jamie is still there somewhere, to run tests, to see if..." She closed her eyes, and more tears went racing down her cheeks, mascara marking her grief in their wake. "To see if Jamie *died* in that house." She opened her eyes. "Will you help me, Ray? Please?"

"I…" Ray swallowed hard, then shot a bitter look at Ionia McAdams. "Nice ambush."

"Ray? I need your help. I need you to help Agent Connelly find my baby. Dead or alive, Ray, I have to know. Not knowing is killing Danny and me. It feels like we're drowning in the unknown, like the possibilities are leaden weights attached to our ankles, pulling us down to Davy Jones."

Ray closed his eyes, his mouth working silently for a moment. Finally, he said, "What do you need to know?"

That's when Meredeth circled around, pulled out the chair next to Jenna's, and sat. She didn't smile, and she patted Jenna's hand. "Here's what we need to know, Rad."

CHAPTER 24

SATANIC PANIC

Ukiah, CA

THINGS HAD CHANGED at Kahin's house, and not for the better. The open-door policy Kahin had previously maintained, which resulted in a steady stream of both familiar and unfamiliar faces coming and going at will, had turned into something more akin to entering a seedy downtown club.

When Rad showed up a little after three in the afternoon—as soon as the jerks at Ukiah High let him go for the day—he found the front door locked and a new hand-written notice pinned over the ones that were already there. It read:

> *Knock to get in.*
> *Prove yourself to stay.*
> *Interlopers and spies will be dealt with.*

Rad stared at the notice, disturbed by both the paranoia it displayed and the implied threat of the last line. After a few moments of staring, of dithering and shifting from foot to foot, he gave the door three short raps and was rewarded with the sound of the locks disengaging. The door swung open a couple of inches until a silver chain stopped it.

A single, dark-colored eye—almost black—peered at him through the gap. "ID."

"Huh?" That was the last thing Rad was expecting anyone to ask for. "I don't have any."

"Then you don't get in." The guy on the other side of the door tried to close the door, but Rad shoved his boot into the crack and shifted his weight forward to block the door from shutting.

"Get Kahin. He knows me. He'll let me in."

"Don't need to." The guy was still pushing hard to close the door, pinching Rad's foot. "No one comes in without ID. New rules. Either show me some identification or get lost."

"Look. Just talk to—"

"Move your damn foot." The guy slammed his weight against the back of the door. Rad was about to give up and go around the back to see if he would have more luck there, when a voice he recognized spoke up from inside the house.

"Let the kid in. He's all right." It was Anya.

The doorman hesitated as if he wasn't sure, but then he undid the chain latch and pulled the door wide with a dissatisfied grunt.

Rad shoved past him into the living room.

There were fewer people lounging around than normal. The house had a different feel. It was darker. More claustrophobic. The people inside seemed sullen, scared, maybe.

Anya snaked an arm around his waist. "Hey there, lover boy."

"Where's Kahin?" Rad asked, ignoring Anya's fingers that were dropping lower and probing inside the waistband of his Lycra Stars and Stripes pants.

"He's around," Anya replied. "Probably in one of the bedrooms smoking dope or communing out in the woods with the Master."

"I'm right here."

Rad pulled away from Anya and turned to see Kahin near the kitchen doorway. His hair was more ratty than usual, and his skin was even pastier than Rad thought possible for a living person. There were dark bags under his eyes. His skin had a waxy sheen that look positively unhealthy, and his bloodshot eyes appeared raw.

But it was the pistol in his hand that alarmed Rad the most.

"What do you need that for?" he asked. An image of the dead guy in the basement with his face blown off strobed in Rad's mind like the memory of a gruesome slasher film.

Kahin held the gun up and looked at it. "Insurance."

"You don't think it's dangerous, waving that thing around?" Kahin was unpredictable at the best of times, but now he looked positively insane.

"Need the gun. Can't trust anyone."

"You look like crap," Rad said. "When was the last time you got any sleep?"

"Hard to say." Kahin's eyes danced around the room, flitting between the few disciples that had made it past the front door thanks to his new rules. "Got to watch my back. Too many people want to take all this away. Put a stop to our fun." His eyes shifted to the front door. "They're out there right now. You can't see them, but they are."

"Who?" Rad asked. "Who's out there?"

"Feds. Cops." Kahin's face twitched when he spoke. "Infiltrators. Templars."

"The man is out to get him," Anya said, circling around. She stopped and draped herself against Kahin's back. "Can't trust anybody, can you, honey?"

"Nobody but the faithful," Kahin told her. He looked at Rad. "Someone's been telling tales. Whispering in ears that shouldn't be whispered into. When I find out who they are..." He lifted the gun, pointed it at Rad's face, and feigned pulling the trigger. "Boom."

"Hey. Easy there." Rad stepped out of the gun's line of fire. He didn't trust Kahin not to pull the trigger, even if only by accident. "Watch where you're pointing that cannon."

"Why?" Kahin's voice was croaky. His eyes were watery and dull. "Got a guilty conscience? Maybe you did some whispering of your own."

Rad couldn't stop the guilty panic that flooded his mind. *How does he know?* a panicked voice in his mind screamed. *Does he have people watching the damn high school? Or...* But no, that was impossible. *There is no Satan, no God. It's all fairy tales.*

The guy at the door who had challenged Rad took a step toward him. Things were getting out of control.

"Nah. Nothing like that." Rad shook his head quickly. "I'm worried about you, is all."

"Kid's worried about you," Anya echoed. "That's sweet."

"Or maybe he's worried that I know more than he thinks I do." Kahin shrugged Anya away and stepped close to Rad, so their faces were inches apart. "You tell anyone about our little secret in the backyard?"

"No! Never. I do that, and I'm in as much trouble as you." Rad leaned back to avoid the worst of Kahin's foul breath, which was more pungent than normal.

"You swear you didn't squeal? Not even to that dorky friend of yours." Kahin clicked two fingers of his free hand. "What was his name?"

"Mick," Anya said.

"Ah. Mick. That's right. You confess your sins to the dork?" Kahin asked.

"I told you already. I didn't mention the body in the backyard to anyone." Rad darted a glance behind him at the sullen stoners in the room. The vibe in the house had changed from one of easy dope and sex-induced relaxation to paranoia and untethered anger. Rad's home life was bad, but this had turned worse. And because of what he'd done, Rad was trapped in Kahin's world, whether he liked it or not, no matter what that prick Marine FBI agent had to say about it.

"Tell me where your friend Mick lives." Kahin had lowered the gun. It was now pointing at the floor.

"Why?"

"I need to pay him a visit. See what he knows and how he knows it."

"Mick doesn't know anything. I said that already."

"Then you have nothing to worry about."

"And Mick?" Rad asked. "You'll leave him alone?"

"Can't promise that." There was a hard edge to Kahin's voice. "Course, if you'd killed him in the beginning like I asked, none of this would be necessary."

"This is nuts." Rad didn't want to be there anymore. He turned and walked as fast as he dared to the front door, praying that Kahin wouldn't put a bullet in his back on the way. The guy was floating in an ocean of his own paranoia, with no land in sight.

"Where are you going, Rad?" Kahin called after him in a singsong voice. "Are you afraid of me?"

Rad didn't answer. He brushed past the guy at the door and pulled it open. As he stepped outside, Kahin taunted him.

"Go on then. Run home to mommy and daddy. You want to turn your back on me? Fine. I don't need you. I don't need anyone."

Rad barely heard him. He made his way across the front lawn, which was more weeds and trash than grass. But before he could reach the road, he heard the door open and someone pound out after him. His heart leaped into his throat. Kahin was going to shoot him, after all. And right out in the open, on the street.

But it wasn't Kahin, the footsteps were light. *Anya*.

She caught up with Rad and grabbed his arm, seemingly oblivious to the fact that she was on the front lawn in nothing but a pair of dirty panties. "Hold up there, kid."

"Get away from me." Rad tried to shake her off but failed. He turned to her. "It's not safe here anymore. He's losing it."

"Boo-hoo." Anya sneered at him. "It ain't safe anywhere. You walk out on Kahin now, and he'll never look at you the same way again. He'll always think you're the kid who snitched on him. That what you want?"

"I don't care what he thinks."

"You should. He's looking for someone to blame."

"I didn't do anything. If someone spoke to the cops, it wasn't me."

"This ain't a courtroom, kid. There's no innocent until proven guilty. Kahin thinks you did something, you did it. He loses respect for you, that just makes it worse."

"What am I supposed to do?" For the first time since his father whaled on him with a belt when he was nine years old, Rad was close to tears.

"You get back in there and make him respect you. You grow a pair."

"He'll kill me."

"No, he won't. Just the opposite." Anya released Rad's arm. "But if you run out of here like some kind of pussy... well... Don't say I didn't warn you."

Rad hated the thought of going back into the house, but he also didn't want Kahin to hunt him down and make him pay for some imaginary indiscretion. "You sure about this?"

"No one knows Kahin better than me," Anya cooed. "I'm doing you a favor."

Rad hesitated, torn between taking the easy way out or trusting Anya. In the end, he swore under his breath and stomped back toward the front door.

Anya didn't move. At least, not until he'd gone back inside. Then she went to the front window, which provided a splendid view of the living room, and lingered there waiting for the fireworks to start.

CHAPTER 25

RED FEATHERS

Ukiah, CA

MEREDETH DRUMMED HER fingers on the small circular table in her room while Kevin's phone rang. After they'd finished with Ray Michaels, Bobby had dropped her at the hotel so she could get some rest while he and Al worked on the no-knock warrant. Ray had come through—outlining several occasions in which either Kahin himself, or one of his women had given him alcohol or drugs, and better yet, he'd told them the story of Kahin hitting his mother. She had no doubt they'd get their warrant.

"Yo, FBI," said Kevin, sounding a little out of breath.

"You take up jogging, Chief?"

"Nope."

"Are those red feathers still on your windowsill?"

"Let me look." The sound of curtains dragging open sounded like Velcro ripping over the phone. "Yep. Still here."

"What are you doing in Quantico, Kevin?"

"What? Why do you think I'm in Quantico?"

"Red feathers. Northern Cardinal. The Virginia state bird."

"I kind of thought it was too obvious."

"Well, it did take me two days to put it together."

"You were distracted."

"Come on, spill."

"Spill what?"

"What are you doing in Quantico?"

"Okay, I get the Virginia part, but how did you get from the state of Virginia to one specific town?"

"There's nothing else in Virginia."

"No? What about Colonial Williamsburg and Mount Vernon?"

"History. Boring."

"Okay, then what about Arlington? I've got friends buried there."

"There, not here."

"Dammit," he muttered. "Maybe I'm at the beach."

"Not likely."

"Okay, what about the Shenandoah National Park?"

"That one is at least your style, but no, you wouldn't go there without me."

"And that canvas chair."

"And that," she agreed. "Before you start listing the civil war battlefields and whatnot, I don't buy those either."

"Maybe I'm in Richmond at a convention of police chiefs."

"No such event, and you'd hate it if there was. Now, quit this obvious evasion and tell me what you are doing in my backyard."

"How's the case going? Have you found Jamie?"

"Nice try, buckwheat. Spill."

"You can be quite demanding, FBI."

"You ain't seen nothing yet, Saunders. Don't make me call Richie and use my FBI tricks on him."

"You wouldn't do that. And besides, why would he know where I am, let alone why."

"You tell him everything. Everybody knows that."

"Not this."

"No?"

"No."

"Then tell me. The weight of the secret must be wearing you down to nothing."

"No, I think I'm okay."

"Trust me, Kevin. Keeping this from me is wearing a thin spot in the middle of your fat head."

"My head's not fat."

"Says who?"

"Me, of course. Besides, teasing me about the size of my head won't change anything."

"Tell me, Saunders."

"Nope."

"Please?"

"No."

"I'll cry."

"I don't believe that for a second."

"I'll *pretend* to cry."

"Yeah, but we'll both know you're just pretending."

"Fine. I don't want to know your lousy secret."

"Good, because I'm not telling you."

"You can be so stubborn, Saunders!"

"Me? *I'm* stubborn?"

"If you weren't you'd tell me."

"Then I guess I am."

She rolled her eyes and sucked her teeth. "You're just lucky I'm in California and you're in Quantico, Virginia."

"Why's that?"

"I'm not wearing much, and I know I could get it out of you if I were there."

"Then hurry back."

She sighed. "Yeah, okay. Don't tell me. I'll find out soon enough."

"Yeah?"

"We found our way in. We have a raid scheduled for zero-dark-thirty tomorrow morning."

"Ew, that's early."

"You bet, the early bird gets the worm-infested Satan worshiper. Speaking of which, I'd better go rest up."

"Well, good luck, and be careful tomorrow."

"Oh, I will be. After all, I have to get back to Virginia so I can start denying you sex."

Kevin laughed. "I bet when you get back here, you'll change your tune."

"Maybe. Maybe not."

"I guess we'll see, won't we."

"Fine."

"Fine." He chuckled. "Listen to me, Mere. Don't get killed, okay?"

"I won't. I promise. I love you."

"I love you, too. Get some rest."

CHAPTER 26

EVIL TRIUMPHS

David Branch's Farm, NY

ALEX STOOD OVER Jonathon's cooling corpse with a look somewhere between hunger and relief. Cutting a man's heart out was not as easy as one would expect, and it had taken Carl the better part of fifteen minutes to accomplish the task. Not that Jonathon was still present for most of that time. When the knife plunged into his stomach, he'd thrashed and screamed with renewed vigor, the pain and realization of his own impending death flooding his body with enough adrenaline to counteract the effects of the god-awful beating he'd already received. But he couldn't get away, it was far too late for that. His screams and cries had ebbed to whimpers before he fell silent together.

Lucy wasn't sure when he died. For a while, as Carl hacked and cut, she thought his chest was still rising and falling in shallow breaths, but it might just have been the quiver of his flab against the jerk of the knife.

But it was finally done, and all that remained was to dispose of him.

"Go get a shovel from the barn," Alex told Carl as soon as he'd regained his breath.

He nodded and rose wearily to his feet—cutting out a man's heart was far harder than he'd thought. His shirt and pants were slick with blood. So was his face. He looked like some ghastly demon risen from the bowels of hell. He looked down at Jonathon as if summing up his handiwork, then turned and trudged out of the courtyard toward the barn on the other side of the house.

When he was gone, Alex turned to Lucy and fixed her with an icy stare. "Jonathon didn't do this to you."

Lucy wet her lips. "No. You did."

"Yeah. But I sure as hell didn't rape you."

"As if you could," Lucy said, wincing as she spoke because it hurt to talk. It also hurt when she didn't talk.

"That's a good way to get another beating, Squirt," Alex replied, taking a step toward her.

"You already did a good enough job the first time," Lucy said. "But that's okay. I made it serve my purpose."

"And what purpose was that?"

"What do you think?" Lucy's gaze flitted from Alex to the bloodied corpse sprawled on the floor in front of them. "Jonathon is gone. The pig is dead. He won't be around to bully me anymore. And my boyfriend did it with your approval. Now we're all in this together. The three of us. Father won't question it because you sanctioned it. No one gets in trouble. No one gets punished, and Jonathon is still dead."

"Taking an enormous risk there, Squirt." Lucy pushed his hands into his pockets. "Dangerous game."

"Maybe. But it's a game I'm going to keep playing. This is how I'm going to make my way in the world."

"By manipulation." Alex nodded slowly. "Why commit murder when someone else can do it for you?"

"Something like that." Lucy pulled her foot away from the widening circle of blood around Jonathon. "Who could hold me accountable for murders someone else commits? People are easy, stupid. You pull their strings, and they dance."

"You sure pulled Carl's strings."

"Not just Carl's."

"Yeah. You're not as dumb as I thought."

Lucy grinned. "I'm not as dumb as I *wanted* you to think."

"Touché." Alex returned the grin. "You'll go far, Lucy. I think I'll retire your nickname."

CHAPTER 27

WHEN GOOD MEN DO NOTHING

Ukiah, CA

RAD OPENED HIS eyes to inky blackness, and while, as he swam back to consciousness, an overwhelming wave of disorientation seized him. His head hurt worse than any pain he'd experienced in his life, and he couldn't move his arms or legs. He tried to make sense of his predicament, even as he struggled to draw breath through an avalanche of panic. The last thing he remembered was talking to Anya on the front lawn. She had urged him to go back into the house and confront Kahin. That didn't explain how he had ended up blind and immobile with the mother of all headaches.

But when, a few moments later, his eyes adjusted to the gloom, and he realized where he was.

The basement.

The reason he couldn't move was that he was hogtied with his hands and feet bound behind his back and tethered together by a short length of rope. There was a cloth stuffed into his mouth and held in place by another cloth strip tied around his head. He was lying on his stomach, trussed up like a Thanksgiving turkey waiting for the oven.

"Hello?" He tried to force the words past the gag, hoping that maybe the noise would at least bring Anya or some other member of Kahin's inner circle down the steps to his rescue. But he could only produce a low mumble—worse than a whisper, a susurration of sibilants and not much else. Then it occurred to him that drawing attention might not be the best thing, anyway. If Kahin had put him down here, no one was going to defy the man in the state he was in. No one was coming to set Rad free.

He was better off keeping quiet and trying to work his bindings loose before Kahin asked some other disciple to prove himself and do to Rad what he had been expected to do to Mick and that guy who defended Kahin's mother. Better get free and run. He could leave through the back, run into the woods, run straight to the sheriff's office, and ask for protection from the FBI chick.

An image of Kahin flashed in his mind. A sudden recollection—disjointed and unmoored—of the man pressing his gun into Rad's face, the muzzle cold and hard, and screaming at him. *A memory or my imagination*? he asked himself.

A memory, Rad decided. He groaned as more fragmented memories surfaced. Kahin waving the gun around like a madman while others looked on. Kahin pacing back and forth, his face twisted in uncontrollable rage. And then, one last memory. Kahin lunging for him and bringing the gun down in a sweeping arc.

That was why his head hurt so bad. Kahin had pistol-whipped him.

After that, he must have dragged Rad down into the basement and tied him up. There was only one reason he would do such a thing. This hypothesis was borne out by the fact that he was lying on the same tarp the guy with no face had previously occupied. Worse, there was more kitty litter to supplement what was lying loose around him on the floor. Fresh tubs of it standing off to one side. Despite his predicament, Rad wondered when Kahin had time to go shopping for so much of the stuff. And why no one in the store thought it was strange. How many cats did they think the man had?

Raised voices filtered through the floor above—a ruckus starting up. Kahin bellowed something unintelligible. He was walking back and forth, his heavy footfalls making the floorboards above Rad's head creak and groan. Someone else was talking, too. A voice he didn't recognize. He couldn't make out the individual words, but it belonged to a male, and it sounded like the man was in a panic.

And there was Anya—not talking but laughing—the sound of it hollow and frightening, devoid of mirth. To Rad, it came across as almost hysterical. The laughter died down, and then she was egging Kahin on and telling him to 'get on with it'. Rad could mostly understand her because her voice was higher pitched, and the sound carried better through the insulation and flooring.

With a sinking feeling in the pit of his stomach, Rad realized Anya wasn't his friend. She never had been. She'd never really taken Rad's side. She had pushed Rad to kill Mick. She encouraged him to take care of the guy who stood up to Kahin, promising to sleep with Rad if he went through with it. And then the final betrayal. She had played on Rad's emotions and sent him back into the house when he was out the door and on his way to freedom. She knew what Kahin would do. How he would react. It wasn't about respect or standing up to Kahin. It was about Anya manipulating everyone around her. Maneuvering them into confrontations like pieces on a chess board. But to what end, Rad couldn't even guess.

The disagreement, whatever it had been about, appeared to be over upstairs, and the house had settled into an uneasy quiet—much the same way his own house went still right before his father's rage exploded. Rad held his breath and listened. The lack of voices was almost more unsettling than the argument itself. He wondered if Kahin was even still up there.

The sudden boom of a gunshot answered his question.

A heavy thud sent dust floating down from the rafters, and someone screamed. Kahin roared for everyone to shut up.

And everyone did, swaddling Rad in more silence.

Until the sibilant murmur of Anya's voice reached Rad's ears. She was talking in hushed tones now, which made it impossible to understand what she was saying. And there were fresh footsteps, too.

A renewed sense of dread gripped Rad. He squirmed and tugged at his bindings, struggling to loosen them, to free himself so he could at least make a last stand, could fight his way free, maybe, maybe. For the first time in his short seventeen years, Rad sensed the fragility of his own mortality. His eyes bulged. His heart thudded against his ribs. He thought about his parents, and even though he'd never been close to them, never even liked them, he would have given anything at that moment to be back at the decrepit block house with his mother passed out on the couch and his father skulking around in a black mood. This only made him all the more determined to escape. He flopped around on the floor, straining at the ropes that bound his legs and arms.

Then, the basement door opened.

Then, footsteps on the stairs.

Through his terror, Rad guessed it was his erstwhile host, but from his vantage point on the tarp, he could not see. When the basement light clicked on, Rad was forced to scrunch his eyes shut against the sudden glare. He forced them open again, slowly so his pupils would become adjusted to the brightness.

Kahin loomed over him, for once wearing dirty jeans and a white flannel shirt unbuttoned and hanging loose. Flecks of crimson spread across his bare chest and onto the shirt as if someone had flicked paint at him. There were more red speckles on his face and arms.

He stood statue-still and stared at Rad without speaking, without so much as blinking. His face was a blank canvas devoid of emotion, devoid of humanity.

Rad looked up at him and waited for something to happen. When it didn't, he started to think Kahin might have had some sort of mental break. That he had finally flipped and was in a semi-catatonic state, but then a smile spread across Kahin's face. A smile so innocent and full of warmth, he might have been looking at a newborn baby or a playful puppy.

Kahin came closer to Rad and kneeled down in front of him. "Wow. I mean, wow. I'm so sorry. I don't know what came over me. Treating you like that. My house guest, my friend."

Euphoric relief surged through Rad, and he tried to say that it was okay, all was forgiven, that if Kahin would just release him, there was no harm done. But of course, he couldn't do that because of the gag. All he managed were a bunch of incoherent grunts.

"Here. I'll set you free." Kahin reached into his pocket and pulled out a folding knife. He opened it, the steel blade glinting in the glow of a bare bulb hanging from the basement ceiling. He leaned forward over Rad and reached toward the ropes. But then, his other hand landed on Rad's forehead and forced it back.

The knife flashed.

Rad felt a peculiar sensation, like someone running an ice cube across his exposed neck. There was a momentary sensation of pressure before the chill was replaced by a sudden flowing warmth.

And a surge of nauseating pain.

Rad's neck was on fire, and he found it impossible to draw breath as if some monster had him by the throat, squeezing, squeezing, squeezing. He looked up at Kahin, bug-eyed, and at the vermilion-painted knife blade.

Kahin wiped the blade on his pants, first one way, then the other. He snapped the knife closed and pushed it back into his pocket. "Better luck next time on the wheel, kid," he said, standing up.

Rad struggled to speak, but now it wasn't the gag hindering his efforts. It was more that he couldn't catch a breath. Worse, everything felt distant, removed, like his view of the world had collapsed to a slowly darkening tunnel. At the end of that tunnel was Kahin, watching Rad's life ebb away in an ever-widening pool of blood. Standing behind him, near the foot of the stairs, was Anya. The grin on her face was wider than any Rad had ever seen. And as the last image of his life faded into eternal darkness, a final stray thought flitted through Rad's mind. That Anya looked practically... orgasmic.

CHAPTER 28

DAWN'S GRAY LIGHT

Ukiah, CA

TO MEREDETH'S SURPRISE, her headache had disappeared by the time her alarm went off at four in the morning. She felt rested, calm, pain-free, and she got ready in a sort of daze at the unexpected luck. She met Bobby down in the lobby, and together, they headed out in the pre-dawn gloom and found a place open for coffee to go.

They arrived at the staging area at quarter to five in the morning and parked next to the Mendocino County Sheriff's Office triple-C and piled out into the early morning chill. Al Saville beckoned them inside, and they climbed the steps and took seats near the door as the SWAT briefing started.

The no-knock warrant had been signed by a county judge, and that meant they were free to break in without announcing their presence. Meredeth considered that a stroke of good luck—and if it continued, they'd find Alshaytan and everyone else inside sleeping.

The houses to either side of Alshaytan's were too close to allow proper coverage of the B and D sides of the home, and there was the stockade fence to contend with as well, so the assault was planned as a straight-forward A-side entry, with multiple teams stacking up and making entry through the front door. A single sniper unit would cover the C-side from the woods beyond Jefferson Lane to the rear of the place. Community outreach deputies had already been deployed to rouse and remove the neighbors to either side of the house in plain clothes and unmarked cars.

The entry teams boarded their vehicles, while Meredeth and Bobby climbed into Al's cruiser to follow the SWAT APC to the house. They'd decided to follow on the entry teams' heels, staying back just enough to keep out of the way, while assisting and providing cover as needed. Meredeth hadn't wanted to wait for the teams to clear the house, she wanted to be there, to be in the thick of it all, in the hopes that if Jamie were still alive, if Kahin was holding him against his will, she, Bobby, and Al could secure his release and spirit him away.

The APC turned hard right into the front lawn of 1408 Rosemary Lane, exploding the brick steps into a cloud of red dust and climbing up the hill with a roar and a cloud of black diesel soot. The passenger side door banged open, and a SWAT member rushed out and drove a harpoon through the front door, then sprinted away. The driver of the APC gunned it in reverse, more roar from the engine, more black smoke belched skyward, and the metal winch cable snapped taut with a *twang*, held for a moment, then the doorframe exploded into kindling, and the door went bouncing out into the yard.

The SWAT teams deployed, stacking up behind their respective shield specialists, and Meredeth, Bobby, and Al left the cruiser behind at a dead run to fall in behind the last team to enter. Everyone wore N95 respirators and nylon jumpsuits to avoid any contamination from the scene.

Once inside, the teams moved with quiet precision, each team clearing its assigned areas. The entry team found people in the living room—all groggy with sleep—and took them all into custody while the two other teams went their separate ways. The team Meredeth, Bobby, and Al followed had the bedrooms and the back of the house, and they piled into the dark hallway, checking closed doors as they went. They cleared the first two bedrooms—pig sties with mattresses lying on the floor, no sheets, no other furniture, and no people.

They moved on, breached the locked door into what must have been Kahin's room, and found it in little better shape than the guest rooms, but Alshaytan was not in the bed, not in the closet, not in the room. Only two females were taken into custody—one giving her name as Claire

Mastrantonio, and the other refusing to give her name, but she was not the woman Meredeth and Bobby had met on their previous visit. That meant she was Steph Andrews, and that Anya Seneca and Kahin Alshaytan were elsewhere.

They backed into the hall, where the SWAT team leader had found a door that had a deadbolt and a splintered doorframe. Moving slowly, the team made entry into the master bedroom, where they found Roberta Black lying face down in a congealed pool of her own blood. She'd been shot, point blank in the back of the head.

Meredeth keyed her mic. "All teams, all teams, the primary suspect has not been located. Continue to clear your assigned areas. The FBI and Detective Saville will move to the basement." She nodded to Al, and they turned back to find the door that led downstairs. It didn't take long, but when she flicked the light switch, nothing happened.

Bobby took point, moving down the steps with his Glock drawn, cocked and ready. Meredeth followed in his wake, and Saville followed her, each shining a Maglite in a different direction. The basement smelled of dust and bleach and blood. A lot of blood.

At the bottom of the steps, Bobby swiveled and moved to the left, and Meredeth followed, covering his six. Al moved to the right, playing his light into the corners and darkened spaces on that side of the stairs. Bobby's light moved toward the stairs, then he stopped. "Dammit!"

Ray Michael's body lay face down in the center of his Maglite beam, an island in a red sea of the boy's blood.

"Why did Rad come back here? Didn't he know it would be dangerous after talking to us?"

Meredeth grimaced, playing her own Maglite over the empty cartons of kitty litter and the fresh, unopened packages. She flicked the beam beyond them, settling on the bottles and bottles labeled "bleach" that stood behind them. "Alshaytan's been storing bodies here for a while," she said.

"But where do they go from here?"

She lifted her light and played it across the far cinder-block wall. "Bobby," she said, Ankou's Celtic Knot clear in the center of her torch's circuit of bright white light.

"Dammit," Bobby muttered. "Michelina was wrong. Alshaytan *is* Carl. Roberta Black must be cover"

Meredeth didn't answer, her stomach churning, her temples starting to pound. "Al? Got anything over there?"

"Junk. Animal waste. Who's Carl?"

"How did he know?" asked Bobby. "He cleaned house last night. How did he know we were coming?"

"Better question," said Al, joining them, "is how many has Alshaytan killed? He's lived in this house for years. He's been doing the same nonsense for over a decade. Has he been killing people the whole time?"

Meredeth turned away from Rad's corpse. "The most important question for right now is, "Where has Alshaytan gone? Where has Anya Seneca gone?"

"In the wind," said Al.

The sniper team in the woods broke through the radio chatter. "Suspect on move. Heading west up the hill."

The three of them broke for the stairs and pounded up them, bursting through the door at the top, wheeling left, skidding through the kitchen, then out into the mess of the backyard. Meredeth put her head down and sprinted for the back fence, then tripped and almost fell over a mound of loose earth,

Bobby leaped over the mound and shot past her, running flat out for the fence.

Meredeth recovered her footing and raced onward, keying her mic as she did so. "We need cadaver dogs to the backyard." Her gaze shot here and there, and her lips moved as she counted mounds of dirt. "There are multiple sites that may be graves back here."

She ran for the fence, her heart racing, Al Saville puffing along behind her.

CHAPTER 29

IN A BLAZE OF GLORY

Ukiah, CA

MEREDETH CLEARED THE fence and slammed to the ground on the other side, taking up the shock with bent knees and a muttered curse, just in time to see Bobby dart into the trees across the narrow lane running behind Alshaytan's house and up into the heights. She moved after him, already breathing hard, her belly starting to ache where Dr. Atallah had repaired her guts, but not slowing, not holding back. She knew she didn't have long at that level of effort, but she was determined to give it her all and be there in case Bobby needed backup. As she entered the woods across the road, Al clattered over the fence behind her.

Bobby ran on, leaping over downed trees and rocks like some kind of mountain goat, and Meredeth grimaced at the prospect of following his bouncing, jumping path. He seemed to be following a run-off gulley cut into the hill by an eon of water and mud slides.

"Can you see him?" she shouted into her mic.

"Ten-four," said Bobby. "I'm in pursuit. White male, dreads, jeans, white shirt. No visible weapons. Headed west."

Meredeth curled her lip—he could at least have the good grace to sound out of breath. She ran on, forcing herself to keep the pace, her feet slamming into the earth, jarring her brain, her guts, her knees. Al huffed and puffed behind her, falling farther off the pace with each passing minute.

On they ran, Bobby leading them deeper into the forest, higher and higher up the slope of the hill. Every hundred paces or so, Meredeth caught sight of a flash of white up ahead with Bobby hard on the trail. She glanced over her shoulder.

Al was far behind, his face beet red.

"Stay back, Al!" she called. "Meet you back there!"

Al stopped his shaky jog and lifted his hand to indicate he'd heard her. Then he hunched over, hands on his knees, and lost his breakfast.

She turned back to the chase in time to see Bobby streak around a boulder that was easily the size of a bus standing on end.

"Freeze!" he bellowed.

Meredeth poured on the speed, ignoring her aching guts, ignoring the hitch in her side, the burning in her lungs, the pounding sickness in her head.

"FBI!" Bobby yelled. "Get down! Get on your knees, Carl!"

Mocking laughter echoed down the gulley. "You forget my name already, FBI-man?"

"LET ME SEE YOUR HANDS!"

Meredeth drew her Glock as she approached the boulder, clamping her jaw shut against the sick feeling in her middle. She slid around the boulder, and her feet skipped out from under her, dumping her ass-over-teakettle into the soft loam of the gulley. She rolled and jumped to her feet, then sprinted toward the sound of Bobby's voice.

"I *will* shoot you! Get your hands out in front of you!"

"No, FBI-man. You have no authority over me. I'm Kahin Alshaytan!"

"Don't move! Stop! Stop!"

Meredeth pulled out her last stops and poured on as much speed as she could. Her breath came in ragged gasps, and she was more than a little dizzy, but she came on anyway, ignoring her discomfort, wanting to get there, wanting to back Bobby up.

"DROP IT!" Bobby thundered. "DROP THE GUN, ALSHAYTAN!" The air was rent with the sound of three gunshots—two the abortive sounding pops of a nine-millimeter, followed by the louder boom of a larger caliber round.

"Bobby!" she shouted. She ran on and came up behind him. He stood in the classic move-and-shoot stance, his knees slightly bent, his feet spread, chin tucked down, arms tight, elbows stiff. He was moving forward, moving toward the body twenty feet in front of him. "It's me, Bobby. I've got your six."

"Ten-four." He moved forward.

"Did you shoot him?"

"He offed himself. I fired to try to stop him. Two shots, one hit, one wide. He fired last."

"Okay." She moved to the side but stayed behind Bobby, creating space, creating an angle between them. She centered her sites on Alshaytan's prone form. For each step forward Bobby took, she took half a step forward and half a step to the side. "Alshaytan! Show me your hands!" she shouted.

Alshaytan didn't move, didn't acknowledge her commands. He lay with his arms thrown out to the side. His pistol lay eight inches from his right hand.

"He's down," said Bobby.

"You sure?"

"Reasonably so. I don't see respiration, and his shot was under his jaw, level. Brainstem, most likely." He glanced at her. "Hold there. I'm going to approach and check for vital signs."

"Go." She stopped moving, setting her feet, stiffening her arms, locking her Glock's sites on Alshaytan's center of mass.

Bobby moved in, taking his time, taking small steps, then holstered his own Glock and sank down on one knee. He pressed two fingers to the side of Alshaytan's neck, then shook his head. "He's dead."

"Was he the only one?"

"Yes."

Meredeth keyed her mic and paused for a moment. "Suspect down. Repeat, Kahin Alshaytan is down."

"Ten-four."

"Roll a bus to Jefferson Lane."

She holstered her Glock. "You okay to stay here? I'll go back for the bus and bring them out."

"Yeah, I'm fine."

After she returned with the rescue crew, she and Bobby returned down the gulley, leaving the rescue crew to bring Alshaytan's body down on their own. Bobby was quiet, and Meredeth was content to let that lay. He'd done his best to stop the suicide, but he'd failed, and failure was not something Bobby Van Zandt was okay with.

They reached Jefferson Lane and walked around the ambulance. She looked into the trees, trying to spot the SWAT sniper team but could see nothing but leaves. She turned away, looking first north on Jefferson, then south. "We got Alshaytan, but where is Anya? Rad said she was pushing Kahin to take action."

"Maybe she was ahead of him."

"I don't think so," said Meredeth. "I think she sent him on his own."

"A distraction?"

"Could be. But where is she?"

Bobby shook his head. "In the wind? Up the road?"

Meredeth shook her head and crossed the road toward the fence. She came up on her toes and looked over the fence. "Al?" she called.

"Right here, Meredeth."

"Anya Seneca?"

"In custody—she was hiding in a cardboard box in the garage."

"I want to talk to her. Can you arrange that?"

"Absolutely. Let's head back to the station and get her in a room."

CHAPTER 30

MANIPULATION

Ukiah, CA

ANYA SENECA SAT with her bare legs pulled up onto the seat of the chair. She was small enough to make that work. A deputy had given her a jumpsuit to cover up her nakedness, and she'd put it on against the air-conditioned chill but had immediately set to work rolling up the legs as far as they would go.

Meredeth watched her a moment, through the mirrored glass while she sipped her coffee and tried to ignore the chatter behind her. Bobby had made it his mission to tell joke after joke—well, she supposed it was his way of dealing with the shooting. Laughter was the best medicine, after all.

Anya seemed a bit of a cipher. From Rad's statement, she was controlling, manipulative, even, though the boy hadn't realized it. The question that kept rolling around inside Meredeth's head was: who painted the Trinity Knot on the wall in the basement? Had it been Alshaytan? Was he really Carl? Or was it someone else, and if so, who? Anya? Could she be Lucy?

As she considered these thoughts, these questions, Anya got to her feet and came over to the mirror. She stood there, head cocked to one side, the orange jumpsuit hanging off her sparse frame like a tent.

Meredeth lifted her phone and, on a whim, took Anya's picture. She sent it to Michelina with a priority flag and the caption, "Do you know this woman?" Then she put her coffee down on the table in front of her and turned her back on the woman.

"Well, Bobby, you or me?" she asked.

He stopped talking mid-joke, and the smile melted from his face. "Up to you, Mere. I can give her a run if you're not feeling up to it."

"Good cop, bad cop?"

"Think we'll need that?"

"Maybe. I'll go in first, and if I start to play bad cop, that will be the secret signal that I want you in the room."

"Got it, boss."

Meredeth nodded once, then glanced at the technology specialist who was coming back to sit at her station. "I want a tight close-up of the suspect at all times. As tight as you can get on her face. I may want to review the footage frame by frame for microexpressions."

"I can do that."

"Good. I'm counting on it." She turned back to the other officers in the room. "I want the rest of you watching her closely. I don't want to miss a single thing she does, and I won't be able to catch everything." The officers came over and gathered near the one-way glass, all signs of joking and laughter gone. "Good," said Meredeth. "I'm going in."

She strode out of the room broadcasting confidence she wasn't sure was real. She turned right and walked down to the next door—the interview room's door—then paused with her hand on the doorknob. She dropped her chin and closed her eyes for a moment, focusing her mind on the task ahead. She drew a deep breath to a four-count, then held it for four beats and exhaled for four beats. She repeated the process four times until she felt at ease, and her brain felt full of oxygen. Then, she took one more deep breath and pushed the door open.

Anya whirled around at the sound of the door, half-dropping into a fight-or-flight stance. Meredeth pretended not to notice as she walked in and stood beside a chair that put her back to the mirror. She wanted Anya facing the officers observing through the window. There were enough cameras in the room to make it unnecessary, but there was something to be said about seeing a suspect's reactions live rather than filtered through a camera, a computer, and an LED monitor.

"Take a seat," Meredeth said.

"Who are you?"

"You don't remember? We met at 1408 Rosemary Lane just the other day."

"Oh, right. The butch FBI chick."

Meredeth shrugged. "An apt description, I guess. I've never been girly." She pointed at the seat across from her. "Sit."

"I want to sit on this side."

Meredeth shook her head. "No, sit opposite me."

"But I don't like facing this pretend mirror."

"Tough titty. Take a seat on your own unless you'd rather I handcuff you to the table here." Meredeth turned her back on Seneca—a calculated risk—and sat down. "Come on, Seneca. The quicker we get started, the quicker we finish, and you can move over to the jail before your arraignment."

"Arraignment? For what? Hiding in a box?"

"What kind of a name is Seneca?"

Anya strolled around into her field of vision. "I don't know. You'd have to ask my foster parents."

"Oh, you were in the system? Here or elsewhere?"

"With a name like Seneca, you can't guess?"

"Western New York, then?"

"Bingo." Anya continued around past the chair, her hands clamped together behind her back. She walked to the corner, then spun on her heel and started back the other way.

"Take a seat," said Meredeth.

"No, thanks. I was all cramped up in the box for an hour. I need to walk it off or I'll cramp up."

"You need to take a seat. Otherwise, I'm going to cuff you to the table like I said, and you'll have to worry about cramps in your arms, too."

Anya rolled her eyes, but she came to the table and pulled out the chair. She spun it around, so the back rested against the table, then straddled it. "Who died and left you queen of the universe?"

"Thank you," said Meredeth. "When did you leave New York?"

"A while ago."

"And you moved out here to the west coast right away, or did you make a stop elsewhere?"

"What's all this have to do with Kahin?"

"It's basic background information on you, not Alshaytan."

"To what end?"

"For one thing, I'm interviewing you, not him."

"He got away, did he?" A small, snarky smile dawned on Anya's face.

"No, he didn't."

"Then why aren't you interviewing him instead of me?"

"Because he blew his brains out up on the hill."

Anya's face went through a series of contortions that ranged from raw rage to suspicion, then back to fury. "That cowardly asshole," she muttered.

"Why? Was he supposed to do something else?"

Her face went blank, and the small woman shrugged.

Interesting, thought Meredeth. *No sadness, no sense of loss, only anger at being disobeyed.* She took a deep breath and shifted in her seat. "Why does that anger you? What did you want him to do instead?"

"To survive! To live! Kahin was a visionary! One of today's great thinkers. His death is waste."

"Kahin Alshaytan was a paranoid schizophrenic, and we both know that."

"That's not mutually exclusive to what I said. Einstein was schizotypal and had a schizophrenic son. Don't you consider him a great thinker?"

"He also displayed traits consistent with high-functioning autism, and his son's schizophrenia supports that diagnosis to the exclusion of his schizotypal features."

Anya narrowed her eyes. "Sir Isaac Newton, then. He was psychotic."

Meredeth shrugged. "Perhaps. It doesn't matter. Both those men were productive members of society. Your boyfriend was not. He was nothing but a poser. In fact, I have it on good authority that his so-called Satanism was, in fact, an affectation designed to garner attention."

"What do you know about it? You spoke to him once. He believed enough to change his name."

Meredeth nodded and waved her hand. "Priest of Satan. Yeah. Let's get back to why news of his suicide made you angry."

"I told you. His death is a waste."

"You don't seem sad," said Meredeth. "Yet he introduced you as his fiancée."

Anya shrugged and examined her fingernails.

"Did you not plan on spending your life with him? Was the betrothal a sham?"

The woman sighed and rolled her eyes. "No, or I wouldn't have agreed to it. Kahin was..." She shook her head. "In many ways, Kahin was like a child. He could be incredibly sweet one minute and dumb as a bag of sticks the next. He was unique and, at the same time, like any of a million other men."

"Yet he was *your* man."

She shrugged and flicked her bleached blonde hair. "And he's dead by his own hand. There's no coming back from such a stupid mistake."

"Why did you send him up the hill? Was he a distraction? Did you plan on escaping while he kept our attention?"

"Hardly. I only hid in the garage because Kahin said you were coming to kill us. He said you—you, specifically, Agent Butch—were tasked with our murders."

"And you believed him?"

"Why shouldn't I?"

"Because he was a paranoid schizophrenic."

"Back to that?"

"Who killed Roberta Black?"

"Kahin. You made him paranoid. He lost it. He thought she was trying to have him committed."

"And who killed Ray Michaels?"

"Who's that?"

"Rad."

"Kahin."

"Why?"

"Why did Kahin do anything? His demon-guides told him to."

"His demon-guides?"

"Yeah, that's what he called the voices in his head."

"Do you believe he was a true Satanist?"

"Kahin believed he was."

"That's not what I asked you, Anya."

She shrugged her shoulders and went back to examining her fingernails.

"Well? Did you agree with Kahin's religious beliefs?"

"Sure, why not? It calmed him. It gave him something to think about."

"Is that all? It seems like he'd have been better served if you'd insisted that he take his meds."

"No. The pharmaceutical industry invented his illness, *caused* half his symptoms then wanted to treat them with yet more drugs. Kahin found a way to function without those pills, to live without the medicinal cornucopia prescribed by those hacks at the mental hospital. He didn't need drugs."

"And yet he had a psychotic break by all appearances and was responsible for the murders of his own mother and an innocent seventeen-year-old boy."

"Innocent? Rad? Did you ever talk to him?" Anya chuckled low in her throat.

"Did Kahin kill Jamie Wenstrom?"

Anya rolled her shoulders and closed her eyes as she yawned.

"Why did you choose Jamie Wenstrom? Was it because of his uncle?"

"Who's his uncle?"

"You don't know?"

Anya tipped her a wink. "Do I?"

Meredeth's phone chirped. "Excuse me a moment," she said, pulling the device from her pocket. Michelina had sent her an email, and she swiped it open. The message read:

> *BE CAREFUL, MEREDETH!*
>
> *I do recognize her. That's Lucy!*
>
> *-M*

Meredeth nodded to herself and put the phone away. "Let's talk about something else for a while. You grew up in Western New York? I've spent some time there recently, and I have to say, I love it there. What brought you out west? Kahin?"

"Hardly. I met him here in Ukiah."

"Ah. You didn't grow up with him then?"

"Obviously not."

"Have you ever heard of a small town called Jonodot? It's near Letchworth."

Anya raised an eyebrow. "Never heard of it."

"How about Yoagoh?"

"Nope."

"Hanable's Valley?"

"Sorry."

"Where exactly did you grow up?"

"Cuba."

"That's in New York?"

"Yeah, the Southern Tier."

"Oh, I've never been there."

"You're not missing much. It's a wide spot in the road."

"Have any brothers or sisters?"

"Not real ones. Foster-sibs? Sure. Loads."

"Like Carl? How's he doing?"

Anya cocked her head to the side. "Who?"

"Oh, come on, Lucy. The game's up."

"Lucy? My name's Anya." The muscles around her eyes twitched and danced.

"Do you even remember the name your mother gave you?"

Her shoulders bumped up and down inside the voluminous jumpsuit. "It's Anya."

Meredeth shook her head. "No. It's Stephanie Milneaux. A serial killer who subsumed the identity of David Branch murdered your mother and brother. He took you to his farm outside Yoagoh, New York, and used a process called psychic driving to twist your mind."

"You've got quite an imagination, lady."

"Did you tell Kahin why he had to paint the Trinity Knot on the wall, or did you do that task yourself?"

"I have no idea what you're talking about."

"Was Kahin named Carl when you lived on the Branch Farm?"

Anya leaned to the side and stared at the mirror. "Someone should get in here. I think this lady's slid off her nut."

"What's the point in continuing the game, Lucy? Not even Alex continued to pretend once I found her out."

"I heard she gutted you like a fish."

Meredeth spread her arms wide. "Yet here I am. Answer my question about Carl."

"Sure. Kahin was Carl."

Meredeth narrowed her eyes. "Then who was Roberta Black?"

"Just some bag lady. We convinced her to play the role by offering her free room and board."

"Is that so?"

"Sure."

"Is that why you got so angry that he killed himself."

"Yeah. Carl wasn't supposed to do that. He had work to do."

"And you? What was your role in Ankou's grand plan?"

"I just rode herd on Carl. Once he had his schizophrenic break, Father told me to take care of him. We didn't have a role in the plan to put you in your place. Taking care of Carl was a full-time job, and Father never did believe I could do anything."

"Why did you two kill Jamie Wenstrom."

"I have no idea what you're talking about."

"We'll find the body, you know. Cadaver dogs are back at the house as we speak, searching the backyard and the woods beyond. We'll find all the bodies."

"Goody. On that note, I think it's time for me to exercise my right to counsel."

"Oh, come on, Lucy. It's just us girls talking."

A snide smile broke across Lucy's face. "Yeah. You, me, the camera, and the room full of penises with badges beyond the mirror."

"This is your chance to help yourself, Lucy. Tell us what you know about the plan, and maybe I can convince the DA to accept a plea bargain."

"Lawyer."

"Don't waste this chance. Once I leave this room—"

"L-A-W-Y-E-R. Lawyer."

"I know how it's spelled, but it's a mistake to stop—"

"Lawyer. Lawyer. Lawyer."

Meredeth heaved a sigh and locked gazes with the woman. "Was Kahin really Carl?"

"Lawyer-lawyer-lawyer."

"Fine. Enjoy your time in CCWF or Folsom. When you feel like talking, tell your prison counselor to get in touch with me. If I have time, I'll come out and talk to you."

"Don't hold your breath, Connelly."

Meredeth shrugged and stood. "I won't. Instead, I'll go on with my life, enjoying my freedom. You enjoy your incarceration, Lucy."

CHAPTER 31

SURPRISES

Quantico, VA

EXHAUSTION AND FATIGUE warred for possession of Meredeth's brain. Her past couple of days had been a whirlwind of activity, and unfortunately for the Wenstrom and McCutchins families, it had included the exhumation of Jamie Wenstrom's body from a shallow grave in the backyard of 1408 Rosemary Lane back in Ukiah. Worse still, his murderer had obliterated his face with point-blank gunshots.

It was ugly. Her interview with Lucy hadn't satisfied her, and neither had the answers the woman had given her. She didn't know what to believe about Kahin Alshaytan. On the one hand, Al Saville had told her that Benjamin and Roberta Black had lived in Ukiah for most of, if not all, of their lives. Then again, given Ankou's penchant for subsuming identities, it was possible that Carl had subsumed Benjamin's identity, and that could be why he'd changed his name to Kahin Alshaytan—another layer of obfuscation. Saville was running DNA from Benjamin's psychiatric hospitalization when he was eighteen, and that could put the matter to rest.

Michelina was certain Anya Seneca had grown up on David Branches' Farm in Yoagoh, New York, that she'd been the girl known as Lucy. Of course, there were no DNA records to check her identity against. Whoever the woman was, there was no doubt she'd made her way through life through manipulation of the people around her. That much fit with what Michelina described at any rate.

Meredeth shook her head as her Uber driver pulled up in front of her home in Tacketts Mill. She looked up at the dark house for a moment, wishing she was in Hanable's Valley.

"Is this the place?" asked the driver.

"Yes. Sorry, I'm just exhausted from the trip." She glanced at her app and made her payment. "Thanks," she said as the driver popped the trunk so she could get her bag.

She got out and pulled her suitcase from the trunk, then closed it and rapped on the trunk lid. She turned and trudged up her front walk to the front door. She unlocked it and stepped inside, dragging her suitcase up over the step, then slammed the door and leaned against it.

"Need some help?"

Meredeth gave a little cry and dropped her purse, grabbing for her holstered Glock.

"Don't shoot, FBI. It's me."

"Kevin Saunders!" she shouted. "Are you trying to get me to shoot you dead?"

"No, I was hoping for a more enthusiastic welcome."

"Christ, Kevin! What are you doing here?"

"Well, you wanted me to tell you why I was in Virginia, so I waited for you."

She closed her eyes and tried to slow her galloping heart.

"Sorry I scared you."

"Did you ever! Didn't your mother teach you never to hide in a single woman's house and then scare her half-to-death?"

"Well, not in so many words, no." He appeared out of the darkness of her family room, carrying a dozen red roses. "I must admit I hadn't thought this all the way through. How was the flight?"

"Well, it was commercial, so..."

"Yeah. Did you almost shoot anyone on the plane?"

"No, but then again, no one scared me out of my wits."

"Sorry." He held his arms wide, and she stepped into them. He kissed her soundly, then stepped back and held out the flowers.

"They're beautiful."

"Like you."

"I bet you say that to all the women who almost blast holes through your thick skull."

"Only the ones who work for the BAU."

She took the flowers and turned toward her kitchen to find a vase or a water pitcher or something. She turned on the tap as she looked, then settled on an empty orange juice bottle from the garbage can and filled it with tap water. She shoved the stems of the roses through the bottle's opening and set the container on the counter. "Well?" she said.

"Looks great. Who needs a vase, anyway?"

"Not that, bozo. I meant why are you here? Why did you risk a bunch of holes in your skin to scare the crap out of me?"

"Ah. Why am I here in Virginia?"

"Yeah, that."

He flipped a business card onto the counter.

"What's this?"

"Read it."

She crossed the room and picked up the card and read it, her eyes growing wide as she did so. "Is this for real?"

Kevin nodded.

"But why?"

He shrugged. "You said it yourself back in New York. Spending every night together was kind of good."

"But I—"

"This is my decision, Mere. I couldn't ask you to give up the Bureau, so this seemed like a good compromise. Besides, it's like you said. I want to be doing everything I can to beat back the evil in the world, and being the police chief in Hanable's Valley doesn't exactly allow me to do that."

"But, Kevin..." She shook her head. "This is so sudden."

"Not for me, FBI. I've been thinking about it since we got serious."

"Wait a minute. When did we get serious?"

He grinned and shook his head. "Very funny."

She looked down at the card again. It read: Special Agent Kevin Saunders, Special Weapons and Tactics Instructor FBI Academy, Quantico, VA, then went on to give his contact information. "Are you... I mean..."

"Listen, Meredeth. I wanted something where I can make a difference. Something where we wouldn't have to fight to get our schedules to align. A teaching spot fits the bill, and I can still deploy with HRT when the need arises. I get to stay sharp and facilitate knowledge transfer to incoming agents. Plus, with HRT I can make sure you're not taking stupid risks."

"But, Kevin...you're giving up everything."

He pulled her to him and kissed her hard. "Not the most important thing. I'd like to move in with you, Meredeth, if you'll have me."

Meredeth found that her eyes were wet, and she threw her arms around his neck and hugged him close. "Of course, you big idiot, but only if you promise not to hide out in the dark when I come home from travel."

"Deal," he said and kissed her until they needed to leave the kitchen.

I HOPE YOU'VE enjoyed *Sticks and Bones* and would kill to get your hands on the next installment. The next book in the series is titled *Rhythm of the Knife*, and you can find it on Amazon: https://ehv4.us/4rhtythmoftheknife.

To be among the first to know what I'm up to and when the newest book I write goes live, please subscribe to my newsletter at https://ehv4.us/vvjoinehv or join my online community at https://ehv4.us/discord. You can also support me on Patreon at https://ehv4.us/patreon.

You can find my complete thriller bibliography at https://ehv4.us/booksehv. I also write supernatural fiction, and you can find my bibliography under the name Erik Henry Vick at https://ehv4.us/books.

Books these days succeed or fail based on the strength of their reviews. I hope you will consider leaving a review—as an independent author, I could use your help. It's easy (I promise). You can leave your review by clicking on this link: https://ehv4.us/2revsab.

AUTHOR'S NOTE
9/21/22

SOMETIMES, MY MONSTERS just don't care what my plans, what my needs are. This book—no, this year—has reminded me of that. Starting in April, it's been one thing after another, starting with a surprise five-and-a-half-hour surgery leaving me with a temporary ileostomy (yeah, just like Meredeth), two months of horror and disgust, a surgery to reverse all that, and then, just when I'd finally recovered (at the end of August!), we attended a book signing where Melissa and I acquired COVID—after four doses of the vaccine—and since we'd avoided getting it until then, we were really sick—the kind of sick where you get up and eat breakfast, then need a nap. As I write this, almost a month later, I'm finally leaving the symptoms behind and able to get something done.

But what my monsters didn't count on was my friends and my wife. Despite having to write this book while sick, I got it done in the nick of time. I couldn't have done that without Paul, Ryan, Tony, Sonya, and, of course, Supergirl all pitching in and handling other aspects of my business so I could do nothing but write while I had the energy to do so. And without Tony's awesome contributions to the effort, I couldn't have finished (despite having written thirty thousand of this book's sixty-five thousand words in the last forty-eight hours). I'm not good at asking for help. I admit that, and usually, when people offer me help, I tell them I'll manage, and somehow, I usually do. But in this case, I couldn't have completed this novel without help.

There, I said it.

The next book, I'll do better because I'm finally feeling as though this COVID infection is slinking off into the darkness of bad memories.

This book is a little different than the others in the series—to mention just one difference, Meredeth and Bobby don't even know they are dealing with a serial killer until the last few chapters. And they don't know that serial killer is a product of Ankou's special programs until the second to last chapter. I hope you've enjoyed this slight break from the expected because the next novel, *Rhythm of the Knife*, returns Meredeth's need to profile an unsub with a vengeance. But who will it be? Will it mark the return of Mack? Will it be another of Ankou's creations?

I'll stop there because it's starting to feel mean to ask you those questions when I know the answer. You'll have to read the novel (release date: 11/1/22) to find out!

In the meantime, I hope you'll consider joining my online community. If you'd like to support my writing, please check out my Patreon page at: https://ehv4.us/patreon. And please join us on Discord (it's free!) by following this link: https://ehv4.us/discord.

Until next time, my friend!

PATRON RECOGNITION

A BIG VIKING hug to all my patrons!

Special thanks to Dawn Bogue and an anonymous patron for being the first of hopefully many patrons of the upper tiers.

ABOUT THE AUTHOR

E.H. VICK ¶is the pen name for critically acclaimed best-selling and award-winning horror author Erik Henry Vick. He specializes in pulse-pounding stories filled with nail biting tension—usually involving serial killers as villains and psychologically-flawed protagonists. As an author disabled by autoimmune diseases (also known as his Personal Monster™), Vick writes to hang on to the few remaining shreds of his sanity. He lives with his wife, Supergirl; their son; a Rottweiler named after a god of thunder; and two extremely psychotic cats. He fights his Personal Monster™ daily with humor, pain medicine, and funny T-shirts.

With a B.A. in Psychology, an M.S.C.S., and a Ph.D. in Artificial Intelligence, Vick has worked as a criminal investigator for a state agency, a college professor, a C.T.O. for an international software company, and a video game developer.

He'd love to hear from you on social media:

Website: https://ehvick.com
Facebook: https://fb.me/ehvick
Amazon author page: https://ehv4.us/amaehv
Goodreads Author Page: https://ehv4.us/grehv
BookBub Author Profile: http://ehv4.us/bbehv

Made in the USA
Monee, IL
13 April 2023

31806283R00184